PENGUIN BOOKS

THE GREATEST SORROW

'An unusually thoughtful first novel, original and persuasive' Anita Brookner

'Ovenden has a natural flair for description . . . *The Greatest Sorrow* presents real life in stark relief to musty academia . . . [and] manages to be both compelling and profound – a must read'
Big Issue

'A novel which goes beyond an intimate study of a male friendship to explore the interconnections between biography and life, knowledge and wisdom, relationships and identity' Rachel Campbell-Johnston, *The Times*

'A bold and ambitious novel that elegantly marries meditations on friendship, love and the life of the mind with an absorbing narrative' Penelope Lively

Keith Ovenden was born and grew up in London, where he attended what was then Wanstead County High School. He took university degrees at Keele, Michigan and Oxford, after which he lectured for a few years in the Department of Government at the University of Essex. In addition to several works on political economy, including (with Tony Cole) the influential *Apartheid and International Finance: A Programme for Change* (Penguin 1989), which clarified for an international audience the dramatic political and social changes that were shortly to follow in southern Africa, he has previously published two novels in New Zealand: *Ratatui* (1984) and *O.E.* (1986). He is also a biographer. James McNeish wrote that Ovenden's biography *A Fighting Withdrawal. The Life of Dan Davin: Writer, Soldier, Publisher* (1996) was 'one of the most elegant and compassionate biographies', and that it brought Davin 'triumphantly alive'. Keith Ovenden has lived abroad for many years, in New Zealand, France and the United States. He currently lives in Warsaw.

THE GREATEST SORROW

KEITH OVENDEN

PENGUIN BOOKS

PENGUIN BOOKS

Published by the Penguin Group
Penguin Books Ltd, 27 Wrights Lane, London W8 5TZ, England
Penguin Putnam Inc., 375 Hudson Street, New York, New York 10014, USA
Penguin Books Australia Ltd, Ringwood, Victoria, Australia
Penguin Books Canada Ltd, 10 Alcorn Avenue, Toronto, Ontario, Canada M4V 3B2
Penguin Books (NZ) Ltd, Private Bag 102902, NSMC, Auckland, New Zealand

Penguin Books Ltd, Registered Offices: Harmondsworth, Middlesex, England

First published by Hamish Hamilton 1998
Published in Penguin Books 1999
1 3 5 7 9 10 8 6 4 2

Set in Monotype Bembo
Printed in England by Clays Ltd, St Ives plc

For Piers

'. . . I believe what I write to be the truth, and every man who is not indifferent to the truth has a weakness for spreading it abroad.'

Alexander Herzen

1

Sunday night: December 1996

'Friendship between young men has all the fervour of love and all its characteristics – the same shy reluctance to profane its feelings by speech, the same diffidence and absolute devotion, the same pangs at parting, and the same exclusive desire to stand alone without a rival.'

Moser killed himself last night. Mrs Wharton found him when she came in this morning. He was in his bed, pyjama'd, respectable, very tranquil-looking, she said. There was an empty aspirin bottle on the bedside table, a drained glass, and a letter addressed to Vita. Vita will never read it.

Mrs Wharton, Edith, Moser used to call her, though her name is Elizabeth really, and she dislikes anyone else calling her anything other than Mrs Wharton, burst in on me minutes after she arrived and sent me down to his room. Moser looked as though he was asleep except that he had that greyish-white colour people go when they die, and his hands, on the coverlet, were too tense for live, sleeping hands. He looked as gentle as ever, and just as kind, but the intelligence was gone. I used to think that intelligence was discernible in the eyes, but Moser taught me that this isn't so. He said you could tell intelligence in people with their eyes shut, blind, or asleep, if you knew how to look at hands and feet and posture. How people hold themselves. We used to play guessing games – IQ scores (which are a nonsense anyway) estimated from visual clues – testing one of his theories. But there was no intelligence left in Moser this morning. He exuded only wooden emptiness, like a wardrobe in an hotel.

Mrs Wharton stood in the doorway crying, then she went and came back, went and came back again, unable to tear herself away, looking for him, hoping he might be back each time she returned, and finding only the same unmoving, greyish-white emptiness. Moser's void is the space left by having known Moser, and it is a void known only to those of us who did. The void of Moser is nothing to others.

Herzen is just the same. Moser was my friend for twenty-two years, and Herzen has been my constant companion for the past twelve. There seem to be moments in life, how I notice it today, when you realize afterwards, only afterwards, that threads were somehow being drawn together, the pattern completed, something concluded, a part of the canvas finished. Last night, while Moser was downstairs, draining his glass, ebbing away, dozing down into irreversible sleep and out through that into space, I was up here in the room above, just as I am now but in the small hours, writing the preface. Various views about the character of biography, how much we can know, love and forgive in a subject, whether empathy is possible (certainly not), how the times force a pattern of events on even the most unwilling of us, biographers and our subjects alike. How captive we are for writing the good, and how free to employ the energy of destruction in the service of malice. The acknowledgements and thanks for this and that: librarians in Moscow, St Petersburg, London, Geneva and Rome; municipal authorities in Vyatka, Putney and Nice; fellow scholars in Stanford, Princeton and Paris; the desire to be thought honourable; responsibility for failings that remain; hope of expanding Herzen's reputation and influence among a new generation of today, one hundred and nearly twenty-seven years after his death. And while I wrote, signing and dating the final page, Moser lay back on his pillow, came up to the moment, touched and then embraced it, gave himself to it, and was gone. Now, here on this side sits *Alexander Herzen. A Life*, a counterfeit made by me in 865 pages of typescript stacked on the corner of my desk, below the picture of him on the wall, held down by his Piedmont medallion, a gift from Garibaldi, the light of his ambitions still bright in his words, though long since faded by the many deaths in his eyes. And there, on the other, downstairs under the swan-white college coverlet, lies the dead Moser. The one brought to life just as the other expires, a life for a life, a past for a future, a launch for a wreck.

It is important not to exaggerate, something biographers should learn early. Moser's body isn't down there in that room any more. The coverlet has gone to be cleaned, the bed is stripped, and the harmony, the symmetry of that moment in the night, has been broken and corrupted. Only I will know.

I have no experience of dead bodies, what to do with one. I rang my doctor and he came round and supervised things. By the time he'd finished, Mrs Wharton and the news had spread through the college like a water ration through an irrigation system. By now, tonight, it will be the conversation of Oxford drawing rooms, high tables, and SCRs. An ambulance came and took Moser's body away, and there was some talk of relatives. Next of kin, they said. An archaism reserved only for this occasion, bestowing gravity, solemnity. Next there will be an autopsy, a coroner's report, an inquest. Before Moser can be satisfactorily dead there has to be an explanation and a verdict. My doctor took Vita's letter and said he would have to forward it to the coroner's office with the death certificate. Moser would probably have laughed at all this. Perhaps he did laugh as he poured the water, unclipped the cap (one of those child-proof snap-off ones), laughed at the idea of procedure somehow keeping him alive, bureaucracy as life support. I suppose they will say that the balance of his

3

mind was disturbed. An oxymoron that would have made him smile. He used to say that equilibrium was something unknown to parts of the system. There was homoeostasis, but only in the system as a whole. The mind, he reckoned, was bound to be unbalanced, like the liver, or the testicles. It depended on who you were, and where you happened to be in the process of living, becoming.

I came back here when they had all gone, taking him with them; came back to my study, the bedroom, the deep-set lead-lighted windows, the familiar smell, and the silence. The Master came to see me later, alerted by the Dean, his Sunday morning suddenly upended. Sir Philip is one of those establishment men who always look grave, even when merry. It is the weight of their bearing that carries them to the top. On gay occasions they appear to be seeing more than the rest of us, to be in touch with history. On sad ones their gravity is reverential, establishes imitable tone. He comes and goes at doorways as if they were theatre wings, making his entries and his exits, imposing silence as he appears, leaving whispers as he departs. I wondered if he paused at the door before knocking, adjusted the fall of his jacket, checked his fly, took a last quick look at his make-up. He has silver hair at the temples, a sharp nose beneath gold glasses, and exquisite teeth. We call him, or rather we called him – past tense now Moser is gone – Sir Philip the Smooth. He told me how sorry he was, what a dreadful thing, for Moser, his friends, his colleagues, his college. He did not, he said, know Moser well. Moser took little part in college affairs and was perhaps difficult to approach. But he imagined the business with Vita, her last illness, 'even, paradoxically, her stoic acceptance', must have exhausted him, brought him 'low with grief'. Sir Philip put his hand on my shoulder and said he understood how close we were, Moser and I, and what a sad day, what a lonely world, this must seem for me now. He said if there was anything he could do . . . that I must not reproach myself.

Of course there isn't anything that anyone can do. Not now. Not from here, where we stand today. Being here, at the end of several lanes where they come together in a square, a *place*, one of Moser's beloved piazzas, is a condition, a circumstance. This is not a board game, a *jeu de société*, for each in turn to make a move. This is a state of affairs, and for the moment we can only handle it in whatever way we know how, caress it perhaps, roll it around for the experience, write it down. This is because *doing* is an intellectual matter, a question of will, and decay is beyond its reach.

I didn't say any of this to Sir Philip. Moser and I had a code of college conduct, and item three was Never Tell Anything to the Master. It would be wrong to break the code just because Moser is dead. But shouldn't I say something to someone? Those next of kin?

I lay on the daybed by the window all afternoon, watching the autumn walkers near the river, the trees limp in the misty, damp, still air, trying to recall some particular detail of Moser's family. There was Vita of course, but they had no children. I rarely heard Moser speak of his parents as if they were still alive, though I did meet them once. Brothers he rarely mentioned, though there was a rather older sister, whom I met on the same memorable occasion that I met his parents. I doubted I could find her again, however, as it was a while ago now, and he had never talked of her. 'Since we are all related to everyone else, what does my family matter?' he said once. Didn't he? I seem to remember so. He grew up somewhere in Cumberland, a once real place now suppressed into the geographically and historically incorrect Cumbria, and best designated in our age by wriggles of the pen on an envelope – CU9 2BO. I invent. He hated this sort of progress, denaturing he called it, abolishing

5

history to facilitate an unwanted future. He said that if they could reinvent his past, then so could he. And he did. He had one version of his curriculum vitae that might well have been largely untrue, although filled with plausible possibilities, what he called his 'branch lines'. Not taken, but perhaps crossed, and full of enchanting destinations. Best not to deprive others of the possibility of your having been to them. What was true in this CV and what was not, I have no idea, and neither eventually, or so he liked to claim, did he. 'You're the biographer,' he said. 'You tell me.' He went to the local school in CU9 2BO, and six years later they sent him, unmanageable village boy genius, to a distant grammar school, on a bike. The primary-school teacher, a man called Jenkins, or sometimes in the telling a woman called Conyers, promised him a great future.

This he has now had.

The grammar school, confident, public, uniformed, one of those places where they nurture brilliance conscious of 'the long tail' that drags behind it, was a universe to itself, so the juvenile Moser (perfectly equilibrated, though thought to be headstrong and body-weak) devised a chart, and navigational principles for travelling round it. First principle: make sure you are thought to be good at everything. No holes in the façade. No tears in the fabric. Excellence is seamless. Second principle: never crawl. Third principle: never accept anything without testing it yourself. And so on. He was very precocious long before he won his scholarship to university.

This is where we met, on opposite sides of a long refectory dinner table on the first evening of the first term, thankful for a conversation in which to hide our nervous embarrassment.

Our oppositeness was pleasing. I came from the city, Moser from the country; I was to read philosophy, Moser natural sciences; he was tall, craggy, with dark blue eyes, and a mass of wiry black hair that shot sideways off his head, and that went grey early, making him look occasionally like an Edward Lear drawing. I was nondescript, thin, average in height and agility, with narrow brown eyes and hair of the same colour, hair that may hang limp on my neck, although I usually keep it cut. We were not made for each other, but we loved each other from the beginning, and today, or rather last night, is the first time since that first dinner that Moser has gone anywhere without telling me first.

I do not wish to imply by this that we have lived these last twenty-two years in each other's pockets. Undergraduate life kept us apart a lot of the time, Moser in the laboratories off Parks Road, or on expeditions here and there, North Wales, or the coastal marshes of the southern Veneto, while I moved in my sedentary circuit from Bodleian to Schools, from college to suburban parents. In student days we never had rooms on the same staircase because I preferred the new building with its central heating and functional design, and Moser jumped at anything old, however uncomfortable and draughty. He liked things to have some history in them, and to involve ritual, though he was completely free of superstition. This is what drew him to Herzen I think, once I began my biography. Moser sensed a kindred spirit, someone who was free of the cant of present conditions, yet had a feeling for what is true elsewhere, unexperienced but as if waiting for its awakening kiss. It is an outlook that leads inexorably to exile.

Are all exiles also victims, whether willing or not? Until recently, nobody had, I think, ever victimized Moser, at least not in the sense of wanting to do him harm, but he was certainly one of those creatures we call life's victims. His life resembled a cone, or better yet a pair of compasses, not quite symmetrical in the manner of a pierrot's cap or a metronome, but its downward leg cut off just below the knee. For almost thirty years or so his life had been upward: growth, luck, ability, all matched. Then for ten it had been downward: illness, distress, misfortune, conflict, leading to this. It is tempting to try to locate the moment, the day, the hour, possibly even the second, when the peak was reached, the apex passed, and the upward trajectory turned to descent. The two paths seem quite smooth to me, no rough patches on the up, not much in the way of remission on the way down. Except for last night. Moser was entitled to last night's remission, given that there were to be no others. Anyway, he believed in self-ministration. People should make their own way in the world, free of the chains of inheritance. Property, like repu-tation, makes only prisoners, when what we seek, sought, are free men. 'Just an approximation must do,' he said once. 'You can get close to freedom, but you can't actually inhabit it, or possess it.'

As undergraduates we were, of course, unaware of this, and went about our lives in the safe anonymity of student disguise much as others do. Moser told me a little about his work, most of which I couldn't understand, and I told him everything I could about mine, all of which he grasped rather better than I did. His mind was naturally attuned to philosophical thinking, and he read his way through the syllabus of Western thought for pleasure, as relaxation. Moser also loved food, and was a great eater, making time every day to eat something special, or at the very least to think about doing so. Anything in life which he really enjoyed, like reading hard philosophy, was quickly assimilated into his culinary and dietetic vocabulary. Slices of Kant were delectable as a main course, Descartes was too starchy, Hegel pure *mousse au chocolat*, Wittgenstein battle rations, and so on. He had no time for moderns, Hare, Strawson, Flew, those people. He called them *cuisine minceur*. Lacan, read more recently, was a diuretic. Bhasker tofu. Ayer the sort of fare he imagined got served in the maximum security wing of Broadmoor. The Greeks, antique philosophers, gave him the same pleasure he got from reading an excellent menu. You could keep going back to it, even though you already knew exactly what it promised, because the savour of anticipation was mouth-watering. Things still lay ahead. There was much to live for.

It was at one of our generally late-night conversations about philosophy – we had been discussing, I think, Locke's view of property as arising from labour. *Oeuf dur mayonnaise* was Moser's judgement. Bound to cause trouble later on – that we first talked about liberty, freedom of expression and choice. Or rather, we didn't talk. Not much at any rate. Instead, there was an instant identity of interest which was exchanged between us more like a lover's glance than audible discourse, and we both knew we were as one.

I had known for some time that my own views were unusual because they did not fit under any of the popular labels of the day: not Liberal or Marxist Revolutionary Group; not Labour or Bow Group; nor yet Conservative or Workers' Revolutionary Party. To me, these were all engaged in a side-show, a sort of political professional wrestling – all for show and the results determined in advance. Their juvenile equivalents at Oxford, preparing in rehearsal the variety of acceptable roles for tomorrow, were of no interest to me. My feelings, because they could hardly be described as rational or coherent beliefs, arose from circumstances which I had first thought common enough, but which, until this moment when I felt Moser shared them, I had come increasingly to suspect were unique. They came out of the past, like memories or diaries.

Both Moser and I were born in 1956, the year of Suez, Budapest and Khrushchev, to parents more anxious to forget the past than to invent the future. Sure evidence of the loss of confidence that signals the end of empire. I grew up in a suburb on the Northern Line, a closed world, as secretive, as conscious of the power of magic and the demands of kinship, as a primitive African village. Children from such places must either conform or leave. When Moser and I arrived at Oxford in 1974 we were too late for the sentimental passions of the late 60s, and too early for the fashionable intellectual extremism of 1979. What we had was our work, which we enjoyed, our mutual company, and the empty space which urban primitives bequeath their offspring in lieu of history. We discovered that the children of the upper and upper-middle classes conceived of the world in individualist terms because they had learned to do so at their parents' knee. History for them was what their ancestors, literally, uncle this and grandfather the other, known to them by name and lineage, had done. The children of the lower classes saw history collectively for very similar reasons. Having no personal past, no oral record, they put their intellectual eggs in the basket of movements, classes, currents and forces. There were no exceptions to this. Moser proposed it as his first general law of English society, and he claimed it to be impregnable to argument – a fact which displeased him, naturally. Upper-class Marxists – an English breed, exempt by their own fiat from moral scruple – paid lip service to the inexorable force of history, but thought exclusively in individualist terms. Lenin or Trotsky, Austro-Marxists, Lukacs, heroes all. Masses, material in theory, remained unapproachably ideal. The others, lacking the personal tuition of family, and even when apparently invoking the spontaneity and originality of the individual, could never free themselves from the grip of sociology. There are no working class biographers in England. Moser and I looked at the two sides of this coin and wondered if there was enough space between them for us.

Our crisis came with Iran. Just as for Herzen and his childhood friend Ogarev it came with the execution of the Decembrists, so with us a hundred and fifty years later it came with other though different oppressions, this time in Teheran from the mid 70s, first with the Shah and then with the Ayatollah. We felt for the ancient peoples of Persia as we felt for ourselves, trapped between the irrelevance of two different political conceptions that competed in bigotries and lies, torture and murder, passed from hand to hand like coupons at a supermarket. We used to walk together on Wytham Hill, the woods and views invisible to us, though bleak if we had looked, our minds far away in the colds and deserts of Asia Minor, imagined lands. Perhaps it was Czechoslovakia, crushed while we were still schoolboys, that had made us secretive about our beliefs. So too the murders in Gdansk on 16 December 1970. All this may seem unreal or improbable. I can only refer – biographer that I am – to the testimony of others. To the despair of the liberals at Napoleon's execution of the Duc d'Enghien; to those who lost their shabby faith at the Nazi–Soviet pact, or when Masaryk fell, or at the invasion of Hungary; to those who aged overnight at Munich or Sharpeville.

So we would find ourselves on Wytham Hill, reflecting on the torturers and murderers of one supposedly objective view of freedom, subsequently being themselves tortured and murdered by the adherents of another, and ourselves disgraced in some sort by the indifference towards these events of some of our fellows, and the enthusiasm of others. In our largely silent communion about them, we pledged to devote ourselves to the rectification of these great wrongs.

Strange promises of youth, far larger than the future can allow and, like Herzen and Ogarev on Moscow's Sparrow Hills, never repented of and never abandoned, though never much honoured either – too recklessly implausible for that.

Moser said then that the way forward did not lie in political action as traditionally conceived, bartering in secret while ranting from the platform, organizing coalitions for manipulating as yet unforeseen events in darkened arenas. But neither did he think it possible to achieve the good simply by leading exemplary private lives. Private morality Moser thought a contradiction in terms: morality only had substance in actions, and it is hard to keep most actions private. What Moser proposed was that we should embark on a programme of work which, without being directed at specifically libertarian ends, would have the effect of expanding everyone's liberty. What he called 'making room at the table'. He compared our work, and its future impact, to the great works of art: buildings and symphonies mainly, but pictures, poems, plays and meals as well. Without falsehood, we thought, art revolutionizes civilization. Our life's work would be like those works of art, breaking new ground, compelling attention.

Grand projects. Now Moser is holed up in the black of a box waiting his turn for the autopsy's drill and electric saw, his ultimate private act having freed him from all considerations of morality. People say that suicide attempts are all cries for help, and successful ones those that have gone unheard or been strangled. That wouldn't be true of Moser. He was not in need of help. He saw it, I'm sure, as putting himself down. His was, after all, a terminal case of life exhaustion, and it began with me, on Wytham Hill, just as Herzen's did with Nick Ogarev. Herzen lived to be fifty-eight, born in the year Moscow burned, an exact contemporary of Charles Dickens; died in the year of the Paris Commune, as modern Germany came to life. His dates open and close the nineteenth century, but his spirit was a hundred and fifty years ahead of his time. Moser is – or was, I should say – his modern equivalent. He will only be appreciated far in the future, and many will work to damn his reputation before he is vindicated. People live longer these days, but are burned up sooner.

It was shortly after the start of these events, material in Teheran, ideal in Oxford, during the Christmas vacation, that I had a piece of luck hitch-hiking to London, and it gave us an idea for the coming summer. I got a lift from a lorry driver who turned out to be one of those British originals, a man from no obvious mould. After a few minutes of conversation with him it was as if we might have known each other all our lives: my nineteen years against his, how many, forty-five?

He only drove lorries in the winter, he said. Six months a year. For the money. His wife did the same, working as a secretary, and they lived in a cheap unfurnished flat in south London. They had no children. 'You have to make up your mind what you want from life,' he said, a distant Scottish brogue nudging the surface of his accent. 'All this rubbish,' and he flapped a hand at the mud and devastation of motorway earthworks, the crawling traffic, a thin drizzle, the filth thrown up from the road. 'That's not for me.' He fished in his pocket for a bit of paper and passed it over. 'This is what I call living. Any time you're down there, drop in and see.' The paper was headed with an address: *Elvira Madigan*, Camping de la Plage, Domaine de la Napoule, Mandelieu. Just my reading it was like switching on a current that brought him to life. Speech spilled out of him. *Elvira Madigan* was a yacht, a fifteen-metre keeler that he and his wife had saved for years to buy, second-hand, and then renovate. They moored it at La Napoule and for six months a year lived either on it or on the campsite beside it. In May and October they sailed the Mediterranean. From June to September the boat was let, and they lived in their tent, brown, idle, greeting and dispatching their tenants, doing running repairs, sailing away for a week or a weekend as bookings and cancellations allowed. 'The French have a word for it now,' he said. 'To lizard. You should give it a try.'

When I told this to Moser he agreed. He said we should write to my lorry driver, Fenner he was called, and see if we couldn't go and stay. He'd heard you could rent tents at these campsites, and if it wasn't all fiction in Fenner's head (and perhaps even if it was), then he'd be an intriguing type to talk to. In the end Moser wrote the letter, pretending he was me, and in the middle of May back came the reply. We'd be welcome any time.

Moser and I set off south as soon as the academic year was over. Fine weather, and not too many unspeakable English people about because it was still only late June. Ideal for unwinding. We probably looked a bit picturesque: Moser in shorts with braces, and carrying a stout walking stick; me wearing my floppy cricketing hat that I'd had since the fourth form. Wearing it in the summer began as an adolescent affectation, but grew (or shrank?) into an adult habit. We had got as far as Lyon, hitch-hiking, when something happened that changed the course of our history. We had been dropped at night in the heart of old Lyon, on the hill, and had found a room in a cheap hotel somewhere off the Rue St Jean. We ate cheaply in a brasserie, and then walked up to the Roman amphitheatres behind Fourvière. It was a longish haul up the Montée du Chemin Neuf, and we had already come a long way on a tiring journey throughout the day. Also it was very hot and sticky, one of those nights that make you think you are not fully alive, but only waiting between known and unknown events, suspended between an inconsequential past and an important future – a moment the looser sort of fiction writer would call pregnant. Inside the bigger theatre we sat down on stone benches to recover our breath, and as our hearts were stilled we listened to the black silence, imagining, as I suppose most visitors to such places must do, the roar of a pagan crowd, blood spurting in the sand, the salutes of those about to die.

We had been like this for some time when, through the impressive dark stillness, a figure seemed to move. We were both conscious of her at exactly the same moment. A girl, perhaps a woman. She was dressed in something very light, a whiteness that reflected the moonlight, and she appeared to us on the floor of the arena as though by stage craft, like a *sylphide* through a concealed window, a floor trap, or on an invisible wire. One moment we were alone with our thoughts of the games, murderous tournaments, the next we were aware of her together, the focus of the night. We held our breath, letting in the noise of the cicadas for the first time, and seeing her walk as though she was the first, the original, the model of all that was to come. Perhaps a minute later, one full eternal minute, a minute that didn't just seem to last a long time, but was the sort of minute in which you might cross from one state to another, adolescence to maturity say, or indifference to passion, that minute later she was gone, the space behind her empty and dark.

This apparition made both of us uneasy. Moser was not often silent. He had a quicksilver conversation that licked every topic and every gathering with its speed and precision. But he was quiet after this. For some reason I became aware of the noise of distant city traffic superseding cicadas scratching in the air, as though the world of things was trying to reassert itself over a possibly greater world of spirits.

I must re-emphasize: Moser was not a superstitious man. He had the scientific instinct, an experimenter's nimble fingers, an empiricist's luck. He thought the sort of muscular Christianity often encountered in scientific circles, the Christianity of astronomers flabbergasted by the eternity of space, or crystallographers numbed by the beauty of nature, or of mathematicians hypnotized by the elegance of proof, sometimes silly, sometimes funny. Emotional immaturity he called it. In the process of human evolution intellectual man has reached adolescence. This was another view that we later saw we shared with Herzen.

His reaction to the arena girl/woman, therefore, was wonder mixed with inquiry, not fear or worship. Where had she come from? Where had she gone? Why was she there? These were questions that had answers. She had posed them, and Moser felt that he had to respond. We clambered down to the floor of the amphitheatre and went through the main entrance, where she had gone, or so we thought, moments before. Outside everything was dark, quiet and empty. She was not there. We retraced our steps. There was no entrance on the side from which she appeared to have come, merely shadows. She must have been there before we arrived, and we had been sitting for some time. Perhaps more than an hour. Had she really been sitting still and silent, unmoving, uncoughing, barely breathing, waiting? For what? For a moment to arrive, a moment in which to stroll across this antique space and be gone? Suddenly Moser declared in a loud voice that echoed, as though addressing the tribunes: 'Voyeurs, we are all voyeurs.' And he started to dance, as if with a partner, ballroom style, something between a quickstep and a foxtrot, round and round in the grit and sand, singing as he went:

'Found together, in love from the start.
Seen together, arenas apart.
Bound together, never to part:
Voyeurs, voyeurs.

Crown'd together, science and art.
Thrown together, acting the part.
Ground together, sand in the heart:
Voyeurs, voyeurs.'

Then he sat down in the dust, sweating, and beat with the palms of his hands on the ground. After that he was silent.

'I suppose she means something,' I said eventually, pretending to a weariness that I did not feel, 'this reincarnation of Wilkie Collins's woman in white?'

'Might do,' said Moser, still breathing heavily. 'Anything can have a meaning if you give it one. But everything is part of a pattern, whether you can see it or not.'

The next morning we continued our journey south. After an early start that took us quickly to Avignon it became oppressively hot again, the horizons all around lost in a shimmering, painful white haze, dancing before the eyes. Our rucksacks chafed our shoulders, sweat dripped in our eyes, feet, loins and throats were raw. I have memories only of pain and discomfort. It still wasn't the end of June, and there was very little traffic off the main roads. We stood in the roadside dust through the full heat of midday until eventually an old upright Renault stopped to pick us up, and drove us up into the hills. The car was a black and maroon leather-upholstered roadster, just post-war, I should think, and even under its coating of dust in splendid condition. Its driver seemed to have no independent existence, independent, that is, from his vehicle, to which he was the perfect accompaniment. He said he was going to Cannes, and agreed to take us all the way to Mandelieu so long as we didn't object to his travelling via the back roads, over the hills. He had, he said, a horror of main roads. We were delighted, longing for nothing better than the shade of a country drive.

Moser climbed in behind, laid his head on the high leather seat back, pushed his sunglasses away from his face and closed his eyes. I sat in the front and talked to our benefactor. He gave little away, one of those people who prefer to listen rather than to talk, and with the knack of imposing the preference.

Perhaps he just knew what I have since learned for myself, that young people like to hear themselves talk, and he was happy to have my prattle fill the silence of the stifling afternoon's drive. He said he had come from the Sancerre, but I record this simply because it was all I could remember about him afterwards, and the name stuck in my memory because it sounded mysterious, and I had no idea then where it was. Of the rest, I discovered later that I had been completely unobservant. Asked to describe him, there was not a feature I could recall, not a colour, a texture, a bulk or a plane. I could picture the car, the countryside, the quality of the day, but the man was a blank.

'Rich,' said Moser, improving on my ignorance as I pulled my floppy hat down over my nose, and we shouldered our rucksacks up the path to the Mandelieu campsite in the evening. 'Rich, forty, brown eyes, long white fingers, greying hair at the temples, an impeccable but slightly dated dresser – double-breasted summer jacket, cravat, sock suspenders, tweeds in the winter, I shouldn't wonder. Romantic type. Some poetry in him. Music too. An idealist. Also a spare pair of bloody sunglasses.'

'What?'

'I left them on the back seat, damn and blast, and I shall suffer for the rest of the summer.'

This was true. Moser had poor eyesight, and his sunglasses were a tinted pair of his normal thick lenses. Without them he'd be squinting with pain in the Mediterranean light.

'Too late now,' he said disconsolately.

'How did you know about the sock suspenders ?'

'Instinct. Today he wasn't wearing any socks at all.'

We found Fenner in a corner of the campsite by the river. He had four or five tents organized in a square, in the centre of which he stood cooking at a big trestle table. He greeted us like old friends, though he had never set eyes on Moser before, shouting to his wife as we all shook hands, and we dropped our gear among the pine needles.

'Moll. Vagabond's here, and his buddy Moser. We've been looking out for you since Wednesday.' He drew a pan off his gas range, wiped his hands on the towel which, worn as an apron, barely covered the swimming costume that was all he wore. 'We thought we'd put you in there,' he said, nodding towards one of the tents, a big green ridge-poled thing that formed one corner of the square. 'With the spares. If you hurry and shower we'll eat. *Saucisson sec*, *barbue* in cream, mushroom and olive sauce, green salad, camembert, peaches, coffee. Bellet. Appeal?' Here was a man after Moser's heart.

This was the beginning of an entire month of Fenner's lizarding. The campsite filled up to overflowing on 1 July, but in our well-squared-off corner we barely noticed. We swam in the river, lay in the sun, ate Fenner's evening meals – always a combination of the simple and raw with the complex and rich – and when we were not reading, we talked. Fenner was the first person I had met who could out-talk Moser (though there were to be many later on, as Moser withdrew into his silences) and their conversations raced ahead, generally late into the night. Moll hovered on the edge of these, contributing her devotion like a moth, darting in and out of the danger, while I suppose I may have said rather more than I now recall. In the memory the black nights were full of the sound of Moser and Fenner arguing, arguing, arguing. They couldn't even agree on what to call the subject about which they argued most. Moser said it was nature versus nurture, whether the gene is mightier than the scene. Fenner said that this was a mere sub-field, an offshoot of the more general topic of freedom versus necessity. Moser said Fenner shouldn't try to draw nature into metaphysics. Fenner said you couldn't keep it out. Sometimes the debates were very funny, occasionally they flared into anger. Moser, the natural scientist, was in those days a convinced Darwinian, an evolutionist to his fingertips. Fenner, a man who had broken out of the mould, was a determined anti-genes man. He believed in the will, the conquest of wants and wishes, achievement as learned behaviour.

'Environment,' he'd say. 'Environment. If you'd had a mother like mine, you'd understand. It's mothers that make worlds possible, not genes.'

Moser was not a passionate debater, but a subtle and patient one. I rarely saw him lose his temper. His favourite method was to wait for an opponent to state a contradiction. Then he would use that as a way to open the discussion in his direction. There were no contradictions in Fenner, however. He was an unread man, had, by his own admission, no formal education beyond the age of thirteen, which was his age when the Second World War broke out. But he was acute, sensitive and observant, and he reflected a lot on all that he had heard and seen. His method of argument was much like his physique, strong, supple, weathered by experience and exposure. He held what he'd have called Skinner's theory, if he'd known who Skinner was, ever read *Walden Two* or had behaviourism explained. It was an interpretation of mankind that he'd arrived at on his own. Infants were *tabulae rasae*, and the adults they eventually became were moulded wholly by social forces. Freedom lay in recognizing this fact, and exploiting it to your advantage. He might have been the inventor of consciousness-raising. Moser said his slogan ought to be 'Heaven is other people'.

Fenner was hard for us to argue with because he would allow no abstraction. To any statement he attributed a cause lodged in the experience of the speaker, and he could be ruthless in seeking it out. 'But *why* do you say that?' he would ask. Or: 'You say that because it suits you, not because it's true.' One evening, when Moser was trying to explain how the Darwinian principle of the survival of the fittest had been misinterpreted, and made to apply to human social and economic interaction (when in fact it had nothing to say about such things), Fenner suddenly said, 'You only say that because you are a Jew. A Jewish male. Circumcised. Bar mitzvahed. And you're frightened of pain and humiliation.'

This sort of no-holds-barred sparring was new to me, rather shocking and exciting, but even as he was saying it, I realized that it had never occurred to me that Moser was a Jew. The thought had never entered my head, and the question of religion had never arisen. Now that Fenner had said it, it seemed obvious, but its obviousness implied that it mattered, which surely it couldn't, and didn't. All these thoughts passed through my mind while Moser was answering.

'My father's a Catholic who has lost his faith, my mother an atheist in the Anglican manner. When I was at school the household was agnostic.' Denial of this sort, categorical as it was, never constituted refutation for Fenner.

'You see, that's my point,' he said instantly. 'The bricks and mortar may have been agnostic, laddie, but once a Catholic or a Jew – let alone both – always a Catholic or a Jew. Look at all those German Jewish Marxists and Italian Communist priests. It's the need for the security of a system. You're a Darwinian for the same reason Lenin was a Bolshevik, because your upbringing makes you need it. You can't live without it. Have you ever tried to kick the habit?'

Moser's science made little impression on this kind of all-in wrestling of the mind. He would explain about genetic potential, about the gene pool, about random distribution and mutation, multiple inheritance and significance tests, phenotypes and identical twins. It made no difference. Fenner was impervious.

'You only go on about distribution under the normal curve,' he said, after one of Moser's particularly brilliant expositions, 'because you're trained to believe those sorts of statistics meaningful. But if you'd been brought up to see that man is infinitely adaptable, you'd argue instead that the stats are conditional, and that any one of us, at any time, can choose his future, and thereby be free.'

'But what sort of freedom is this,' said Moser, 'that we must be trained to choose it? You can't choose to be free of biology or the laws of physics.'

'Up here I can,' said Fenner, tapping his bald, brown head.

This pattern of life went on until the end of our third week – we were to stay to the end of July – when the *Elvira Madigan* arrived back at the river harbour with her cargo of satisfied cruisers. This was a Friday, and Fenner's next clients were not due until Tuesday. He and Moll moved through the boat like locusts, clearing and cleaning, and then like bees, repairing, patching, stocking and tending. The next morning, at six o'clock, the four of us put to sea for a three-day cruise, the tents zipped and laced behind us. 'Not time enough to go far,' Fenner said, dipping his shoulder to lean into the wheel as we chugged out into the Mediterranean, 'but time enough for some quiet, and some sightseeing, and the best fresh fish in the world.' Moser said he'd man the jib, though where he'd learned this I had no idea – perhaps in the Lake District? – and he went forward and stretched himself out on the deck, awaiting orders. The sea was glassy flat, and without a breath of wind near the coast. Slowly, however, as we put first a hundred, then a thousand, then several thousand yards behind us, a breeze puffed along, the sails went up, the engine was cut, and we were absorbed into the unrivalled sounds – the creaks, hisses, moans and whistles – of a wooden sailing vessel ploughing through water.

Moser had his head face down over the prow, watching the water swish under the hull. The morning was deliciously fragrant and clear, no spray to speak of, only the emerald, turquoise, mild and blue clarity of the sea, eddying, glancing, drifting and stroking past us. You could see down into it for what seemed infinity, there being no point at which you had to say beyond there all is black, eternal night, and as he looked down, mesmerized by the water's movement and the dancing of the early light upon it, Moser had an overpowering sense of his mortality and his insignificance. There was a rhythm in his head that was the slap of the sea on the boat, that mingled and coupled with the mesmeric effect of the sea in his eyes, and that together linked him directly, so he felt, to the eternity of nature, and man's temporary place in it, as a species without special merit or importance. He was momentarily uplifted by this, as though transported in ecstasy, as a saint, after fasting, mortification and sleep deprivation, achieves visionary insight. And then he was exhausted by it, tired and depressed, bad-humoured and uncongenial.

The future is worse than the Ocean – there is nothing there. It will be what men and circumstances make it.

Moser appeared to have fallen asleep on the deck, and we woke him when the sun got up to prevent him burning. He said nothing of his experience at the time, explaining his groggy state by saying that he felt like someone who had just eaten an English Christmas dinner, so that naturally he had indigestion, heartburn, flatulence, and a bad temper. Later, when we were back in Oxford in the autumn, he told me the rest of what had happened. He said it was a turning point, a

23

definite, living experience, whose origins must lie, he thought, in some aspect of human biology not touched upon before. Experience of this sort had its roots, he believed, in the chemistry of the nervous system, activated by a trigger, probably also chemical, whose workings are obscure to us. It is the heart of human experience, our ultimate mystery, both the nature and sensation of passion. And the scientific explanation of it is the key to the universe. I now realize that I did not then fully understand what he meant, but I think his approach to his work changed thereafter.

Something else happened while we were on the *Elvira Madigan*. The next day, or perhaps the one after – we were being lazy, fishing and swimming, and the days ran into each other – we put in to the harbour at Cannes. This was tourism, a sight Fenner said not to be missed. We were not planning to moor the boat: the idea was just to take a look. We had gone in to the inner harbour, holy of holies for the solemn religion of money and visible consumption, and were put-putting past the prows of about three-billion-pounds worth of floating gin palace when Moser, who was sitting on the port gunwale by the cockpit, suddenly leapt to his feet and ran down the deck to the prow, pointing, jumping over a heap of ropes, and shouting. 'There she is, there she is. It's her. It's her.' I knew who he meant instantly, and ran forward to join him. 'Over there, on the quay. You see, you see. In white trousers and a sort of yellow shirt. Look.' He shoved me in front of him, pointing over my shoulder from behind. 'There. You see? There.' The inner harbour at Cannes is also the street, the heart of the town. It was mid morning in the height of the season. All I could see was a dense crowd of milling people, at least half of them wearing white trousers. It was impossible. The girl or woman from the Lyon amphitheatre seemed to be for Moser's eyes alone. 'You must put me ashore,' he said suddenly, running back to Fenner at the wheel, but Fenner laughed, said something I couldn't hear, and pointed ahead to the end of the quay. I guessed he was saying there was no way ashore till we got to there, and nothing more he could do to help. Moser came back to me in the prow, looked once at Fenner over his shoulder, then all of a sudden climbed over the wire and jumped. It seemed a vast chasm, but I don't suppose it was really more than about five feet to the prow of an enormous playboy cruiser we happened at that moment to be passing. Moser clung to its prow fairing like an acrobat, shinned over, ran straight through a party of six or so surprised-looking aperitif drinkers who were sitting under the awning to be looked at, burst past a flunkey in white jacket and pressed sky-blue trousers, knocking, in the distorting mirror of my memory, a silver tray from his hand to the water (or was it the next-door yacht, for this is terraced millionaire accommodation?), sprang across the gangplank at the stern, and disappeared into the thickest part of the crowd.

There was some confusion in the wake of this exploit. Fenner stood at the wheel of his yacht, his head thrown back, laughing a loud barking laugh, while Moll traded insults with the millionaires who had had their awning pre-prandials disturbed. Apparently they were not used to hooligans. Moll wanted to know why the hell they had come to Cannes, then. Various portholes and hatches on adjacent yachts opened at this, and heads and shoulders appeared to see what all the commotion was about. Some one of these late arrivals sent Fenner into further peals of laughter while he pointed at something I couldn't see, at which Moll began a new dialogue with another contender. There was, it seemed, solidarity among millionaires on the issues of piracy and illegal boarding parties.

Meanwhile, on shore, Moser's progress through the crowd, initially testified to by a straggling line of tussling, struggling people marking his attempts to force a way through the ruck, rapidly became impossible to follow. On *Elvira Madigan*'s deck we were too low down to see, and the crowd swallowed him. In probably not more than thirty seconds we had passed the moorings where greatest offence had been taken, and in thirty more we had ceased even to be a subject of immediate controversy. Fenner turned the prow on to the public quay, set the engine to idle, and after a brief wait nosed in sufficiently for Moser to jump back on board. He was disgruntled and red in the face, his hair more wiry than ever, as though it had grown more obdurate, and he oozed disappointment, despite an attempt at a carefree smile.

'Missed her,' he said, as Fenner swung the boat round and lined up the rows of marker buoys that would return us to the sea. 'Lost her in the crowd.' He sat down on the cabin roof.

'Somebody important?' asked Fenner.

'Was it really her?' I asked simultaneously.

'Could be,' Moser said.

Was the girl's importance to Moser at that time really ambiguous? I had been struck by her myself, of course, as who wouldn't have been? Her appearance in the theatrical setting of an historic monument on a hot, still, silent summer's night had the kind of drama I then associated with John Fowles. Indeed, the romance and mystery made her seem more like an apparition, fictional rather than real. There is no one, I imagine, who has not, at least once, thought him or herself close to touching the heart of another, and being touched to the heart in return, and yet has, for reasons of inexperience, shyness or misfortune, failed to take the necessary first step. Later we reflect on the difference this encounter might have made, of a life lived differently, of other places and experiences, of sudden wealth perhaps, or vast areas of emotion, suspected but never prospected, suddenly opened up, traversed and settled. Everyone I dare say carries a face, a moment, through life, having failed to speak, or been deprived of the chance, that represents the world they have lost, from timidity or adversity, and that lingers on into old age as the last and eventually only reminder of the part played in life by chance.

Moser was unique and original, but he shared this with the rest of us.

Then there was the extraordinary fact of his seeing the young woman twice. To have seen her, as if she were an actress, in Lyon, and then almost four weeks later, hundreds of miles away, to have glimpsed her again, this time in a crowd on the waterfront at Cannes, seemed a coincidence of a very high order.

'Are you sure it was her?'

'Sure, no. But I'm confident it was.'

'Extraordinary coincidence.'

'There are more remarkable chances in nature,' he said. 'But they may not all be chance. We simply have to learn how to look at them.'

Perhaps it was then that I began to see what was to become the most salient of Moser's intellectual characteristics, for me at any rate. And the one that our friendship was witness to over the following twenty years. That Moser was incapable of conceiving of life without pattern. He was utterly opposed to ideology, all the cant and mysticism of politics, but he sympathized with people, like Alice, who got trapped into theories of history, or social conflict, or whatever, because he thought they were natural allies who had merely taken the wrong turning, and couldn't, infuriatingly, be brought back. His idea of pattern was against system because he knew that there was no system in nature. 'Systems are human inventions,' he would say. 'Nature is unsystematic. It abounds in pattern, and patterns have outcomes, but there are no intentions, and nothing is systematically ordered. There is no controlling hand. Nature simply is.' This young woman of the arena and the quay he did not think *intended* for him. But he saw that she was part of his pattern, and he was alive to its possible regularities. This is another reason why he is dead, and why I am now alone in my room to mourn him.

I write this because I had another visitor this evening. At around the point where Moser appeared to fall asleep on the deck and we, Fenner, Moll and I were wondering when to wake him, Benjamin Gould dropped in. He had been to Sunday evening high table, which is a guest night with us during term, and so he was dressed in black tie. With his long, drooping, sallow face, deep-set eyes beneath heavy eyebrows, and sad, almost lugubrious manner, he looked a cross between a basset hound and an Italian concert pianist. Ben is a history fellow and, in his own way, may have been fond of Moser. His way, however, is riddled with contradictions because Ben is an insatiable gossip, and can spare no one, friend or foe alike, when there is a titbit of a story to pass on. Like many historians he is fascinated by detail, and takes an historian's delight in knowing the most intimate details of others' lives. And because he is an open-minded sort of person there is no outrage, no grotesquery, no immorality, excess or deviance in which he is not prepared to believe, or at least offer credentials to for a while. When he is being an historian, no doubt he sifts the evidence and discounts the unreasonable. When he is being a gossip he rejects nothing. If I told him the Master was up on a rape charge he'd repeat the story, relish doing so indeed. Everything is always passed on by Ben, and always with the same enthusiastic air of the privileged informant. It has made him the main conduit for college communication: sometimes an air lane; sometimes a sewer. For this reason I was surprised, not that he should come nosing around, but that it should have taken him so long to do so. Had he looked in earlier he might have collected some scraps for high table.

He raised his eyes when he came in, seeing me writing at my desk, but I covered the pages over, and pretended not to notice his gesture of inquiry.

. . . remember that I am in England, where of all the dull days Sunday is the dullest.

I guided him to the sofa at the other end of the room, the end from which you can see the meadows in the daytime.

'I am disturbing you,' he said, subsiding among the cushions, and agreeing with the pinch of thumb and forefinger to accept a small scotch. 'Herzen still?'

'Yes,' I replied. 'And no. Herzen is finished, but there are things round the edges. You know the sort of thing . . .'

'We missed you at dinner.' I didn't reply. 'Look –' he seemed to me suddenly older and heavier than I remembered him. Perhaps Moser's dying has aged us all. Or perhaps it was the dinner jacket. Everyone looks older in evening dress. 'Maurice and Felix and I wanted to say to you how sorry we are about poor old Moser. Very sorry.' He paused. 'The whole college is in mourning.'

He didn't seem to mean it much. Ben came, years ago, from Kenya – though he used to like to pretend to being a South African, in exile from apartheid. Such exile carried status in some circles in the 70s and 80s – and his accent is still that flat, white African one that kills emotion in the mouth, deadening conversation with menace. He said 'very sorry' as I imagine a Soweto policeman might have said it to a woman whose son he has just shot dead in the street. I had this image in my head, put there by his accent, and displacing Moser, so that I couldn't reply. He carried on anyway, perhaps not noticing.

'We hear it was suicide. A terrible thing.' These were questions, and he looked to me for answers, but I gave none. I wanted to speak, as I did this morning when the Master came, just a few conventional observations, but the hurt of wanting to was in my throat, and I remained silent. 'I talked to him only yesterday,' Ben went on. 'Or perhaps Friday. And he seemed composed enough, still rattling on about his survey results and his mutants. A terrible thing.'

Everybody was agreed, then. It was a *terrible* thing. Moser's taking leave of us this Sunday morning was high-table tested and agreed, a terrible thing. Perhaps this is why it is hurting so much. After all, you can count on Ben to have the word for it, know what's right to say. Anywhere else he'd be the public orator. He has a fund of sayings suitable for every occasion. Witty high table: 'I used to fear I was schizophrenic, but now I'm in two minds about it.' Drawing-room amusing: 'We are all agreed, Lady Olga, that the weather is perfect. Now we must agree on what it is perfect for.' Seminar argumentative: 'Irrespective of content, you'll agree I'm sure that Dr Trix-mire's delivery was as immaculate as the conception that preceded it.' Disappointment in defeat: 'You are a God to me Moser. I worship you, pray to you, have faith in you. Now you fail me. That is true deity.' Guidebook knowing: 'In Oxford all the big talk is small talk, all the small talk big talk.' Sunday-paper review-page whimsical: 'This partisan book is on a highly contentious subject, so you must allow me to get my retaliation in first.' He deals out these familiar sayings like a casino banker with a worn pack. You know that, when it comes, you'll have seen the card before, but you have no means of knowing in advance which card it will be. Now it is a terrible thing Moser being dead. How terrible? Wait for it.

'A death is like an opening into eternity,' he said, eyeing me gravely over his whisky. 'Looking through it we can see everything, but say nothing.'

So that was it. The Queen of Diamonds. If Felix were here he'd trump it.

I am bitter with myself now for feeling so acerbic at the time. Moser did mean something to Ben. Death is so intimate. We cling to our bereavement, waiting for the others to go away so that we can be alone with it. It's hard to think what Moser could have meant to Ben Gould, however. After all, they fought over just about everything. Gould wanted more classics students, Moser more scientists; Moser was for statistics for all, Gould against 'number crunching'; Gould for keeping women out, Moser for admission: any college topic you named they were on opposite sides. And Ben is a college politics man, a resourceful and tireless opponent who is remorseless in either assembling majorities for his views, or manipulating agendas until he is ready. Moser was not skilled at these things. He had the intellectual's irritating habit of winning the argument but losing the vote. This was especially true of college appointments. We have recently elected several new fellows, all without Moser's support. His vote always went to candidates of outstanding intellectual merit and little else. Ben isn't much impressed by arguments about academic excellence. Certainly appointments should go, other things being equal, to brainy people, but there were other considerations: one had to place one's pupils, protect one's subject, purchase favours elsewhere, honour debts. Then there was high-table compatibility. Ben understands these things.

'Did he leave any explanation?' Ben asked. 'Any thoughts

about why he was doing it? Any last wishes, even?' I shook my head.

'There was an envelope,' I said. 'But it was addressed to Vita.'

This seemed to shake him, and he gave one of his disbelieving looks before draining his whisky. Poor old Moser, he was saying inside. A loser to the end. Living in another world really. Ah well. He put down his glass and got to his feet, trod heavily to the door. He looked speculatively across the surface of my desk, but there were no hints, no signs, no give-aways in evidence, and in regret he let it pass.

'Maurice and Felix and I,' he said, 'we would like to be associated with whatever formalities there are to be. A service of remembrance, the interment, whatever. We would like to be kept informed.'

'I think the Master . . .' My voice tailed away as Ben nodded.

'Felix was suggesting a memorial at dinner. Perhaps a prize. But my view is that it's early days yet.' He said goodnight as he left.

A prize.

'First prize for you.' The young woman said this with a curling smile that illuminated her entire face, otherwise concealed in the interior. She had one long brown arm hanging from the car window, which was rolled right down. It was a night in early August, that same sticky, unpredictable summer of our journey to Fenner in the south. Now we were on our way home and had got as far as Paris, planning to catch the train to England the next morning. We were almost out of funds, that state late in a student continental holiday when walking the streets is the only diversion left. We were strolling past the Musée de Cluny on the Boulevard St Michel after dinner. This had gone particularly well because Moser had found a tiny restaurant in the Rue Monsieur le Prince which specialized in *la nouvelle cuisine* (very *nouvelle* in those days) and we had shared a dish of *Lièvre à la royale du sénateur Couteaux*, a creation of such succulence and strength that Moser labelled it Humean, and was still talking about it and human reason together when the car, the same black and maroon roadster in which we had ridden from Avignon to Mandelieu, slowed to a crawl at the kerbside, and that arm and that smile and that voice came out to us through its open window. Inside, I glimpsed long white fingers at the steering wheel.

'You lost these, I think.' The arm held out a pair of sunglasses, and the smile was played at, and only at, Moser. I felt myself propelled into the background, a shadow in a theatre, a mere spectator. Moser crossed the few yards of pavement to the car, which had stopped, and crouched beside it. Over his head I could see that it was the girl, the woman, the same as at Lyon, perhaps at Cannes. Now she was in this familiar vehicle, and she had Moser's sunglasses, was returning them, was talking to him. Then she gave him something else, laughed aloud at something he said, and withdrew her arm as the car slid away down the kerb, pulled into the stream of traffic, and disappeared towards the river. Had I seen him hold her hand briefly as the car moved away? Had she squeezed his fingers as he let go?

I was struck dumb by this, it seemed to me, impossible coincidence of events and people. I must have looked a preposterous sight with my mouth agape in astonishment, gasps coming out of it since words would not. Moser appeared to be taking it all in his stride, however. The young woman, the momentary meeting, the sunglasses, the extra whatever it was that she had passed to him: they had all confirmed something, and he laughed at my dumb disbelief.

'Who was driving?' I asked eventually, irrelevantly.

'The same chap. He's her uncle. Wears sock suspenders. Now confirmed.'

'Brilliant.'

Moser took off his ordinary everyday glasses and put the sun ones on in their place. In the summer night light they made him look like a gangster, or a film star, or one of those black American jazz musicians who may or may not be blind. Someone out of the ordinary, to make the heart beat faster.

'That's better,' he said, and we started walking again. I asked him what else she had given him.

'This,' he said, holding up a spectacles case. It was made of leather, and had a cord for hanging round the neck or the wrist. 'She said it might help me not to lose sight of things in future.'

'Really?'

'No, I made that up. She said it would make losing them harder.'

He opened the slim case. Inside was a card that said: Vita Margolis, 7 Ennismore Gardens, Knightsbridge. There was also a telephone number that had been added to the printed card in small, neat handwriting.

2

Monday

'You can no more bridle passions with logic than you can justify them in the law courts. Passions are facts and not dogmas.'

Alice rang from Singapore during the night. I had been in bed probably an hour, but unsleeping. Someone at Scorpion – Rawlinson, I suppose – had faxed her about Moser and she wanted to know if I was all right. She said they had just got in from Bahrain and were to have a day or so's rest before their meeting on Wednesday.

'And recreation?'

She wouldn't answer that, and we had one of our telephone silences. International calls are far better for this than local ones. There is no crackle or buzz of interference, no distant nattering on barely crossed lines, just the great black silence of space waiting for voices to fill it. It was quite a long wait, but it's the bank that pays. Eventually she returned to Moser, so I explained what I knew, how I supposed the Master would handle things once the inquest was over, that there was to be an autopsy first. I told her there was a letter addressed to Vita and she said, 'How macabre.' I suppose it is odd, but I wouldn't have called it macabre. I don't suppose Alice would either if she thought about it, but 'macabre' is one of her expressions, like 'bizarre' and 'bit of a nightmare' and 'sherbert', which is what she calls things she likes.

'Is this going to change Florence?' she asked. Before she left last Thursday we agreed to meet in Florence, next Sunday, she on her way back to London, me fleeing the end of term. It's a sort of anniversary, twelve years since we married, though not the actual day, and the idea was that we should try to talk, to start again. Florence for sentimental reasons, perhaps even superstitious ones, because it's one of the places we'd been happy in together once before. Now I don't know if I'll go. Moser . . .

'It might be good for you to get away from it,' she said.

'I'll only bring it with me.'

'But even the change of air will help.'

'Florence in December?'

There are no paragraphs in telephone conversations. It is one of the ways technology destroys literacy, and literacy distorts reality.

'What was that?'

'Nothing, I was thinking about something else . . .'

'Well, you'll let me know, won't you? I have tickets to arrange.'

'Oh, well, we wouldn't want to let a little thing like Moser's dying stand in the way of the Scorpion Merchant Bank's arrangements, would we? After all . . .'

'Please don't, Philip . . .'

Woe to him who seeks to learn good manners from Englishwomen, or their husbands.

Afterwards I was ashamed of the sarcasm. Why couldn't I control it with her? Did she invite it? I crawled back into bed, trying to place her again, as so often before, in my world. Alicia Beverley Crighton, temporarily of Raffles, comes from the invisible English upper middle class, from the sort of family that is never seen because it keeps to itself, thriving on privacy. Her father owns a string of motel-like hotels which he bought

36

with an inheritance, and which generate an annual income that for all I know is closer to seven rather than six figures. One of the motels is in the Bahamas, which is where the company holds its annual shareholders' meeting. The shareholders are all members of the family.

Alicia's mother, who was a Beverley before she married, comes from Border farming stock, from people who ran sheep where the pastures of northern England and southern Scotland come together. They had borne the title Sassenach for so long that it felt to them like praise. When she was feeling a bit aggressive Alicia's mother would call herself a Borderer, and claim that her mother had had one foot in each country as she gave birth to her. The sort of quasi-meaningful image that Salman Rushdie might do something with. 'There is cultural division born into me,' she would say. 'Schizophrenic citizenship. And I have passed it on to my daughters.' Sometimes she would pretend support for Scottish nationalism on the grounds that Scottish independence would entitle her to two passports, and two passports were better than one. I think this was said mainly to annoy her husband. All the Beverleys were, I imagine, really pragmatists.

Crightons, on the other hand, didn't fit into categories quite so easily. They had been nineteenth-century Nonconformist industrialists when their politics were radical liberal, free trade and home rule. Their philanthropy had been for progressive schools, orphanages, conscientious objection, famine relief in China. You did not find Crightons in West End clubs, or the pages of *Vogue* or the *Tatler*. They had never aspired to the peerage, never stood in line for knighthoods or Orders of Empire, and avoided the possibility of even temporary fame by steering clear of the entertainment, communications and public relations industries. They lived well, privately, and without fuss. There was a biggish country house in Yorkshire, a dull but comfortable farm on the Essex/Suffolk border, a spacious, dusty flat in a redbrick Betjeman building off Victoria Street. I know, for I have stayed in them all. Like Moser, I married well.

For girls born into this kind of financial class Oxford used to function – perhaps still does – as the best finishing school in Europe. For Crighton girls – there were three of them – who had been brought up at the strong-minded end of things, it meant PPE and thoughts of a serious career. Alicia was definitely of this sort. She specialized academically in economics, but she read for her improvement (Crightons were much given to 'improvement') in those areas of the modern world where her conscience was touched. She was rather too young – only eight in 1967 – to be of the Vietnam generation, and her interests went, like those of many of her contemporaries, into the politics of economic dependence in Latin America and Africa. Here they wolfed a course of ill-prepared Marxism early in the academic meal, and suffered the effects of intellectual indigestion thereafter. There is something peculiarly addictive about nineteenth-century social philosophy: even those who manage to kick the habit of one invariably get hooked on another. Moser said it had to do with predispositions, and that the degree of conviction – whether lukewarm, like Ben's Spencerian social Darwinism, or impervious to argument, like Fenner's mixture of Nietzsche and Samuel Smiles – was proportional to the will's resistance to genetic effects. He said once, very gently, that Alicia would make an interesting case study. Anyway, such undergraduate characters as Alicia find plenty of endorsement for what they already want to believe in the writings of Baran and Sweezey, in the theories of periphery and centre, post-colonialism and the power of finance capital. Such stuff is readily understood by intelligent but inexperienced minds because theory brings order to what are otherwise disorderly and unconnected events of the day. Everything has a place, and can be tidied away.

In her second year at Oxford Alicia moved out of college into a flat on the fourth floor of a house in Walton Street. She shortened her Christian name to Alice and started going out with a draughtsman from the ASTMS who was studying for a diploma on a trade union scholarship at Ruskin College. She met this man, Peter Mackleby, known as Mac, so she told me, during a demonstration in St Aldate's organized to prevent a prominent politician from making a speech to the local Conservative Association. Thrown together in the crush of the crowd, they went afterwards for a drink together at the Bear. Mac introduced her to regular meetings of a group that called itself the Tricontinental Revolutionary Movement, where there were earnest discussions of revolutionary praxis in Central America, Mozambique and Thailand; where Alice met young dons and graduate students from St Anthony's and Nuffield; and where famous intellectuals came occasionally from other countries to present and explain their ideas: Nicos Poulantzas on concrete structures in the class system; Marcuse on the special character of alienation under late capitalism; Althusser on the logic of Marxian textual exegesis. This was just before Marcuse died, Poulantzas committed suicide, and Althusser killed his wife. Such coincidences may consign us to one generation rather than another without our being aware of it at the time.

None of this seemed either strange or extreme to Alice. Nor did it to me, in the way that she described it. She had been raised by a family of wealthy free thinkers in a home where intellectual independence was encouraged. The fact of their wealth, in the context of Alice's beliefs, was strictly irrelevant. What counted was honesty of thought and a serious commitment to the improvement of mankind, especially those substantial parts of it less privileged or advantaged than the rest. Paradoxically perhaps, certainly little understood, the space that separates radical philanthropy from revolutionary extremism is rather small, generally no more than a generation.

As far as I know, Alice's parents were not troubled by her conversion from agnosticism to fervour. It was the sort of thing one had to expect would happen at that stage, and they claimed to find Mac a nice enough chap. 'A rough-cut ruby,' Mrs Crighton called him. 'A beautiful red.' In any event, Mac did not long survive his acceptance. His role was transitional. I think of him only because when Alice came to me she was no longer a virgin. I find myself now, sixteen or so years later, sandwiched between two acts of transparently vacuous copulation, like a fly trapped in the double glazing, waiting for death and for dessication.

Perhaps this is putting it too strongly. I am not the one to tell. I don't think you ever can, when it is happening to you, even if there have been confessions, the taking of guilt. And there have been none in my case, our case. Alice travels with a man called Gradle, a little older than me, forty-five perhaps, who is on Scorpion's business development side. They make an investment analysis team, Alice the economist and policy-maker, Gradle the industrial and business analyst. Together they assess projects in what Gradle calls the developing world, Alice calls the Third World, and I call poor countries. Bangkok, Seoul, Bogota, Ibadan, La Paz, Dacca, Mombasa: she rings me out of the distance as they arc backwards and forwards from project to project, here today, back on Saturday, 'a papaya for you specially for breakfast', duty-free perfume, yesterday's edition of the *Straits Times*, the scent in the background of Gradle. When the deals are too big even for Scorpion, the banks get together. Then the circuit is Frankfurt, Bahrain, Singapore, Manila, and the satellites bounce and rebound acronyms: IMF, ADB, SDRs, IBRD. Alice is away about ten days out of every thirty, a third of our lives, and even when she's here it's mainly head office, the Barbican flat, Oxford only at weekends.

It wasn't, is it ever?, like this at the beginning. Alice walked into my study, my life, one afternoon in the middle of October sixteen years ago. She was going, having just dropped Mac, through an intense feminist phase, rejecting contemporary opinion, contemplating street theatre, a crew cut. She had taken up a then fashionable brand of Oxbridge rejection, for it was considered chic in some circles to rent damp and unappealing lodgings off the Cowley Road, to live in a mess of radical broadsheets, unwashed cups and scratched records, and to affect contempt for the university and an inability to complete the chosen degree. 'Worthless when you had it anyway.' Affectation easily grew from imitation to truth, and the best years of many lives crept past in ugliness, unthought opinions, the waste of atrophying talent.

She came to my study because her tutor thought she should take some extra tutorials in philosophy before Schools, and she'd heard on whatever grapevine she then hung that I was a possible candidate for her patronage. I readily agreed. She was very beautiful. I can't now remember what philosophy we did together. As I say, I found her very beautiful, and much of each of the first few hours she spent in my study went, while she read her essays in that crisp, clever voice, into reflecting on her beauty and contemplating its details. She had an almost perfectly oval face, almond-shaped, with clear, rather hard, brown eyes – I would say hazel but it implies a kind of softness, whereas Alice's were flinty – and small ears. Her complexion, pink in the cheeks, white in the throat, gave off that fresh girlish innocence that foreigners call typically English, but which is actually pretty rare. There are wild roses in it, and a summer's breeze on the South Downs, and nursery rhymes – Miss Muffet, Jill on the hill, I do like a little bit of butter with my bread. Moser thought love was a sensation induced by some powerful reminder of childhood, something adored and forgotten, reactivated by the loved one. He said this was why most people thought their loves beautiful even though the vast majority, by any commonly agreed standards of beauty, clearly were not. Alice was certainly beautiful to me, but not to me alone. She was quite tall, with long legs, and could wear more or less anything: short skirts, a caftan, culottes, battered faded jeans.

I was intrigued by her, a little intimidated too, so that although I wanted to invite her out I didn't know how to set about asking, and hovered for weeks on the edge of my own indecisiveness. Eventually I solved the problem by shifting the tutorial to the late afternoon, suggesting that we continue the topic over a pint at the Lamb and Flag, and graduating from there to a Jericho cinema and a Dildunia curry afterwards. Each succeeding station of this processional was a success. Intrigue and intimidation softened over evening into love.

Through the fog of recollection of the past sixteen years I remember her first kisses as I imagine a dying Catholic remembers Confirmation. Bliss is not too strong a word. I had had adventures before, liked to think of myself as pretty jaded, as the young like to do, at twenty-three or -four. But Alice was an experience altogether fresh. After our first kiss she looked at me with a dramatically inquisitive eye, her brow furrowed as if troubled or uncertain. And then she kissed me again, very deliberately, exactly the same as before, as though testing for the truth of something. Somehow this implied assent. I was heartily grateful for it. It was a night in November, wet and strewn with fallen leaves, and with a high wind in the trees. Hardly a time for walking. But we paced for hours through the semi-suburbias of Oxford, circling from north to east until she was back at the flat, and we parted for what was left of the night.

When two people fall in love they see it, or rather experience it, as a passage from a solitary circumscribed world into a world infinitely enlarged through merger with the other. The family suddenly expands, a new circle of friends is acquired. This is one reason why love is so refreshing when it is new. All the horizons expand, and there is originality again. Alice brought with her a complete universe, a universe of relatives and friends, houses and places, opportunities. One sister, older, married to a barrister, living in a London town house, doing up a barn in Normandy, children called Harriet and Emma, friends all interesting on the *Sunday Times* or 'in designing'. Another sister, younger, musical, living mainly in the Victoria flat with a housekeeper and studying the violin six hours a day, back and forth to Hampstead for lessons, preparing for a competition in Venice, and after that the Curtis Institute. Parents thoughtful and intelligent, novels by Iris Murdoch, David Lodge and Gore Vidal, war studies by John Keegan, paperbacks on Euro-communism, prison reform, the abolition of whaling, copies of *Private Eye*, big houses and cars, but unaffected, not posh in that agonisingly stupid English way, and without the vulgarity of Belgravia and Sloane Square. Not like parents at all really. Despite the wealth, I felt at home.

The same, it must be said, was true of the impact of Alice's ideas. Outside of the purely mechanical side of philosophy – logic, the meaning of meaning, materialism and dualism in the debate about consciousness, games philosophers play – she was a firebrand, not just in the day-by-day sense of siding with the PLO, or thinking well of China, or opposing American interests wherever – because to tell the truth I don't think current affairs ever interested Alice all that much, and she rarely, before going to the bank, read ephemera at all – but in the far more steadfast and intellectual sense of holding a world theoretical explanation of current conditions. This she had thought through, both by herself and in the company of her friends from the TRM, and it had a rock-like substance to it.

This didn't trouble me. It was not what first, or even mainly, attracted me to her, and in any event I was accustomed to the company of people like that. When we met I had been working for two years on a doctoral dissertation about nineteenth-century anarchists. I had just won a junior research fellowship, which gave me a further year in which to finish the study, and I had reached the point where the pattern of anarchist ideas had established itself for me, and I was beginning to find it easier to write. When Alice walked into my room looking for a tutor, her head full of theories of repression and domination, the pile of paper that was to become my first book was thickening on my desk, and I had already been living for two years among ideas about and arguments for total social transformation. When you have come to know Nechaev well you are not much frightened of Alice Crighton. When you spend so long reading Kropotkin, P.-J. Proudhon and Bakunin, the company of revolutionaries comes to seem normal. If Alice Crighton wanted to overthrow capitalism, well, after all, didn't almost everybody? Graduate social scientists, at least in those days, used to chat about such things much as I imagine children talk about the hit parade, or retired clubmen discuss batting averages. It was part of daily life, not something to be taken seriously. For all the fire in her conversation Alice surely thought so too, even then.

One of the things I now recall most clearly is that she was the perfect sounding-board for my thesis, since there is no one the convinced Marxist likes less than an anarchist, and she could debate against my accounts of their views with a welcome ferocity, demolishing and ridiculing simultaneously.

It was precisely here, in the context of a discussion on whether a proletarian revolution led inevitably to tyranny, that we started going to bed together. This may seem, on reflection, inauspicious. At the time it was not so. Alice was a wonderful lover, and I was wonderfully in love. She brought to the physical plane of our affairs the same tough mind and tender sentiment that she gave to social analysis and philosophy. It is an unusual and highly erotic combination, and it has kept me enthralled in the years since.

It did not solve our disagreements, however. Moser and philosophy together had taught me to have at least a partially empirical mind, and Marxists despise empiricism because of its emphasis on facts. The application of correct historical reasoning is far too important to be impeded by factual evidence, or to be allowed into the hands of fact collectors. At first, and for some years, this stood as a joke between us, something to bat backwards and forwards in play. But as time passed it hardened from soft plaything to solid impediment, and since I wasn't an anarchist, but merely a student of their ideas, I let the issue drop. The surface and substance of Alice's political convictions then became for me a field of social observation, and I ceased trying to argue with her.

This was surely a mistake. Anyway, it happened only slowly, and total withdrawal lay some way off. Meanwhile, we were busily preoccupied with our work. Alice took a good degree – missing a first because of a poor politics paper – and got a job as a research assistant at the Institute. I managed to win election to a fellowship here at the Court, where Moser had preceded me by a year, and after making the adjustment to teaching fourteen or fifteen hours a week I got back to my thesis and finished it.

It was during this time that I first came across Herzen, and began to fall under his spell. His name cropped up several times in connection with Bakunin – whom he knew, and helped on a number of occasions. He was an incredibly generous man – and I had read E.H. Carr's book *The Romantic Exiles* because it had a chapter on Bakunin which I needed to have read. When I got hold of it I found it all rather amusing, although I read it without thinking about it much. It was enjoyable as a novel may be enjoyable. There were no fresh ideas in it. Carr's view seemed to be that Herzen didn't have any ideas. Alice thought Carr among the best of the (then) living historians – she had read him on the Russian revolution – and applauded my reading him – albeit on a nineteenth-century topic – as though by doing so I had raised what she called my MQ (morality quotient – broadly speaking, morality increases with class consciousness; it follows that a wholly working-class consciousness is incapable of immoral acts, etc.). It was in this state of unpreparedness that I then came across a second-hand copy of Duff's 1923 translation of Herzen's *Childhood, Youth and Exile*, the opening salvo of what was to grow into his monumental work of autobiography, *My Past and Thoughts*. I read this book in a state of very great excitement. It seemed to me to be not just a masterpiece of literature, but a remarkable social document that had lost none of its force or point in the one hundred and thirty years since it was written. Somehow, as a writer, Herzen transcended the century that lay ahead of him, and seemed to have lived not for himself, but for all of us, and to have done so quite naturally and unselfconsciously. When he wrote down what he did and thought, he enabled us to share in and to profit from his experience, and not just to comprehend it.

I realize now, today, in my darkened rooms, the curtains drawn against the quad's many eyes (though my mother would

46

have drawn them for Moser) and the night far, far advanced in Singapore, that living with Alice and Herzen simultaneously could never have been easy. Herzen is a warm and vibrant figure, but he has a cold eye to match the warm heart. He sees as a sceptic sees, doubting. He gives money to an indigent Russian seaman so that he may reach and join his ship in Portsmouth. The man returns the next day, still slightly drunk, the ship missed, the money gone. Herzen expected it, lectures the man, but still gives him more money. And so on. Herzen's scepticism and his compassion were attitudes that he acquired amid the torture and fire of personal tragedy and political failure, not once but many times over. This is why his humanism and his charity are blessed with such peculiar force. You cannot love Herzen and hypocrisy at once. Rationality tells me that I cannot love Herzen and Alice together either.

But rationality plays no part in love. It is the region of behaviour dominated by inheritance, without the sway of will. Moser thought that this was why, in primitive economies with elaborate cultures, love was allowed no part in marriage. The will was brought to bear, partners selected by assessment and bargaining, deals struck. The survival of the tribe and its cultural pattern took precedence over other considerations, mere feelings or passions. The irony is that the apparent chance of human affections is more efficient at ensuring social adaptation than any alternative method involving intervention or compulsion, and the Western world's attachment to the chemistry of love – what we then thought a genetic response – as the basis for organizing procreation has made it more rather than less likely to survive. The fittest, Moser was fond of saying, survive because they are more closely in harmony with necessity, not because they (think they) know best how to resist it.

'Perhaps I would have done best to resist Alice from the

beginning,' I said to him once, when we were on one of our walks. 'She is just evidence of my weaknesses and inadequacies.' He gave one of his deep-eyed smiles.

'From the point of view of the gene pool,' he said, 'your weaknesses and inadequacies are potentially beneficial.'

'The gene pool has no point of view. It is devoid of morals, convictions or intentions.'

'Oh quite so,' he said. 'And that way power lies.'

I was about to slide into cliché, and write that it is easy to be wise about Alice after the event. But what event would this have been? Even reading *Childhood, Youth and Exile*, tumultuous as it was, did not constitute a decisive event. No, there was no event, only a process, a process that has gone on for sixteen years, fitting us both into habits of expectation, desire, need and dependence, that even when denied by neglect and breach still grind away at the millions of points where we touch, rubbing, chafing, scuffing and grazing, turning us raw. There were doubtless moments – her decision to join Scorpion, for instance, or the business with *Vom Anderen Ufer*, or our visit to Nice to see Herzen's tomb – but these moments were not events in the sense of happenings that had a core of logic, they were not facts in the way that affection, love and passion are facts. And it is facts that cannot be changed. These were happenings that varied, like all human happenings, according to the point of view of the participant or observer, so that what was true in them varied from one to another, and posed perhaps insuperable problems of interpretation. It is the dilemma of all biography. Even if the participants are agreed on some sequence of events, they may each have made something different of them, yet the biographer has to take a stand somewhere if there is to be any narrative to a life at all. Alice does not accept this. She lives, or so she says, and I think it's true, according to her principle that facts are insubstantial compared with theory. There is no point in worrying about the past. It is over, and there is nothing that can be done about it. And in any case, everything (culture, ideology, patterns of belief and affection, everything) flows from the level of material development achieved. Nothing survives the city.

I find these ideas deeply disturbing. But I love her. And my love continues, indeed intensifies, despite everything that she and I have done to it, maltreatment and degradation together. After her phone call, on into the darkest point of the night, despite the sourness of our conversation and our silences, despite that other great fact of Moser's lifelessness, I lay awake in my bed, tormented with desire for her, imagining her love, her legs, her climactic embrace. And I imagined her too with Gradle, at breakfast in his lightweight tropical suit, jaunty with his thin pointed fingers, his glasses hanging from a strap at his neck, man of the world, seasoned traveller. 'Tell me, Gradle, is business class a class in itself, or a class for itself?' 'Business class is a class by itself, old man,' he replied out of the darkness and the distance. 'And its ideas are the dominant ideas of our age. And don't you forget it.'

This morning, when the early December mists were clearing across the meadows, and after discovering that Maurice had put up a notice cancelling my tutorials, I thought of going for a walk. But it was a morning crisp with frost, mouths puffing steam, the last late autumn leaves clinging lifeless to the trees, waiting for a sufficient wind to carry them away, a morning that was made for walking with Moser. Without him I couldn't go. A hundred years ago I would have had a fire in my rooms, prayed to God for Moser's eternal soul, have been warmed inside and out by the beneficent times. Now my rooms are centrally heated, the grate holds a gas fire, and God is an empty, sterile, echoing chamber of the mind. 'An idea whose time has gone,' as Alice put it.

I read through what I wrote last night, wondering how I might go on with Moser's life. There is a gap where he wooed Vita because I wasn't there, alone in my undergraduate world, and although I came to know her well eventually, and loved her in the time that was given to us, it remains a fact that the Vita of that first winter is unknown to me, must be in some degree imagined, invented, though Moser told me of it as things developed. I have no desire to invent the past. That is something that one does with the future.

These matters naturally had the effect of coming between us a little. Such spare time as Moser had went to Vita, and we were not to take a long summer holiday together again for ten years. However, as substitute we began walking together, just the two of us, and adopted the pattern of going away for a week in the early autumn, late September, when the sun may still be warm, and before the trees turn. One year we went to North Wales, another to Hadrian's Wall, a third along Offa's Dyke. Moser never wanted us to go to the Lakes together. After that we started on France, and followed various *randonnées* in the Touraine, the Morvan, the Aveyron.

These were really excuses for conversation. We would have been apart the whole summer, holidaying in different places, or more likely he not taking a holiday at all, but roaming his American circuit between Ann Arbor, Princeton and the NIH in Bethesda, Maryland, so these were occasions for catching up. I had to tell him everything I'd read and why it mattered, and he would try explaining to me the point he had reached in his ideas about inheritance. My role here was to pose what he called 'hard unexpected questions', but even if they were unexpected he never seemed to find them particularly hard. He was straddling several fields at once in a bewildering assault on the literature – genetic theory, human physiology, reproductive biology, demography and fertility, and what he called his 'ifrs': insects, frogs and rats. He would run several laboratory experiments at once. For a while he even talked about taking up sociology. Steadily he was edging towards the theory of dynamic selection – although its outline was only hazy to us at this time – which was eventually to get him into so much trouble. It never occurred to either of us that this might lie ahead. I suppose we were innocents really.

Afternoon

I had been thinking about this, turning over some old photographs of the two of us together – anoraks, boots and packs, Moser with his hair sticking out sideways, his eagle's eyes glinting behind his glasses – when Maurice came in to see me. He said he was worried about Thursday, and wanted to find out if I'd be there. The Court is having its Founder's Dinner on Thursday night, the last full night of term, and there's quite a queue of guests lined up to be looked after. Maurice Singleton is our bursar, and a great worrier.

'We'll all understand if you want to pull out,' he said. 'But things'll want reshuffling if you do.'

I like old Maurice. He used to be a chemist, a chess enthusiast who struck me as being a rather too gentle person. I've never really understood why he knocks around with Ben and Felix, except that the three of them are keen on bridge, and that makes a bond of sorts. Every Oxford college has a trio of bridge players looking for a fourth. Maurice is seventy now, due to retire at Christmas, and he walks with a stick and a pronounced limp. Ben said Maurice got the limp at Goodwood when he was an eighteen-year-old private in the Northamptonshire yeomanry. 'Good Kettering boy, you see.' According to Ben, instead of a kneecap on his left leg Maurice has a hinged steel plate. I have no idea whether this is true. Maurice certainly has a pretty pained look on the broad, veined, hairless spaces of his face, but I've never heard him talk about the war. Still, he is a worrier. And he is also a slow and deliberate man, choosing his words with a sort of austere prudence. I told him that I thought I would 'in all probability' be at the Founder's Dinner.

'I think, if you don't mind my saying so, that will prove a beneficial decision,' he said. 'A help to you.'

He is thinking of drawing me out, dulling the pain by diluting it in society. Is that what was done to him, I wonder, when he was in pain? Perhaps he does understand these things.

'Also,' and he coughed, as if excusing some imminent audacity. 'Also there is the question of Governing Body.'

I raised my eyebrows. Was it a question? Maurice knows I dislike GBs, attend reluctantly, try never to speak, usually fail. Alice says I'm too iconoclastic. 'It never matters in the slightest who wins or loses trivial issues of the sort that surface in college politics.' But I can never bring myself, especially not once the meeting has begun, to agree with her.

'On Wednesday afternoon. Our last match of the season.' He smiled at his own manner of speaking. 'The Master thought that what would be appropriate would be a brief statement about Moser, which he would make naturally, and then no other comment. Until we know about the inquest verdict, you understand. Then, perhaps, a proper tribute to be made at our first meeting in the New Year.' He looked at me with his big, round, yellow eyes, flecked with white, the irises the colour of distant summer clouds. 'He wants to do the proper thing, and is hoping for your cooperation. There is the faint possibility of some public embarrassment, and he felt it would be for the best if the college agreed to say nothing for the time being.'

Ah, so it is a question. Not one that I'm to ask, but one I'm to answer. Will I behave myself? Will I be a good chap?

Help to ensure that the boundary's not crossed? Good taste. Reasonable prudence. Avoid at all costs the frightful faint possibility of the college suffering some public embarrassment. After all, Moser's only dead. Nothing serious . . .

There is something about bereavement that makes us combative. It is that feeling of everything being raw, the surface flayed as if after a two-pipes flogging, so that we cannot bear the touch of anything fresh, not even the caress of the air. Our emotions rise to this tortured surface and lie upon it, in wait for the torment of a passing touch, ready to be licked into flame. The Master requires me to behave myself at GB on Wednesday afternoon, or better still to stay away altogether. Maurice Singleton is his messenger. What is my reply? The flames began to recede.

'Maurice,' I said, 'if I come I promise to be good.' I smothered them completely, offering him a smile that felt like torn canvas from my side of things. He closed his eyes in recognition and acceptance of my good sportsmanship, and just for a second, wildly, I thought he might be falling asleep, there on the rug where he stood, in the middle of my study, his cane over his arm, in the middle of our conversation.

. . . among the English [one meets with] the simplicity that is due to slowness of mind, to their always seeming half asleep and not being able to wake up properly.

But he opened his eyes again, and ran a hand through the little that remained of his limp, white hair.

'I knew you would,' he said, and I thought he might be about to shake my hand. Instead, he spoke again. 'The Master also suggested you might like to cancel all your remaining tutorials. He's put a note round about reorganizing Moser's pupils next term, and he thought you might drop things now. It would do you good to be out of college for a while.'

'Did he say that?'

'No, no. That's me. I . . . well, being cooped up . . . not . . .' Maurice's austere carefulness overcame speech entirely at this point, and he lapsed out of my room in silence.

Where would I go if I were to leave college now for a while? To London, and the Barbican flat? The flat Alice bought with her cheap Scorpion mortgage, and where I never go if I can help it because it smells of merchant bankers, claret and Brut, and reminds me of advertisements in the *Economist*? To our house in Jericho? Three floors of tight town house, shuttered, poked away in a brick courtyard, off streets where Jude once walked, where now the BMWs and Volvos jostle for kerb space, and the pubs serve Côtes du Rhône by the glass. The little yellow brick house opens up only at weekends, when Alice comes from London, Kiev, Maputu, La Paz, wherever, and we have Mozart on the CD player, and we air the kitchen, put Harpic in the lav. Domestic life. When Alice stops thinking, or at any rate talking, about exchange-rate movements, profit ratios and commodity prices, or about the glass ceiling and sexual discrimination in management, or about injustice and the inevitability of historical progress: when she at last stops going on about exploitation in one or other of its multitude of forms, she relapses into what is, I think, herself. A person of generosity, simple kindnesses, sympathetic warmth. Someone to sit and browse the Sunday papers with, to be silent with. At peace.

Is this something she also shares with Gradle? I don't know him of course. Have never met him. I've known about him for a while because, for six months or so after he joined Scorpion, Alice could talk of no one else: his sympathetic intelligence; his thoughtfulness; his happy family life – a son mad about cricket, and good too, on the edge of a county youth side, all that sort of stuff. Alice never had the slightest interest in cricket until then, but all of a sudden she took to telling me all about the game, its psychology even. It wasn't hard to see that she was obsessed with Gradle. Alan, his first name is, though I never use it. He comes from New Zealand, supposedly a land of miracles, its landscape glorious, its ecology protected, indigenous peoples respected, wine *nonpareil*, and economic policy an example to us all. We have to visit apparently.

Alice gets seized with these enthusiasms from time to time. Usually they reflect her underlying instinct for generosity. On my thirtieth birthday, before the day had really begun, when we were still in bed and the early April morning dark, she woke me with kisses to give me a present, murmured those words of encouragement we all get then, I imagine, and again at forty, even fifty, before making love. Afterwards she brought us breakfast there. My present was a German first-edition copy of Herzen's *Vom Anderen Ufer*, Hamburg: Hoffman and Campe, 1850. Without German I couldn't read it, but it was the best thing I have ever owned. Herzen's first real book, in its very first edition.

When he went into voluntary exile, leaving Moscow for ever in the January snows of 1847, he travelled with his family through Germany to Paris. Then they went to Italy. But when the revolutions broke out in 1848 he returned by stages to Paris, where he was witness to the collapse and destruction of Republican spirit, betrayed by its government, butchered by the National Guard, finally buried under empire. Throughout this tragedy he wrote a series of articles as letters to his friends at home in Russia, and five of these, along with two open letters to his then friend George Herwegh and to Mazzini, make up *Vom Anderen Ufer*. The title is expressive of his journey, from repressive, slumbering Russia, to a West where revolutionary spirit is kindled, and where free thought is possible; from an isolated and impotent oppositionism to a willing identity with the political struggle of ordinary people; from an innocent, perhaps juvenile, *desire* for liberty to a mature understanding of the need to work for it.

The crossing was not from idealism to cynicism, but from a shore on which it was possible only to gaze about haphazardly in confusion, to one on which it was possible to look forward purposefully in hope, and backwards deliberately in understanding. It is the discovery of history. The new world. Herzen announced his arrival in Platonic dialogue form that crackles with his fireworks.

And what warmth and sincerity amid all those fireworks.

Behind Herzen we see two shadows, one the looming menace of Karl Marx, whose own essay on the events in France in 1848, eventually published as *The 18th Brumaire of Louis Bonaparte*, became a staple of the radical sociology school because of its interesting evocation of the peasantry, though it is bad history, and worse philosophy. Anyone who read Herzen rather than Marx could not fail to have a better understanding of the democratic aspirations of the French urban revolutionaries at mid century. It is a work to set beside Daumier's painting *The Uprising*. The other shadow we see over Herzen's shoulder is the treacherous presence of George Herwegh, our first glimpse of him, supposedly a friend, the recipient of one chapter of the book, Herzen's assistant in translating and editing for this first German edition of his pieces. Already, does Herzen sense it?, Herwegh is betraying him in his thoughts, perhaps even already in his deeds. The smell of Herwegh hangs over *Vom Anderen Ufer* where I lie in our bed and clutch it to my breast.

Alice bought the book in Frankfurt, on one of her visits.

An acquaintance there organized an antiquarian bookseller to search for a copy, and he found it in Munich. I wondered later whether Alice knew about Herwegh and his part in Herzen's struggle. I imagine not. It was just another coincidental part of the pattern. As so often before, I was profoundly grateful to her.

Two years later, thinking of someone else to please, Alice lent my *Vom Anderen Ufer* to a person she met at a seminar somewhere in London. This young woman lent it to someone else, whom she has since forgotten, and the book is mine no more: an expression of how temporary are our possessions, how the times change them and us, and how briefly we experience them. I was tremendously angry when I first heard that the book had been lost, an anger that built slowly from displeasure at learning that the book had been lent, to bitterness when I heard it had been passed on, to spasms of fury when I eventually absorbed that it would probably never come back.

'Why did you give it in the first place?'

'I didn't give it. I lent it.'

'To me.'

'Oh. Well, because I thought you would like to have it.'

'So then you take it away from me again.'

'I didn't take it. I lent it.'

'And without asking.'

'You're so selfish. Why not lend things? And I didn't know she'd pass it on to someone else.'

'I don't mind lending things. But *that*. That book was my birthday present. My favourite. She lost it.'

'She didn't lose it. She lent it to someone else. He may have lost it. It may come back.'

'But this is crazy, Alice. You must have paid a fortune for the book. You gave it to me, on my thirtieth birthday. I thought it was special. Don't these things matter to you?'

'Oh money. Who cares? It was only an object, and anyway you couldn't read it. You're too tied to things. Sometimes I despair of you.'

You imagine that you despair because you are a revolutionary, and you are mistaken. You despair because you are a conservative.

She was always like this. Even in the middle of the most heated of my bouts of anger she would remain calm, continue to talk in that still, small, reasonable voice. She was capable of inflicting the most damaging of wounds, but since she did it in such rational tones somehow it was privileged and permitted. I went out, slamming the door, and afterwards, as always, felt profound remorse for losing my temper, though perhaps mainly because it meant that I had lost the argument.

The problem is, I think, that Alice's generosity makes little distinction between recipients. There are no deserving or undeserving people, no just or unjust demands, no strong or feeble claims. If she has something, and somebody asks for it, the chances are that she will give it. It is some sort of instinct, an impulse, a pulse even, like one of those machines that draws a graph of the heart's rhythm. The heart beats, the pulse is measured, the machine responds, the pen moves and the paper rolls. *Vom Anderen Ufer* came into my hands as a genuine expression of Alice's generosity to me, her husband and lover. And it went out of them as an equally genuine expression of her generosity to a young woman she met once at a seminar in London. The sentiments of receiving, surely different in each case, seem to play no part in the equation of Alice's giving.

Sometimes I am frightened by this. Sometimes I am perplexed as well as angered by it. Sometimes I am touched and held by it, as I am now, here in my room, remembering that perhaps seven thousand miles away she is thinking of me and of how I grieve for Moser, and is suppressing her own grief to pity mine and to think of ways she might alleviate it. I know this and am humbled by it, and feel my shame rising at all the things I have said and done.

Evening

Maurice Singleton will be thinking that I took his advice because I went out for a walk at this point, and I met him as I was slipping through Fellows' Gate. He gave me one of his encouragement smiles as he limped off towards St Giles and I turned down in the direction of Magdalen.

It was late afternoon, night falling grey across the damp face of the city and its gardens, that melancholy that all Oxford people carry ever after in their hearts rising with the shame and the sorrow. On Magdalen Walk, round by the Cherwell, it was cold, still and dead, the waters brown, the fields swamps glimpsed through the ragged unpruned trees, St Catherine's dilapidated across a ditch, its walls discoloured and stained, already old and crippled. Here and there among the trees, on more historic buildings, the scaffolding and balloons of green plastic and canvas protective cloth have all gone, and the ancient stone walls have been restored to honey and white. Beyond everything, the deer are eerily distant, sentinel outposts of an old, tired dream, entirely lacking the menace of their nervous indifference.

I went through the back wall and walked up Longwall to Blackwell's Music Shop, thinking to look for some scores, but I turned away at the door. There was that slightly tawdry taste of refined virtue hanging in the air. It mixes with the shabby gentility of studious good breeding, and I back away from it when we meet, always have done. Alice calls it my fear of tradition. You no longer encounter it much in Oxford colleges, especially not since they integrated, but it lingers still among the city tradesmen, as if they were loath to give up a Dickensian view of the world. I suppose they are encouraged in it by the palatial architecture, and by the Americans who come in the summer.

Finding it like a taste on the tongue reminded me of how hungry I was. I hadn't eaten since Sunday morning, breakfast in my rooms, and now it was Monday evening, many hours and teacups later. The prospect of food depressed me further. There isn't a restaurant in town without memories of Moser or Vita or Alice, and after twenty-two years of residence some carry reminders of all three. I couldn't dine in hall. I will be ready to face that again, but there is this time of doubt to live through, and high tables are not places for doubt. They demand certainty, or at any rate confidence.

In this frame of mind I bumped into Felix in Parks Road, on the pavement outside Lenin's mausoleum. He was carrying his furled umbrella and looking sternly at a tree poking up above the wall of Wadham. When I approached him he said, without shifting his stare, 'There are two things one asks of a tree: beauty and wood. That thing has neither.' Felix lays claim to being our aphorist, the Court's answer to Maurice Bowra. 'The pen is sordider than the might.' 'Two beds are better than one.' 'His mind remains pure. It has never been stained by an idea.' 'He had to become Master. We made him an offer he couldn't understand.' 'Second marriages are like falling asleep while making love. Impossible to imagine at twenty-three. Hard to avoid at fifty.' 'Gould is a moral contortionist. He can put his foot in it and keep his finger on it at one and the same time.'

And so on. These are all Cunninghams, as we say. Remarks that Felix Cunningham has made once, apparently without rehearsal, and left behind for others to repeat. They are his signature, like his umbrella, one of those big, multi-coloured golfing things that he carries with him everywhere, rain or sun. Ben said he had once seen him with it in August in the Mani. These things make Felix unmistakable, but they distract from his other features, leaving him opaque. His field is English literature, where he has specialized in the eighteenth century, and from which he has perhaps drawn a sensitivity that is at once acute and robust. He can be gruff and rough in argument, is notorious for terrorizing his pupils, and yet is a sensitive, even delicate man, with sharp bird-like features, and an occasional, always surprising, capacity for human sympathy. Felix is a lot older than me, possibly over sixty, and someone told me once of his having had a son who died in childhood. His wife left him years ago.

'What you need,' he said, turning from the unsatisfactory Wadham tree, 'is a drink. And a good feed. Agreed?' I didn't disagree, so we went into a pub on the corner and Felix busied himself with pints of beer and orders for plates of food. When he came back he said, as though we had been in the middle of a conversation, and he merely carrying on where it had broken off, 'And then there's Alice too. How's she taking it?'

'Alice is in Singapore.'

'Ah –' and he drank. 'Bad luck.'

'But she knows. She rang up. Someone faxed her from the bank.'

'Rawlinson,' said Felix. 'The Master rang him. There's to be an obituary in *The Times* and Rawlinson's to help get the facts straight. I'm afraid Campbell-Quaid's writing it.'

Campbell-Quaid chairs a committee at the MRC, and is a big wheel in the Royal Society. Moser long suspected him, without being able to produce evidence, of opposition, both to him personally and to his research. At the end he knew it was true. Campbell-Quaid is a biologist at Cambridge. Felix lit a cigarette. He smokes uncontrollably, sometimes a pipe, cigars after dinner, cigarettes continuously, leaving ash and dead matches in his wake, stains and burn marks on his fingers, his pockets baggy with the smoker's paraphernalia. It never seems to do him any harm.

'Was boy Moser a genius?' he asked. I give him a smile for an answer. The question was not offensive because there is no malice in Felix. Somewhere, somehow, he shed it all, a long time ago, and its absence is instantly recognizable as a part of his being, like indolence in a cat. Even when his fun is misplaced you excuse it. You might as well condemn a fresh-water spring for bubbling when you feel gloomy.

'We were all told he was when we elected him. You know how it is for us humanist fellows when there's a scientist to elect. Do as we're told. Honour and obey, that's us. Then he seemed to come unstuck, with that row at the Royal Society, and the Americans withdrawing support, and the MRC inquiry rumours. Jesty was telling me some of this stuff with great relish a couple of weeks ago.' He paused for a moment after mentioning Jesty. Jesty is the college shit. His presence is one of the costs of academic tenure. Like all such characters he is deeply insensitive to others, and utterly impervious to criticism. That he should spread dirt about Moser was wholly in character.

'You'd better brace yourself for the obituaries,' Felix said. 'It could be another case of the scholar's life.' I didn't recognize the reference. 'Sam Johnson,' said Felix. ' "See nations slowly wise, and meanly just,/To buried merit raise the tardy bust." '

'I think they'll all be very happy to forget Moser just as quickly as they can,' I said.

Our food arrived, reminding me ten minutes later, as it worked its effects, of senior tutors' first tactics. If an undergraduate complains of depression, inability to work or whatever, ask him how long it is since he had a square meal. Moser agreed, using it as proof of his indivisibility principle. 'The problem is that what's common sense for daily life can't be admitted to high theory without being dressed up. It upsets the high priests. Like shaving in a baptismal font.'

Felix and I chatted for perhaps half an hour, and then I walked back to the Court alone, to sit once more behind my desk. *Alexander Herzen. A Life* has gathered a little dust in the past two days and I blow it off. I wonder what I should do with it now. Mullens expects the manuscript by the end of the year, a few weeks away. Time to give it one more light edit, check the quotations, proofread the footnotes again. I know I won't really do any of these things. Herzen is quite finished, and Moser's dying seems to prove it. A phase of my life has come to an end, or should have done. I can't help myself thinking that this is a sign. Biography is like this. To write a life is in some sense also to live it, and in doing so you run the risk of either dying with the subject, or being the victim of his ghost, whatever that means. Perhaps, merely, that one is forever inhabited now by his spirit. Hence the idea of a sign. If the pattern of one's own life, crossed with the pattern of another's, is still to be regular, then the ending of one should mean the ending of other things as well, things at the centre of other regions of my life, overlapping with each other, bending them, the way twisting grain pulls timber out of true.

This is another part of biography, like the risk of exaggeration, the temptation to see form in the movement of a life, start breaking it down, consigning this bit to one chapter, that to another, pulling threads together to make neat what was ragged, unformed or frayed. As though at the end of a phase of life one could put out the light, sleep well, and rise the next day to a fresh clean chapter heading and a new departure. The truth is awkwardly different. Things start that way, certainly – childhood, youth. But then they become complex, convoluted. Time's arrow exercises the discipline of each succeeding day, the route from adolescence to maturity, to middle age and senility, but experience and its interpretation does not flow with the same motion. Language applied to experience and mixed with speculation (worlds we do not know, but can imagine) produces a silt which clogs up the stream of conscious understanding, clouding, muddying, occasionally blocking the channels. We experience today in the light of yesterday, and the weight of yesterdays grows heavier with the passage of the years. This is why so many great thinkers appear unworldly: they are not living their lives according to the serial progression of weeks and years, but according to some other frames of reference altogether. Their biographies require radical treatment. For the rest of us, as our lives flow on, the detritus of experience gets both heavier and thicker, and makes no distinctions by category, origins or purpose. One thought bowls into another, releasing a memory, a twinge of guilt, a sensation of something lost, replaced by a desire, wants, hope. The present is clogged with this silt, turning to mud, settling thicker and thicker as the pace of life slows with the loss of force. Scientists, mathematicians, have short research careers not because they are burned out but because they are clogged up. The clarity of mind required to see outline in sharp detail unavoidably blurs with age. Language, experience and speculation, the building materials of life, are ultimately deadly too, poisoning intellect. It is hard, given these certainties, to make shapes or forms out of circumstance, which is what biography seems to demand. It is barely possible to separate one day from another.

Like the day Alice came home from the Institute and said she had had an offer to work for Scorpion.

'Are you going to accept?'

'Do you think I should?'

'You haven't said what they want you to do yet. But I wouldn't have thought finance capitalism was really your thing.'

'Mr Rawlinson explained it to me today, at lunchtime. He was up for the Institute's Board meeting and came to find me specially. He said Scorpion was unhappy about the way they'd been handling Third World investments, and were putting together a new team. Someone called Ellicott, who's been in the PM's think-tank, and one of the Ferguson banking twins. Rawlinson said Ellicott and Ferguson are terrifically bright, but a bit stuffy. Too much Whitehall and City. He said he'd heard a bit about my work at the Institute and thought I might balance them up.'

'And what do you think?' I was feeling wretched. This meant she would be leaving Oxford. She put her arms round my neck.

'You haven't heard the half of it.' Peck on the nose. 'The salary's ginormous.' Broad Alician grin, full of good humour, unselfconscious pleasure. 'And it means travelling all over the world looking at schemes, assessing projects.'

'You really think that will do some good?'

'I don't know. He said to think about it over the weekend, and ring him on Monday.'

'You're going to, aren't you?'

'Would you want to dissuade me?'

'Yes.'

'Why?'

'It'll be dishonest.'

'It'll be good for women.' She let me go, stepping away.

'Which ones? Black ones?'

'And I'll be on the inside. Know your enemy. That was unfair.'

'Alice, I'm not against people in general working for Scorpion. It's *you*. You.'

'That's one of the differences between us. I am against people in general working for Scorpion. But *not* me.'

'I suppose you'll have to go and live in London.'

'Oh that's it. Of course. What price women's independence when the man won't move his job and so the woman must.'

'Now *you're* being unfair. You know I'd never do anything willingly to impede your career, and . . .'

'You talk like a philosopher.'

'Dammit, I am a philosopher.'

'But this is not a bloody tutorial, and I am not an epistemological problem. I have been offered a fantastic job. I'm fed up with the Institute, you know that. Flea-bite scratchers, model builders and procrastinators. And it's a marvellous opportunity.'

'But not for you. I don't understand it. Christ, Alice, you're a Marxist, and now you're proposing to go to work in the engine room of Western exploitation. For years all we've got out of you is the extraction of surplus value from debt-laden, underprivileged, post-colonial wage slavery, and now you decide to go and help in the extraction. Can't you see that's irrational? Only a week ago you were telling me that statistic from Stüffengler about correlations between numbers of microchips produced in Japan and infant mortality rates in East Africa. I *really* don't understand it.'

'I haven't said I'll take the job.'

'You will.'

'What else can I do, then?'

'Get a lectureship, like we discussed. There's that job coming up at York. Oh Alice, please. You can't do this.'

'I think I can.'

And she did. Not instantly. Calmed by the Sunday morning,

we agreed that she should find out more before making up her mind. Rawlinson thought this very sensible – 'in the best traditions of sound banking' or some such – and invited her to spend a day at head office, meeting the team, discussing prospects. After that we talked it over again, and she said yes. I'm not sure now, twelve years on, whether or not she always intended this kind of career, but the contradiction that it poses to her seems to suit her temperament. And it was, indeed still is only more so, a lot of money.

With Alice expecting to be away all week in London from the September, when she was to start, we decided to get married. We moved from the little flat we had in Summertown into a neat little town house in Jericho. We married in the registry office on St Giles's on a Tuesday afternoon in July 1984. Moser and Vita were our witnesses.

A man really does something serious only when he does it for himself.

3

Tuesday

'It mortifies us to realize that the idea is impotent, that truth
has no binding power over the world of actuality. A new sort
of Manichaeism takes possession of us, and we are ready, *par
dépit*, to believe in rational (that is, purposive) evil, as we
believed in rational good – that is the last tribute we pay to
idealism.'

Moser's parents were neither lapsed Catholic nor English
Anglican. Both of them were indeed Jewish, but neither was
devout, and Moser himself claimed never to have heard a
religious word spoken in his home. This may not have been
true, however. Moser disliked talking about his childhood and
youth, and when compelled to do so often invented whatever
might seem appropriate, as with his alternative CV, though
the singular is wrong: he had many of them. Close as we were,
I never went to his home town, nor indeed ever really knew
exactly where he came from. Moser's view was that experience,
especially early experience, was creative and useful, but only
to the recipient. Others, who could never know, let alone
understand, the importance of it, would only misuse it, forming
judgements about character and personality that would be
travesties of the truth, but hard to shift once allocated. In any
event, he said, what people really liked was mystery, and he
deliberately enveloped himself in a variety of strange and
peculiar tales whose exoticism guaranteed notoriety.

Had I not been there to witness it myself, I would have
judged the account of his first meetings with Vita in Lyon,

Cannes and Paris to have been just such a story. When we got back to Oxford he lost no time in telephoning her, and they agreed to meet in London one afternoon for tea. Their rendezvous was at the Albert Memorial, not far from where she lived in one of those spacious late-Victorian apartments with cage lifts and gurgling central heating. They walked in Kensington Gardens under an August sun, and he talked about his work and ambitions, and she talked about her music. Vita was then seventeen, two years younger than Moser, a pianist, studying performance at the Royal College of Music. All of this may seem simple and straightforward enough, yet it has more of invention in it than truth. For the truth is that I have no idea what really happened during any of their courtship, and such knowledge as I think myself occasionally to possess is no more than a second-hand rendition, elaborated in my own imagination, of snippets that they may have told me, and that I may have embellished. Much biographical knowledge is of this kind. I met a military biographer at a conference once and he told me a story about a General's widow. He was writing the General's life, and had heard an amusing anecdote about what they were doing on the day the First World War was declared. When she read this in his manuscript she wrote to him that it wasn't true, this wasn't what she and her husband were doing, but it captured the spirit and the feeling of the day very well, and so should be left.

Courtship is even more difficult. By definition we do it in privacy, yet its importance is rarely superseded by any other experience. When did Moser first make love with Vita? Did he have to persuade her? Was she the one to suggest it? Was it a shared decision, taken without discussion, an impulse? No one knows and no one ever will, yet it was arguably the most important event in Moser's life. I don't believe he ever slept with anyone else, and Vita's devotion to him was legendary.

Would it be enough, in a biography, to write that last sentence as the sum and total explanatory account of the single most important relationship in his life? One would have to go farther, but how? When they were alone together, what did they talk about? Did he tell her secrets? Which ones? It is not just the egotist who wants to know: did they talk about me, telling each other what they thought? Those who enjoy listening to gossip generally forget that they may be the topic, or the target, when they are not there. And what about Moser's family? Did they exist for Vita? She told me once that they liked their obscurity, and she and Moser preferred to give way to it.

On the other hand, Vita's family became very well known to Moser, and he formed several good friendships among them. Vita's mother, Mireille, was French, and the man driving the post-war roadster her brother, Vita's uncle, Lucien Beaumont. He did indeed come from the Sancerre, as did Mireille. The family home was at Bué, a little village that I visited in due course, where there was a wine *négociant* called Pinard who really had christened his son Vincent. Vita would go into peals of laughter over this oddity.

Vita always gave the impression of being rather fragile, though she had a wonderful sense of humour, not in the blunt instrument way of making jokes, but in being able to see the funny aspects of ordinary things. Or extraordinary things. One of these became famous, or at any rate notorious. She was performing the Brahms Second Piano Concerto at the Festival Hall with the LSO and Colin Davies (both Moser and I were there, so at least this story is kosher). Vita could be flamboyant at the keyboard, and on this particular evening was clearly in the mood. In the long and difficult first movement, after the introduction and the first theme, there is a bravura passage demanding great virtuosity, in which the pianist flies up the keyboard, bottom to top, playing huge chords, apparently urging the orchestra to thunderous response. Vita swept upwards with great panache, not a note out of place of course, our senses tingling at her energy and daring. At the top she flung her arms into the air. The orchestra was large, the space on the platform constricted. Her flying right hand swept the first violinist's music stand into the lap of a large lady sitting in the front row of the stalls. A considerable distance. Colin Davies raised an eyebrow to see if Vita was all right, which she was after a fashion. The first violinist huddled closer to his neighbour for the score. The lady in the front row tried decorously not to cause any further disturbance. We couldn't see Vita's face – Moser always sat behind her at concerts – but we could tell that she was laughing by the movements of her shoulders. Davies, who certainly could see her face, started to crack a smile too, and one or two others who could see, like the timpanist at top right, had to get out handkerchiefs to quell the hilarity. Vita carried on playing, as did the whole orchestra, but the first movement turned into a sort of celebration of the absurdity of life, or of high art in life, or of the laughter at the heart of beauty, the temporary movements of the passions, and the passage of grace to old age and the withering of talent. At the end of the movement, Vita swung round to the woman in the front row and asked her if she was all right, apologizing. The woman may have wanted to be sour, but one look at Vita's glistening eyes must have told her the truth, and she began to laugh too. The first violinist retrieved his music stand and his score. Brahms continued, but first Vita had to beg a big handkerchief from the conductor to dry her eyes.

Unusually perhaps, I suspect that this sense of humour came from her French side. Lucien turned out to have a slow sense of irony that could be very attractive, though your French had to be rather better than mine to understand it fully. Mireille was one of those bright and cheerful women who are always determined to see the amusing aspect of things, no matter what. The Margolis side of the family was rather different. Vita's father, Lawrence, had gone through Japanese prison camp with his parents, and although he never discussed it Vita said she felt that it had made him value tragedy above comedy. He wasn't bitter, or unhappy, or depressed, but there was a part of him, something normally present, that in him was simply missing. She had never been able to detect it by name. Perhaps it was just a negation. A hole of some sort. She said he was nothing like either his older brother or sister, both of whom had been at school in England when Singapore fell, and had stayed with relatives through the war. The whole Margolis side of the family was musical. Vita's uncle was musical director of one of the Guards' regimental bands, and her aunt taught the cello. Vita learned to play the piano from the age of two, and could think of nothing else that she had ever wanted to do. She went through a number of different teachers before she was ten, but a repetition of her career here serves little purpose, as she became a famous concert pianist and recording artist, and is safely in the public domain. What I wanted to know at the beginning was: what happened on the evening of her appearance to us in the arena at Lyon, and why wasn't she in the car with her uncle the next day, heading south for Cannes?

Vita liked to tease Moser and me about this. Once she said that she hadn't been there that night at all, and that we must have seen someone else, and subsequently confused this person with her. On another occasion she said that perhaps she had been there, but she couldn't remember on which night, and anyway, there were always people visiting the Roman amphitheatres at all hours, and it might or might not have been her. Once she said, under constant but good-humoured questioning, 'Oh all right, yes. I saw you both going into the arena, and I thought you looked interesting, and that it would be amusing to create an impression.' This account didn't really make sense because what I remembered was that she emerged from the shadows on the side of the theatre away from the entrance, and so had to have been there from before we came in. As to why she hadn't been in her uncle's car the next day, this was because she had not been with him at all, either at Bué or at Lyon, and as far as she could remember was already at Cannes. And yes, it was true that she had been there that summer, but she had no recollection of being down by the yacht harbour. And more of the same.

Moser approved of all this. It suited his sense of uncertainty. It helped to explain, I think, why Vita never made attempts to find out about his childhood or his family. She also preferred the uncertainty of his various accounts. Vita and Moser shared everything, above all story-telling. 'All human relations are just story-telling anyway,' Moser said. 'Falling in love is telling your life-story. Your personal myth, the psychiatrists call it. And it is far from clear what it means, in this sort of endeavour, to tell the truth.' One of Moser's favourite parlour games was what he called 'Life Court'. You drew lots to allocate roles: judge, prosecutor, defence lawyer, juror, defendant. Then the defendant, having sworn to tell the truth, the whole truth and nothing but the truth, underwent an interrogation without charges. 'When did you first fall in love?' 'With whom?' 'What was it like?' This was not an easy game to play because, in the right hands, questioning rapidly became difficult to handle, and nobody ever managed to tell 'the truth' as a father confessor might expect to know it.

Do not forget that man loves to obey, always seeks to lean upon something, to hide behind something. He has not the proud self-reliance of the beast of prey.

Later

It was just as I was thinking about this observation of Herzen's that Alice rang again from Singapore. It was ten o'clock at night there, and she was about to go to bed. Perhaps reflecting on Vita's effect on Moser, how good they were together, had calmed some of the despair that I have been feeling, and I was able to respond to Alice's compassion and concern. She wanted to know if I was 'coping', and whether anyone was being a help. I explained that I was trying to write. I felt a sudden urgent surge of great affection and tenderness for her that took my breath away. I stumbled through a few conventional endearments, broken up by her asking, 'Why, oh why couldn't we just be close like this more often?' I pointed out, unfairly, that she was so often away. 'I so very much just want to have ordinary life with you,' she said. I was silent at this, perhaps a little humiliated. She broke the silence by asking after Moser's autopsy. 'No news,' I said. 'But it seems obvious enough that it was suicide. I don't think anyone's going to challenge that sort of finding.' She mmm'd as though unconvinced. I asked after her work and she said something about routine negotiations in the morning, followed by 'hospitality', and an afternoon plane for Hong Kong. We agreed to keep our rendezvous in Florence on Sunday, and she said she would ring me again tomorrow when she got in to her Hong Kong hotel. She said she loved me before we hung up.

Reminded of Florence, I went out to the High to buy a ticket. It was cold and dry, the bite of frost in the air, the streets already dark at 3.30 in the afternoon. The young woman in the travel agency told me I was silly to book so late, when I could have had a cheaper fare by booking three weeks in advance. Three weeks ago seems an eternity now. I had no plan to go to Florence then. Moser was still alive. Alice had been up for the weekend. I dropped into a reverie of these things standing at the counter, and was wakened by one of those English conventionalities – 'A penny for them.'

Perhaps it was in order to avoid such depressive vacuity that I took up writing. In this sense, writing is mere necessity. Therapy. I discovered this when I finished my dissertation and got an offer to turn it into a book. By then, this would have been 1983 or so, I was deeply involved in learning Russian and reading Herzen, and I didn't really want to take the time to fiddle with a project that had lost some of its interest for me. Eventually, a year after signing the contract, I was compelled by its terms to do the work, and I found, in the summer months that slipped by in this way, a tranquillity that was new. The book – it was called *Eden's Politics* at least partly because the publishers hoped that this might stimulate a few extra and mistaken purchases – was brought out by Mullens, a great London house whose capitalist profits come largely from the labour of socialist intellectuals. It was a dismal flop. The general editor of the series in which it appeared lived in California, I was in Oxford, the publisher in London's West End, and their production department in Ilford. The book was designed in Edinburgh, typeset in Bangalore, printed in Hong Kong and bound in Wantage. It took fifteen months to produce, bore the date 1984 when it actually appeared in 1985, and coincided, when it eventually arrived in the bookshops, with a newspaper and magazine strike. It was barely reviewed at all, and remaindered in 1986. There was a curious justice in this. *Eden's Politics* was critical of anarchism in general, of some particular anarchists especially so, and the failure of the book to reach any sort of popular audience seemed fortuitous, a silent, possibly anarchic judgement on my first attempt to mould opinion. 'Further evidence of negation,' was Alice's comment. 'Pure chance,' said Moser. In the end I decided not to mind.

To see oneself in print is one of the strongest artificial passions of an age corrupted by books.

It was the writing I had enjoyed, and after that the holding of the finished work, the delicious feel of its bulk in the hand, its appearance on the shelf, the order and symmetry of its pages, the typefaces, the binding, the smell, the solidity, the pleasure of reading randomly among its pages, to rediscover the self that has since disappeared. Do all writers feel like this about their books? No answers to the question because these are secret matters, feelings indulged only when the study door is shut, the writer alone in his world. I don't suppose writers ever intend to feel like this. It is simply what happens. And anyway, academics do not write books to have them read, but to add the titles to their CVs so that they can acquire status and win promotion. This is one reason why they are so easily cheated by publishers. Also, to have a book find popular esteem and climb on to a bestseller list is generally a disaster for an academic, as it enables his colleagues to discount him as a mere popularizer. He might as well become a tele-don, or write newspaper articles, both activities widely condemned in academic circles as evidence of intellectual turpitude.

Learning Russian has also brought me the same pleasure that I derive from writing. Until I came across Herzen I had only studied Latin and French to what the English rather grandly call Advanced Level. This enables you to translate Musset but not to argue back in conversation, and it reflects the priorities of the British Foreign Office. This is one reason for the success of a writer like Julian Barnes. He makes his English readers feel comfortable about their knowledge and cultural understanding of France. By getting them to smile, perhaps even laugh at, for instance, Enid Starkie, by means of an unprovoked and unfair attack grounded on nothing but the ease with which the target could be hit, he gives us all a certain *hauteur*.

Speaking French in a bad but 'superior' way is an accomplishment, however, beside our knowledge of German. At most universities in the world you would need to read German in order to study philosophy, but not here. Here we do not encourage our pupils to read Hegel or to wrestle with ontological proofs. Such things may form part of cultural studies but they are not philosophy. Moser and I used to laugh about this, the more so as his German, originally studied as part of a science education, was excellent.

Anyway, despite these impediments, it was obvious to me that if I was to make a thorough study of Herzen, then I would have to master Russian. The Academy of Sciences edition of his complete works, published in Moscow, runs to thirty volumes, and only about a quarter of this has found its way into English translation. Dozens of reviews, hundreds of letters, his novel, numerous fragments, the complete run of *The Bell*, none of this would be accessible without learning the language. I signed on at what was then the Technical College in Headington for evening classes, bought tapes and manuals, loads of children's books, some history and poetry texts, and set about the job for a regular two hours a day.

I am unable to remember what I stopped doing in order to fit this in, but it can hardly have been important because nothing else in my life seemed to change. Alice and I had settled into a routine in which we lived as if married while denying that we were, or saw any need to be. Technically I was living in college, but after 1980 I lived mainly at Alice's flat. When Alice was twenty-one she graduated, received a car for her birthday, came into some trust money through her grandparents, and started work as a research assistant at the Institute more or less all at once. With the new independence that this brought she began buying an apartment at Summertown, on the northern outskirts of Oxford. Here we led a quiet, uneventful and apparently contented life. Alice had a lot of Oxford friends who came and went for dinner, lunch parties, visits to pubs; we read a lot and discussed what we read; I did my two-hour language stint every day. We belonged to a small circle of privileged dons – young, secure, with long careers ahead – who thought they were more numerous than they were, and believed that their lives were normal, even faintly on the dreary side. It was the sort of life which, had we been capable of living it unselfconsciously, would surely have made us supremely happy. Living it from day to day, however, with all its little presumed frustrations, probing at it constantly with the mind, critical and discontented, it appeared and felt at best merely average. It was probably wasted on us, and should have gone to someone else.

This is another of the things that drew me to Herzen. He came from that stratum of Russian society, the liberal, well- and Western-educated aristocracy, that could not play a role under tsarist autocracy, either for the regime or in opposition to it. Since only idleness lay between these two impossible poles, they were condemned to a life of boredom and frustration, prey to all the heartless distractions idleness brings. The existence of these people was apparently superfluous, and they came to see themselves as superfluous people. The solution to the pointless way of life this presupposed, directionless and numbing, lay in action. But action under the Tsar was precisely what was impossible, short of exile and the most strenuous, monumental labours. Herzen undertook this path towards liberation and away from the anaesthetic effects of a superfluous role at home, and the cost he bore for it is one of the things that makes him admirable. His experience suggests that exile of some kind is the pre-condition for liberty, that you must remove yourself completely from your origins, your roots, live as if in the void of unknown foreign lands where the language is impenetrable and the customs new, engage in the terrible task of reconstructing ideas, beliefs, convictions, from a position devoid of what he called tradition, what Alice calls ideology, and what I think of as magic. Our difficulty is that it is not clear how we are to achieve this exile in the dying years of the twentieth century. Herzen's genius is that, from a hundred and fifty years ago, he shows us the way.

Alice took my initial enthusiasm for Herzen fairly seriously. She had no desire to learn a new language herself, but I suspect, without ever saying so, that she thought my learning Russian a step in the correct ideological direction. I was going to emerge from it a better person, more fitted for my historical role. In this spirit she gave me a lot of active encouragement, enduring hours of Russian tape recordings, rehearsing me through tests, buying me books, maps and guides. The flat started to fill up with picture books of the colourful Soviet Union, the people's glorious gymnastic squad, daily life on the Volga, the triumphs of Soviet space travel, and much else besides. We even thought once or twice of going for a holiday to Russia, though this never actually came to anything because I rather dislike travel.

For Herzen himself, however, Alice could grow little hotter than lukewarm. She read *Childhood, Youth and Exile*, but refused to see it as anything more than a first-hand eyewitness account (and evidence of) the repressive tsarist system. 'And Herzen by his birth, his social position, and his ownership of property, was himself a part of the repressive system,' she said. 'But an interesting part. Progressive.'

The word was better chosen than she knew. Some years later, reading the annotated *Complete Works*, I found this was exactly the word the Diamat-Histmat priesthood employed to explain him (away). He was 'progressive'. Translated from Newspeak into common English, what this means is that Herzen must be thought of as having been basically on the right side of history, although most of what he wrote and thought was, as we now in the light of Marx and Lenin see, rubbish. Next author please.

Moser and I saw him differently. Together we formed a sort of Herzen brotherhood. We saw less of each other at this time than previously or since – only now it's afterwards – but there were natural reasons for this and we accepted them. Moser was deeply involved with Vita, who continued to live in London, which took him away a lot. After getting the brilliant first we all knew he'd get he had a junior research fellowship, and after that an MRC research grant for his genetic work. He put in long hours at the laboratory and even longer ones in his study writing up experimental results, planning a succession of publications. His first remarkable paper on the primary theory of evolutionary chains and the genetic pattern of complex organs appeared in *Nature* in 1982, and started him on the road that was to lead to scientific fame, then notoriety, and eventually and finally to isolation. A loneliness in his profession that was matched, ultimately, by a loneliness of the mind, down there on his bed, writing at the end to Vita before lying back, switching off the light.

Before Sunday I thought it was just a phase. His isolation was temporary, and Moser would show them that he was right, that he could make a comeback, impress most, shame some, outclass them all. Moser to me was a star. One of my fantasies was to compose his Nobel Laureate's address.

His heart beat to the same tune as mine; he too had cut the painter that bound him to the sullen old shore.

Correspondence is the biographer's treasure. So much so that in some recent fiction aspirant biographers are portrayed as willing to kill for it. I have long thought this odd. Anyone who has ever written a letter knows that it's an uncertain source of truth, where much may be sacrificed for effect. And literary people are among the worst offenders in this regard. Oscar put it beautifully when he pointed out that writers write their plays and poems for their intimate friends, and their private correspondence for the general reader. Nowhere is this more obvious than in the case of two writers who, without reasons of friendship or common concern, start a correspondence, and continue it for many years, writing about their own and each other's work, spelling out such aspects of daily life and thought as each would like preserved. Nowadays the great and famous, and many who are neither, even lodge their correspondence in the British Library well before they die, 'for safe keeping' naturally!

I have almost no letters from Moser. A few notes and cards from holiday trips, and a small number of longer letters written from the States when he took sabbatical terms there in the late 80s. From the 60s to the 90s people seem not to have written letters, and there is a gap in the record. Once fax machines came in, and then E-mail, the act of correspondence revived, and there is a flow of letter-writing once more. Some think it too 'instant' to be anything more than sub-literate, but I think not. Herzen used to write many notes and letters every day when he lived in London, and they were delivered almost instantaneously – by servant. Some days he would write, receive a reply, answer it, and get another response, all before dinner. Rather like the on-line academic today, writing to California or Canberra. This sort of material is going to be far more to the biographer's taste than carefully considered literate correspondence concocted over hours in peaceful seclusion, and dispatched for the purpose of building another layer of literary remains.

Evening

Moser and I discussed suicide once. He had been reading Camus's *L'Homme révolté* and, if I remember correctly, Sartre's *Esquisse d'une théorie des émotions*. He said these sorts of books were like the *antipasti* trolleys they push around restaurants in Piedmont. There are hundreds of different delectable things to choose from, but unless you are very careful in your selection it is easy to put together an indigestible mixture that spoils the courses that are to follow. 'The problem is far simpler than these word-wranglers allow,' he said. 'And a prime candidate for human sciences analysis. There are two questions to answer: why do people do it? Is it justified?'

You might have thought so in his case. He was under attack for so long, and had so much to bear. But he always seemed to me to be a stoic. Was he concealing the truth? Disguising the tensions he really felt? When he seemed unmoved by criticism they called him arrogant, egotistical, supercilious. None of which was true. But he did defend himself, though in some things this was hard if not impossible to do. The whispering campaign, for instance. Not orchestrated against him, but just the normal workings of the science, perhaps any, community. 'Oh Moser, you've heard of him, have you? One of those brilliant deviants – got a bee in his bonnet.' 'Moser? Mmm, know him well. Who doesn't? Ha, ha, ha.' 'Moser's our modern-day Koestler. Seems to be what these ego-men do.' And so on. One particularly nasty slur was that he was never to be seen, always off in America, or Germany. No one was ever more scrupulous in supervising his pupils or directing the research effort at his lab. Yet somehow the slur stuck. 'Seen Moser, have you? You're a lucky man.'

Moser laughed these things off. He said the little terms and catch-phrases that people employed to condemn competitors and colleagues revealed their true fears and anxieties. The longing to dominate. He asked me once if I knew how Herzen talked. What did he sound like? How were his accent, his turns of phrase, idiosyncracies of speech? I had to admit I had no idea. Before the radio and the recording studio we don't really know what even so public a voice as, say, Charles Dickens sounded like. If you 'heard voices', you were unwell, enraptured or bedevilled. Herzen wrote elegant Russian, in uncorrected correspondence as well as in published work, and I always imagine him speaking as he wrote – measured, balanced, reason and force together.

Each of us is different in a foreign language, however. Personality moves with syntax and cadence. The derivations of words hover behind them, pressing history upon the present, moulding the user. Herzen spoke German and French, by all accounts fluently, if occasionally incorrectly – not so much errors as the fault of inauthentic embellishment – a Second Empire disease, just as it was slightly later in Britain with the gothic revival in ecclesiastical architecture. His Italian was less good, though I doubt it lacked brio. His English, at least according to Mrs Carlyle, was atrocious. I imagine, however, that the standards of speech of the Carlyle household were uncommonly high.

'Guesswork,' said Moser. 'Insufficient for biography. How we speak, the little phrases we employ – the facial tics of language – are the public façade of personality.' We turned over our colleagues: Felix's gags; Ben Gould's weakness, like a *Guardian* headline writer, for the approximate pun. 'Have you been to see the new *Tempest*?' 'No, no. Too much like bard work.' That sort of thing. The Master, with all his *gravitas* and bearing, for some reason always pronounces the *l* in salmon, and puts the emphasis on the second syllable of the word cucumber. Moser invited him to tea one afternoon, hoping to get him to say, 'Ah, splendid. Salmon and cucumber sandwiches', but the fish would not rise.

'You could tell almost all you needed to know about my mother,' said Moser, enriching this story with another, 'by the handful of phrases and clichés that she used. When fed up – most of the time – it was "I'm just about at the end of my tether with you" or "I've slaved my fingers to the bone, and *this* is what I get" or "You're nothing but trouble" and "You'll be the death of me, you really will." When thoroughly worked up at me she would address an imaginary third person in tones of great exasperation. "Nothing's ever right for him, is it? But will he take no for an answer? No, he won't." "Oh yes, it's all right for some" and "He's been nothing but trouble since the day he was born." When reduced, unusually, to laughter at something I'd done, it was "You daft ha'porth" or, more rarely, the mysterious "If you only knew . . ." which was accompanied by a shaking of the head. When confronted with my father's disagreement on some topic – a common feature of our domestic life – she would claim to be "Damned if I do, and damned if I don't", while any riposte at the breakfast table meant you were "a bear with a sore head" such that "There's no peace for the wicked." Any promise to do something later drew "Yes, well, the streets of hell are paved with good intentions", while any reported mishap prompted the incomplete "It's an ill wind . . ." or "If the cap fits . . ." These few terms, along with a handful of catch-phrases from some distant film or radio programme – "Will you 'ave it now or will you 'ave it later" for tea; "Home James, and don't spare the horses" after any family outing in the car; and "I'm faint for lack of nourishment" from a 50s soap opera of some sort – constituted her full range of conversational power.'

Moser said that in this context it proved easy to conceal himself behind catch-phrases of his own, brought home from his own generation. With a cinema German accent: 'Ve haf vays of making you talk.' Or with a Sean Connery burr: 'Nice one Miss Moneypenny.' Or Peter Sellers in American tour guide disguise: 'Bal-ham, gateway to the South.' While 'Gawd it's 'ot in 'ere' was Tony Newley in a fur coat in a phone box, much prized because banned in England.

Moser was right. There is something obscure about people whose voices we have never heard. No matter how famous, prominent, or controversial; no matter how much or how elegantly they may have written; if we do not know them in the vernacular, have not heard their voices in modulation, the tones of anger or affection, sarcasm or wit, then we have not really known them, and may not fully understand them. It is a problem at the heart of historical biography.

With it comes the matter of empathy, a conceptual nonsense that now poisons the air of discourse. From Presidents to social workers, everyone prattles about his or her ability to feel what others feel, to understand them by identifying with them, to share experience by intuition. This is meaningless. Since we cannot recapture the sensation of our own past feelings, it is impossible for us even to deduce, let alone actually to feel, what others are experiencing. The claim that one can do so is an expression of egotism, and takes the form either of projection, or of self-delusion. In either case it is false. Yet writers, readers, even critics, all agree that empathy, and the power both to feel it and to express it, is what makes for good biography.

Perhaps some of this is due to lexical indifference. Some people who use the term 'empathy' may actually intend 'sym-pathy' and are (merely!) confusing the terms. But most seem both to intend and to mean what they say. This is reckless when discussing the biographies of more or less contemporary figures. When discussing individuals from the past it is closer to lunacy. We have no idea what it must have been like to think and to feel in, say, the 1830s, a time pre-dating the looming figures of nineteenth-century thought, Marx, Darwin and Freud. The conceptual map of experience available for use then is inaccessible to us now, not because of their limitations but because of ours. Knowledge, particularly in the form of analytical tools such as Freudian psychoanalysis, or Marxist class theory, divorces us from the past. We may use these tools to try to understand history in the sense of giving it meaningful shape for ourselves, but the content of what we know divorces us, inevitably, from the mental states of those without the knowledge. This is the paradox of history. The more we may think we understand the past, the more divorced we become from it.

This is the main reason why lives can be told and re-told again and again. In a few decades it will be imprudent, if not derelict, to offer biographical accounts of behaviour without knowing, or trying to know, at least something about the anatomy and biochemistry of the subject's brain. How much better we might understand a Byron or a Churchill, a Lenin or a Balzac, if only we had this information about them.

Even so, the additional detail, however much it might alter the design and emphasis of any portrait, would not permit us to know how the individual *felt*. Feelings cannot be shared. They are one definition of the self: that part of it which, when pursued, fades into insubstantiality.

Perhaps what drew me to Herzen in the first place was not his eminence, but his obscurity. He moves like a shadow through the drawing rooms of 1850s London. He was a big man, physically robust, fully bearded in the manner of the day, with a corporation and a waistcoat to keep it in, and a supply of fine hats for each occasion. Yet even so, perhaps especially so, he is hard to see because he is impossible to hear. There is no voice. Surely all biographers discover that, in the same way that much of the sense of taste really comes from the sense of smell, so the appearance of people in the eye is moderated by what we hear from them in the ear. How rapidly beauty turns to ugliness, or the plainest of faces to the most interesting, when someone begins to talk.

It has been common to substitute correspondence for the voice. And I don't mean that we read letters for their content, their information about love or passion, bereavement, child-birth, mortgages, money and matrimony. These things are obvious up to a point. Rather, biographers incline to read letters for the sound of the voice that is writing them, as though the page was a score, and the composer's voice behind it ready to sing in key. Hence Carr's analysis of Herzen and Natalie, when he detects in the style of their correspondence, written in Russian, the voices of romantic Western Europeans in the manner of George Sand, and assumes that the voices he hears are self-evidently truthful, and not either counterfeit, or the product of his own yearnings rather than theirs. One does not have to reflect for long on G.B.S.'s letters and cards, or the correspondence between men like Miller and Durrell, Lyttleton and Hart-Davis, Byron and Scrope Davies, even writers as different as Orwell, Turgenev, Patrick White, Virginia Woolf and Evelyn Waugh, to see the truth of this. The letter is a little performance, and in the pen of the master of the performance art it reflects the writer only in so far as the writer seeks a particular response. And when the letter is to an intimate, its truthfulness or otherwise, particularly in the matter of the voice adopted, is hard, perhaps impossible, to establish.

So it was with Herzen and his Natalie. She fell in love

and eloped with Herwegh, who had insinuated himself into Herzen's company. Only then she discovered that she had made a shocking error of judgement. Herwegh was an impostor. A boring, grubby imitator of the passionate romantic, as true to the history of ideas as a Disney themepark to the history of society. Even his contemporaries used to call him 'the iron lark'. Unsurprisingly, Natalie was subsequently defensive about her error of judgement. The mortification of being doubly deceived, both about herself and about the authenticity of Herwegh, led her to disguise both the nature and the course of her infatuation. Herzen, had he been in a position to read her letters to Herwegh, would surely have recognized what Carr could not, that Natalie needed sympathy and understanding. That her letters were a self-defensive façade behind which she was trying to conceal her humiliation. When Herzen offered her the hand of his love she took it, and returned to him.

In the biography I was tempted to write this part of Herzen's life-story in the form of a film script. Herzen and Natalie go to live in the villa in Nice in late June 1850. Herwegh arrives in August, ostensibly to be Herzen's secretary. He seduces Natalie: poetry by moonlight; warm Nice nights in the garden; Herzen preoccupied with his work; Natalie, pregnant with Herzen's daughter Olga (who will be born on 20 November), neglected by him, so that she is starved of his affection. Natalie gives way to impulse, capitulates to Herwegh, eventually runs away to join him. Herzen is devastated but stoic, the philosopher in life. He recognizes and accepts his own responsibility for the disaster that has befallen him. He doesn't pursue her, but they correspond. Reading her letters, he detects her anguish. In the summer of 1851 they agree to meet in Turin, and are reconciled. They return to the villa in the South of France, Natalie already pregnant once more. Herzen settles back to work, and on 2 September finishes his essay letter to Jules Michelet on 'The Russian People and Socialism'. Shortly afterwards Natalie and Herzen witness the death by drowning of their son Kolya and Herzen's mother, Madame Haag, victims of a ferry disaster outside the port of Nice. Later, in the damp of winter, Natalie contracts pleurisy. She takes to her bed on the first day of the new year of 1852. The complication of illness leads in April to the premature birth of a little boy, who dies, and then three days later, on 2 May, to the death of Natalie herself.

A tragic film, shot in the hard light of the Midi, with landscapes drawn from Cézanne.

I wasn't able to persevere with the idea of biography as screenplay. I mentioned it once to my agent, who pursed his lips the way he does, and then put on his glasses, as if to examine my features for evidence that I'd gone mad.

'It would make a good play,' he said. 'But is biography theatre?'

A good question. One to set alongside the more common: isn't biography fiction by another name? Or at least: doesn't biography appeal to the same longings as fiction once did, but in a post-industrial world, where stories need somehow to be harder and more real, where names and streets and buildings must be seen, described, photographed, to be believed in? One contemporary biographer believes his work to be concerned with 'the kind of human truth, poised between fact and fiction, which a biographer can obtain as he tells the story of another's life, and thereby makes it both his own (like a friendship) and the public's (like a betrayal) . . .' A view now widely assimilated. I doubt that it's true. The people who read biography are, I suspect, the same people who read fiction. And they know the difference. Some of those who write biography also write novels. They can surely tell the difference.

The best parallel, if one has to be found, is drama. It's true that biography isn't theatre, but it satisfies the desire that people have for shaped experience, for comedy, passion, tragedy and denouement.

We live in the West with two models of experience in our minds. On the one hand, everything seems random and haphazard. With no god, life is a lottery. Luck is what shapes experience, and possibilities are defined by the bell curve and wherever you happen to lie under it. On the other hand, everything seems ordered and controlled. The hidden hands of nature's laws, market operations, and social structure, combine to control and determine such opportunities as we may enjoy. The state has us under surveillance when we travel, when we earn, when we are sick. Marketers know what we want, and what we are prepared to spend on it. Popular culture keeps us 'happy' from day to day. We are used, manipulated, soothed and coerced. Biography frees us from the dilemmas of understanding that these two models implicitly pose, by uniting them, by illustrating the singular among the general, by suggesting the locations in experience where the solitary individual might break away from both the constraints of order and the random wilfulness of chance, to impose his will, and thus be free.

Thinking about this, and the importance of drama to life itself, made me realize how close I was straying to Moser's scientific terrain. As I understood it – imperfectly, probably – Moser came to the view that the genetic make-up of any particular individual asserted what a layman might call a 'pull'. He was not referring here to fundamental physical attributes, like skin colour, or number of toes, things that you inherited, and which could not be moulded in any way; nor to what he called 'potential', such as the possibility of being tall, or starting a malignant cancer, or being a great concert pianist, each of which depended on environmental circumstance in some degree. 'Pull' was at work in the arena of what he thought of as 'hidden traits' of character and personality. The evidence for this was not empirical, but derived from the assumption that it was theoretically reasonable to assume that the mind (which has no physical or chemical existence) was the sole structure of life that was free of genetic constraint. He conceived of the will as the mind's principal agent. As the bundle of genetic certainties and possibilities that we call a child is moulded and kneaded into shape by its environment, it may develop a mind capable of, so to speak, standing apart from its biological self, and perceiving alternatives. Adolescence and young adulthood, for reasons he thought had probably to do with the molecular chemistry of the body, offered an opening for the mind to transcend both the necessity of genes and the randomness of luck. A young person, by the exercise of will-power, can overcome the disadvantages of genetic inheritance, quell the inner voices of passion or indifference, rise above the psychological imperatives of parents, and literally be him- or herself. Free, independent, creative.

Escape in this fashion, which is how he thought of it, was hard to sustain, however. The imperatives of genes and environment maintain a crushing pressure. Even the great escapers, Byron, Darwin, Luther, Wordsworth, Wittgenstein, Mozart, Keats – he had such a long list of them – may be exhausted young, ready to throw in the towel, either in death, or in surrender to convention. For many of us, the diminution of the will is the discovery, in mid-life crisis, that we are indeed like our parents, and that there is no escape from the prison of this discovery. It is the reassertion of genetic compulsion and environment together. The rediscovery of death – suppressed since infancy as a distant prospect of no great concern just yet – the emotional and psychological response to physical necessity, loss of powers. I find myself grappling with these possibilities. Am I living, in Alice and Gradle, my own crisis of middle age? Would Moser's ideas constitute scientific endorsement of what I sense, but can only fumble to explain in my reactions to Herzen's life, to Alice, to Moser's death, to Vita? Moser said old age was the triumph of nature rampant, the will shrivelling to nothing at the moment of death, the mind desiccated and empty as the ultimate genetic potential, extinction, is realized.

Unknown to themselves perhaps, readers find release in rehearsing this shape of life in biography. Not only is it terrible how genes follow us around, what is worse is that they get us in the end. The knowledge of this is what accounts for little trivial things, a woman catching herself doing something her mother always did, and of which she had herself once been critical. Or a man, seeing himself, off guard, in a mirror, and detecting the man who had been his father, or was his older brother, and realizing that he bore the signs, the expressions, the hair-line, and, behind the eyes, the same sensitivities, or lack of them, that he had once, perhaps, despised.

But it also accounts for much bigger things. For horror and despair; shame and ignominy; fear and alienation. All the things I feel today.

It hadn't occurred to me before, but I wonder now whether Moser's theory of the 'pull' of genetic inheritance and the struggle of the mind to be free didn't themselves flow from intimations and fears that he had about his own family. Two years ago I met some of these people, and they turned out to be quite unlike the more or less mythical beings he had concocted for me previously. There was to be a celebration, a silver wedding party for his sister and brother-in-law, and Moser begged me to go with him. 'Normally Vita would have come,' he said, by way of sufficient explanation.

We took the train to Keswick, and then a taxi to an hotel on Ullswater where the party was to be held on the Saturday night. It was very early spring in northern England. Presumably the wedding to be celebrated had been one of those pre-Easter tax-reduction ceremonies that social historians will write about one day. No doubt recalling the original day, the weather was cold, with a spitting rain. I felt apprehensive. When I got into my room I lay down on the bed with my coat and shoes still on, and fell into a deep sleep. Alice was away, of course, I think in Valparaiso on this occasion, and I dreamed of her briefly, offering me love from behind, in front of a mirror that for some reason had a steam train engraved on it, puffs of silver smoke contributing some sort of sexual obscurity. This all came to nothing – well it was a dream – because Moser came in and made some herbal tea, and produced two large and quite delicious scones from a brown paper bag.

'Time to abandon the nobility of sleep for the common lot of afternoon tea,' he said.

'Class even in dreams?'

'Everywhere, dear boy,' said Moser. 'As you are shortly to discover. English family occasions are class occasions, and this one is lower middle. You will thank me later for the inoculation of this Scottish scone.'

Moser was right. The party turned out to be a surprise. That is to say, Moser's brother-in-law had organised the event as a surprise for his wife Belinda – or Belle, as everyone except Moser seemed to call her – and had gone to elaborate lengths to ensure that the guests all arrived by 7.00 p.m. and were neatly tucked away in the Wainwright suite before himself arriving with Belle at 7.30, and falling on the assembled company as if in total surprise. The subterfuge may have worked, though Belinda seemed to me more shocked than gratified.

The guests consisted entirely of those who had been at the wedding twenty-five years before, though a few deaths and rather more divorces made the company incomplete – and they raised a cheer, sang 'for they are jolly good fellows', and then fell into an uneasy silence which, the festivities not having been scripted beyond this point, no one felt able to fill with a speech. I could feel Moser beside me squirming with embarrassment. Someone called for 'a few words from the jest of honour'.

'Well,' said Belinda. 'What a surprise.'

I was surprised myself to discover that her voice didn't sound anything like Moser's, but was high-pitched and coarse, like a coin scraped on glass. One of those placeless English voices, cheap and dreary.

'I'm amazed!'

And so she was, since she said not another word. Stuart, her husband, managed a brief account of his experiences in keeping the occasion secret throughout both planning and execution, an explanation that was full of 'phews' and 'close call, that one' type of remarks. For some reason the idea of the event, its quality of surprise, surpassed in importance its specific content, the celebration of a quarter century of marriage, and presumably successful marriage at that. There were, after all, several grown-up children present, Moser's nephews and niece, who looked like a credit to someone, but to whom no one referred, as though the twenty-five years between the event and its celebration were a void, and they had disappeared into it. Some waiters appeared with bottles of something called Sforza champagne-style wine and the party began in, well in what?, earnest I suppose.

In the course of the evening I had an opportunity to talk to Stuart, who introduced himself to me by questioning my presence at the occasion as the only person who hadn't been there twenty-five years before. I explained my connection to Moser.

'Ger always reckons he can go his own way,' said Stuart, laughing, and sucking deeply on his glass of sparkling wine. 'Lovely stuff,' he said appreciatively.

I asked him about his work and home-life, and he told me about both. He quickly emerged as a robust Thatcherite (she had been forced from office four years before, but he still held hopes for her return as 'the only one that's any bloody good') and his conversation, quite naturally it seemed, touched on 'our coloured brethren', 'Argies', 'layabouts' (a euphemism for the unemployed) and 'nitwits' (trade union members, Labour Party supporters, and anyone generally who did not share his views). He worked as a technical draughtsman in an electronics components firm, work that he proudly claimed to having 'learned on the job' without the unnecessary preliminary of acquiring a degree. I think he did actually refer to the school of hard knocks at one stage. He professed some pride in being 'self-employed', a consultant, so that 'I look after the tax end of things, and the firm's freed of all that admin and bumph.' He accompanied this information with a wink. He stood on the balls of his feet, his legs apart.

'What about you? What's your angle? I suppose it's something the rest of us pay for if it's anything to do with Ger.'

This opening implied an unprofitable line of mutual recrimination, but I managed to restrain myself enough to agree that I was a university teacher, and that young people were more interesting and useful than was sometimes supposed. With this we were separated by Moser, who took me on a tour of inspection which he coupled with a discreet running commentary that he somehow poured into my left ear as he steered me around the room.

'No aristocrats of life here tonight,' he said. 'No Fenners

or Felixes. Still the gene pool is less murky than many suppose, and contributes a categorical disaster for every miracle. My brother George, known as "Foxtrot" when a boy because his schoolmates said he was a proper Charlie, and there used to be some sort of NATO alphabet reference that went "Foxtrot-Charlie", well, he's not here tonight because Stuart decided not to invite him on the grounds that he would spoil everything by arguing with Pop. Pop's his name for my father, who is over there.'

Moser's father was a short, stout man with a bald head, and either no social bearing at all, or else a developed sense of social revenge, as he had come wearing a yellow pullover and blue corduroy trousers, and was spectacularly rude to everyone to whom I heard him speak. This included the short speech which he contributed to the proceedings at about 10.00 o'clock, in which he reminded everyone that it had been his duty to make a speech this very day twenty-five years ago, and that he was happy to do so again, the more so as on this occasion he was not paying. There was some laughter here, but a lot had been drunk by this time, and none of it of any particular merit. I had holed up in a corner with one of Moser's uncles while this was going on, and although I searched for Moser in the crowded, smoky room, I couldn't locate him. The uncle, who was some sort of family rough diamond, confided to me that Moser's father was a snob who had never liked his in-laws, whom he regarded as beneath him, and so he always behaved in a vulgar way whenever they were present 'so as to even things up for them'. He claimed that it made them feel more at home, though the truth was, as Moser later explained to me, quite the opposite. He only wanted to humiliate them.

This conduct he also extended to his wife. Later, when Moser and I were having a quiet supper together in his room, and the party-goers had long since departed, Moser told me that his father had, from as long ago as Moser could recall, been repeatedly unfaithful to his mother. He coupled his flagrant infidelities with an equally flagrant po-faced denial of them, so that the family had grown up knowing that what was true was false and what was false was true. His mother had become neurotically ill as a result. His brother had become estranged, and had joined a religious cult in Somerset from which he rarely emerged, and then only in order to tell the rest of the family what to do. Belinda had, he thought, married early and unhappily in order to escape, and he, Moser, had retired to a life of the mind in order to avoid madness. He believed that his father was quite convinced that he had led an exemplary life, successfully raised a fine family despite the impediment of his wife, and regarded himself as a social asset in whatever circle was fortunate enough to have him at the moment. When I said that all this was incomprehensible, Moser said that he thought not.

'This is social reality in the English lower middle class. It is why the word "escape" occurs so often in English biography and autobiography. There is much to run away from.'

There were other features of this silver wedding anniversary that were worthy of note. Three fights occurred towards the end: two in the car park, and one in the ladies' lavatories, where a large porcelain swan ornament was smashed, and several broken shoe heels were additional (though not the only) causes of late-leavers limping from the scene. A number of the celebrants had brought cardboard cartons with them in their car boots, and these were produced to carry away remaining food and drink – keen competition for which was a cause of one of the car park fights. Belinda spent most of the final hour of the proceedings in tearful conversation with three middle-aged women of uncertain temper who had, apparently, been her best friends at school. One of these was heard to observe that she'd give Stu a horse-whipping if the opportunity presented itself, but it didn't (at least not on this occasion), and the last fight was left to two overweight men who scratched each other's car doors leaving the hotel car park, and traded black eyes before being separated by their wives. When Moser said goodbye to his sister, and kissed her on each cheek, she was still tearful, and said that she realized he had never liked her husband, so it was especially good of him to have come to the surprise party. No amount of reassurance from Moser could, apparently, shake her from this opinion, which may, on reflection, have been one of the few accurate things that she knew about her brother.

These details are of indifferent interest were it not for the fact that last night, after a lot of hesitation, but knowing that today there would be an announcement and tomorrow an obituary, I summoned up the energy to look through Moser's desk for his address book and, having found it, telephoned his sister. There were various addresses crossed out before one in Battersea, and I recognized her voice as soon as she came on the line. I explained who I was, and how we had met only once some years previously when I had been her brother's guest at her silver wedding anniversary party, an introduction which evoked a loud sniff.

'Well?'

'It's my painful obligation to report to you some very bad news I'm afraid. It concerns your brother. I'm sorry to have to tell you that he died on Saturday night. Here in college. In bed. Of causes that have not yet been established.'

There was a silence for several seconds.

'What, Ger? Ger dead?'

'Ger' was how he was, or had been, known in his family. It was supposedly short for Gervaise, but Moser had told me this with little conviction, and I had never really believed it. I had the impression that Belinda had been drinking.

'Yes. I really am very sorry to have to tell you. There will be an announcement in the morning papers, perhaps an obituary in *The Times*. I was hoping that you and your husband . . .'

She began to laugh uncontrollably.

'My 'usband? You mean Stuart? He left me eighteen months ago, and I 'aven't heard from him for at least a year, and I shouldn't imagine that he'll care much about Ger. They never got on.'

'Excuse me. I'm sorry. It was rather that I imagined you would want to let the rest of the family know . . .' My voice tailed away. I found her impossible to talk to, and my own grief was an almost insurmountable obstacle to any but the most banal conversation.

'Well, if it's goin' to be in the papers, like you say. When's the funeral?'

'No decisions have been taken. There has to be an autopsy. Tomorrow, I think. And after that the family could make whatever arrangements thought necess . . .'

'The family?' She pronounced the word as though it were an entirely new idea to her, one that might require a definition.

'I could get a day off to come, but Dad's dead now, last year, and wha' a go-round that was, and Mum's been in and out of places with 'er nerves for years, and she's in at the moment. I don't think she could handle Ger's passing right now. What did you say he died of?'

I told her again about the need for an autopsy and said I expected the college could manage arrangements. I gave her my phone number and we agreed to talk again. No sooner had I hung up than Alice rang. She could change her plans if necessary, she said, and get a plane home overnight. Would I like her to? Or should we stick to the Florence plan? I began to weep.

'Poor boy,' she said. 'I really am sorry. I wish I was there to comfort you. Please don't be sad about me to add to being sad about Moser. Call me back later, any time. It's all right to wake me. Just say if I should come.' She gave me her direct line number, and said, 'I love you.'

4

Wednesday

'It is difficult to have a personal quarrel with world history.'

I had planned to write more before bed last night, but was
deterred by the effect of the phone calls, and then by a late
and solitary supper at the Gardeners Arms in North Parade.
This pub is often a cause of, or stimulant to, melancholy, and
I like to go there occasionally when I am alone because it
is cheerful, and thronged with young people who are not
undergraduates, but language students from Denmark or Hungary, or au pairs from France and Norway. Their apparently
carefree happiness is a reminder of much of my own that has
been lost, and I find the sense of forfeiture it stimulates strangely
enjoyable. A bit like a clergyman conducting a wedding, I
imagine. The happiness is not his, and in its simple and
uncomplicated pleasure, with all of the carnal intention it
implies and precedes, stimulates uneasy feelings of time past
and mortality to come. Anyway, the G.A. was relatively quiet
yesterday, and I spent an hour over a sandwich refreshing my
memory of Carr's *The Romantic Exiles*. I had forgotten how
truly awful it is, and began to wonder whether I shouldn't go
back and put something stronger in my biography. Reading
this sort of pseudo-academic work – and there's a lot of it
about in the darkened wings of philosophy – has the interesting
effect of raising my pulse rate. I have often wondered why
this is. It's as if I'm personally threatened by it, somehow, and
can only recover my equilibrium by turning away from it,

putting it aside. It was the excitement of ideas that drew me to philosophy in the first place. Perhaps it will drive me out of it in due course. Maybe it has already. Writing biography is not exactly the pursuit of hard ideas. Anyway, these things must have tired me out because when I got back to my rooms in college I lay down on the sofa in my study and immediately went to sleep, then woke in the early hours and dozed uncomfortably until Mrs Wharton came in at 7.30 and I had to get dressed.

Alice is right, I think. It is difficult to dissociate being sad about Moser from being sad about her. These things have always seemed to go in tandem. Ten or so years ago, when Alice and I had been married for a while, she had some sort of a relationship with a Frenchman, Maxime Vinteuil, who also worked at Scorpion in those days. When she first met him I don't know, but there was a period of about three months when she seemed able to think of no one else. No matter what topic was raised, Max was there: what he thought, what he believed, his background, his family, his wife and children. Maxime — I could never bring myself to call him Max — was older than Alice, quite tall, a little grey at the temples, a pair of half-glasses on a string round his neck, and a strange mouth — a thin upper but full lower lip, slack and somehow dissipated. I met him only a couple of times and can't recall the colour of his eyes. His father was a wealthy Parisian publisher, his grandfather had fought in the Spanish Civil War, his uncles and brothers were all connected to Mitterrand's court. In that comfortable, secure, French bourgeois world, I imagine that he had grown up believing that rites of passage were entitlements.

Alice became deeply interested in him, his generosity, his courtesy, his loyalty. She wanted to invite him to Oxford. I was to meet his wife, to whom he was devoted, etc., though apparently she was his second. I asked Alice whether he was devoted to his second wife in the same way that he had been devoted to his first, but Alice finds my sarcasm contemptible, and this kind of remark never went down well. Sometimes I wonder whether even intelligent women understand anything at all about men. Vinteuil struck me as a saloon-bar socialist, the sort of man whose social conscience rattled like a pocketful of small change. His principles, of the Third World exploitation variety much admired by Alice, seemed to me like a thin veneer. You will say that jealousy makes me a poor witness, but the fact is that Maxime wore his principles like other men wear a watch, or carry a walking stick, for convenience or a flourish. Something to be put down when you come home, or taken off at bedtime. He particularly enjoyed telling stories about Mao Tse-tung and Zhou Enlai, whom he had met as a teenager when he went with his father on some junket or other with Malraux, back in the early 60s. Their understanding of, and sympathy with, peasant culture and the problems of development had so much to teach us. And so forth.

Was Mao still a Maoist in bed, I wonder, thrusting with contradictions? He spent enough time at it, by all accounts. Perhaps that was it: we are all Maoists between the sheets. Sex, not death, is the great leveller. There are no classes on the long march to coitus.

But that can't be true. There are sexual aristocrats and there are sexual slaves. There is a great middle class of sex: *les hommes moyens sensuels*. There are those who own it, those who profit from it, and those who are exploited by it. I belong to the pathetic exploited sexual class, but what is my use value, and what is my exchange value? As with so much else it is probably only lawyers who know the answer.

These digressions often occur when I think of Alice. Somehow she propels everything before her into economic terminology. At one time I used to deal with it by lampooning her subject as 'anycomics', and its practice as 'anycomical'. But the point wasn't funny at all, because her brief infatuation with the French bourgeois radical occurred more or less at the same time that Vita was diagnosed as having a rare form of skin cancer. This was another example of how being sad about Moser always seemed to go in tandem with being sad about Alice. They were linked, somehow, in a pattern of gloom.

At first, Vita's illness had seemed a sort of surprising impossibility. She had gone to her doctor because she thought she was pregnant, although it is also true that she felt tired and lacking in energy when normally, with the autumn concert season approaching, she would have felt her usual vitality. Whatever, blood tests showed that she was indeed pregnant, but that she had a carcinoma, and that behind it, as another cause for concern, she also had Hodgkin's disease, cancer of the lymphatic system. In this way, an occasion that should have announced a new life actually turned into a life-threatening diagnosis. A 'surprising impossibility' was actually Vita's term to describe the experience. The nature of the illness was rare enough, but there was treatment available, and both she and Moser took a positive view of her chances of recovery. The problem had been caught in a reasonably early stage, and her specialist promoted what he rather unpleasantly called 'aggressive therapy'. He said she stood 'every chance' of a complete recovery.

'Chance is my subject,' Moser told her. 'So it has to be on your side.'

She lost the baby during chemotherapy.

My own view was what I had by that time come to call Herzenian. Fatalism tempered by humanism. It is true that Herzen was a fatalist in his private life, and there was much there to provoke his fatalism: the deaths of his children and his mother, betrayals by friends, inconstancy of acquaintances, Natalie's infidelity to him with Herwegh. But outside the arena of the heart and its torments, he was a true man of the people – *all* of the people – and he sensed and willed their early optimism, even when, perhaps especially when, he disagreed with them. After the failure of the Commune in 1848 he moved around from Paris to Geneva, to Nice, to Zurich, and back to Paris. He had financial worries, and was preoccupied, along with his mother, in extracting her fortune from tsarist Russia. But once the Empire came into existence he made his way to London, where he lived for twelve years from 1852 to 1864. It is not the case, as Carr asserts, that Herzen became a sceptic after the personal and public events of 1848 to 1852, as though he had acquired such a close understanding of English attitudes that he could assert them in response to his own circumstances. His scepticism was already fully developed in the final pages of his *Notes of a Young Man*, written probably in 1840, long before he left Russia. In this remarkable work of a 28-year-old he has a fictional Polish landowner, Trenzinsky (a portrait of Chaadayev?) observe, '. . . a man does reconcile himself in some way with life: one by not believing in any reconciliation . . . ; another . . . by believing that it is reason that convinces you of what you believe . . . Believe me, we are all children and, like children in general, we play with toys and take our dolls for reality.' The truth is that he never particularly liked England. He felt at home in France, and he yearned for the Russia which he was never to see again. In this sense he was rather like an English literary intellectual of the twentieth rather than the nineteenth century, despising England, happy in France, and yearning for an impossible utopian homeland concocted from childhood recollections and the imagination. Despite these traits Herzen recognized in dull

English society certain pointers to a realistic future which other nineteenth-century thinkers were incapable of detecting.

Herzen went about in London, both sides of the bourgeois barricades, drawing rooms as well as drinking clubs. He attended working men's reading groups, knew Karl Marx and the circle of communist acolytes that was forming around him, was familiar with Proudhon and Bakunin. Even knew about Nechaev at the end of his life. He understood what these various people were saying, followed their arguments with scrupulous attention, and he came to the conviction that not only were their revolutionary expectations false, but each in his own particular way threatened to impose, out of revolutionary chaos, a new tyranny even more ferocious than any it might replace. Marx's notion of class warfare, and the need to side with history in the 'objective' annihilation of the bourgeoisie under the dictatorship of the proletariat he recognized as genocide. Its 'inevitability' as an 'ineluctable' consequence of the 'scientific laws' of history he considered trite. He called the German revolutionary immigrants to England in the 1850s 'cockchafers of the political and literary worlds, who rootle about every evening, gloating and busy, in the discarded remnants of the day'. An empirical view of Marx rather different from that of his twentieth-century worshippers.

These sorts of opinions don't make Herzen an idealist, someone to contrast with Marx and his supposedly scientific materialism. Herzen was a true revolutionary. He wished to set everyone free, shopkeepers as well as miners, lawyers' clerks and their housewives as well as printers and mill workers. He believed long before it became evident to anyone else that racial discrimination was just as likely to be a source of social conflict as class, and that it would divide classes against themselves. He held and promoted advanced views about the status and liberation of women at a time when such views found expression among only a tiny fragment of the population in even as developed and open a society as Britain in the 1850s. In all these matters Herzen was far, far ahead of his time, addressing our problems as we see them now, speaking to us directly across the many historical tragedies that have since intervened.

Just as he was no idealist, so neither was he a romantic. Perhaps, as his representative, I may be said to have stood in for him at Moser's sister's twenty-fifth wedding anniversary party, an occasion which he would surely have recognized as indicative, perhaps even symbolic, of the consequences of conferring social and political liberty on ordinary people like ourselves. It would not have made him laugh. He sympathized with people and their predicaments. Nor would it have made him despair. Herzen understood that society evolves, and has no final resting place.

. . . every generation lives for itself . . . From the point of view of history it is a transition, but in relation to itself it is the goal, and it cannot, it ought not to endure without a murmur the afflictions that befall it . . .

Each new situation challenges us to find solutions, make decisions, confront change. No doubt he would have sighed, and admitted that yes, it was true, people sometimes used their precious liberty for the most banal of purposes, but it was *their* liberty, to use as they wished, thoughtfully or not as each case may be. Tastes and opinions vary, and the tolerance of variety may be one of the few virtues to be self-interested as well as altruistic.

Some intellectuals find this hard to accept, mainly, I think, because they have to possess ideas instead of just contemplating or analysing them. There should be an economic theory of ideology, explaining how worth is acquired in the market-place of ideas, how they may be purchased and exchanged and in what currency. I must suggest it to Alice. In the hands of a typical contemporary practitioner of the dismal science, *An Economic Theory of Ideas* would be as vacuous as most of mainstream micro-economic theory has become. But I doubt that anyone would notice. This is because it is convenient for intellectuals in our age to believe that ideas are quite divorced from the people who hold them. Even as sound a guide to Herzen as Isaiah Berlin never mentions Herzen's sexual transgressions, his betrayal of Ogarev. He sensed, I suspect, that these matters detracted from the high-mindedness, the generosity and sensitivity, of Herzen's political and philosophical beliefs. Carr may have thought the same, because he revels in Herzen's lapses, discusses little else, so anxious is he to put them at the centre of his story, convinced, presumably, that they prove Herzen's duplicity, his hypocrisy, his lack of serious-ness. This is the only topic (and neither of them refers to it explicitly) on which I think Berlin and Carr see eye to eye. Yet surely they are both wrong. The whole Herzen is the real figure, muddled sometimes, occasionally immoral, now and then lost in his own egotism to the detriment of his friends, but not mostly, not even often. Herzen knew this himself.

In order that an idea which is clear and rational for you should also become someone else's idea, it is not enough that it should be true. The other's brain must be as well developed as yours, and it must be emancipated from tradition.

Emancipating yourself from tradition is not easy anywhere, but London in the 1850s may have been simpler than most places. The whole city was in a state of both expansion and demolition: population, industry and transportation all growing rapidly. It was also, briefly, a truly cosmopolitan city, overflowing with the flood of political refugees in flight from imprisonment and execution after the failure of the European revolutions of 1848. A polyglot city, self-confident, diverse and culturally rich.

Herzen's response to the muddle and excitement of London seems to have been a restless peripatesis. In the twelve years of his residence he rented at least fourteen different properties, half of them in the first four years, when he seemed unable to settle, and moved from Trafalgar Square to Spring Gardens, from Euston Square to Richmond, Twickenham, Richmond again, and then the Finchley Road. For some reason Carr gives all these addresses in an appendix, though there is nothing in his text to indicate why he should do this. Perhaps to bestow a sort of spurious scholarship to his 'research' – look, see how I investigated all of this. He missed one, however: in the autumn of 1852 Herzen lived at 2 Barrow Hill Place, Primrose Hill, which was where he penned the very first preface to *My Past and Thoughts*, titled 'To my Brothers in Russia' – though the fragment was never published in his lifetime. This was also where he wrote the introduction to the first edition of *Prison and Exile*, which was eventually published in 1854.

What is perhaps more interesting even than the frequency with which Herzen moved during his time in London is what subsequently happened to his places of residence. Some years ago I devoted a couple of days to touring London to see each building. One or two of them may have remained, though greatly transformed if so, and renumbered and renamed as well, so no longer identifiably his. There was no 4 Spring Gardens, where he lived in September/October 1853, and such other adjacent numbers as had survived, on the corner of Cockspur Street and facing across Trafalgar Square to the National Gallery, were steak houses and travel agencies. In their turn, these abutted a modern building – concrete and glass, bunker style, overlooking Admiralty Arch from the back and St James's Park from the front – which housed the British Council. Would Herzen have approved of this?

There was no 'Laurel House' in Putney High Street, where Herzen lived, and Turgenev visited. Just beyond where it should have been, where the High Street becomes Putney Hill, there is 'The Pines', with a plaque commemorating it as the residence of Swinburne and Watts-Dunton. High Romanticism, but no evidence that a philosopher and lover of liberty passed this way. On Putney Bridge, with its diagonal churches, the green of the park and the placid, dark river beneath, it is possible to close one's eyes and imagine away the present. But not in Putney High Street. Seifert and his gang had worked their destruction on one side of it – rows of tattered concrete pill boxes that seemed to crush people to the uneven pavement. Opposite, dilapidated late Victoriana, upper windows smashed, the buildings themselves perhaps already grotesque when they were built – they flaunted their dates, 1889, 1893, etc. – and worse than ever when neglected. I have never been back.

Unless one is to become a complete hermit, others are unavoidable, however. My favourite from this catalogue of horrors is Euston Square, where Herzen lived at No. 25 in the autumn and winter of 1853–4, perhaps until June of the latter year. Roughly where his house once stood, there now stands *Piscator* by Eduardo Paolozzi, assisted by Ray Watson, and cast by Robert Taylor & Co (Ironfounders) Ltd. This is a great gleaming lump of silver-coloured sculptural trash. It was commissioned by the British Railways Board; Fluor (Great Britain) Ltd; Sir Robert McAlpine & Sons Ltd; Norwich Union Insurance Group; and Pension Fund Securities Ltd; and was, as it explicitly proclaims, 'presented to the nation through the Arts Council of Great Britain 1981'. Nearby, at least on the day I visited and lingered – perhaps it has all changed again since then – were Rail House and the offices of something called Inmarsat, along with a plaque to commemorate the London walkway. On the handsome statue of Robert Stephenson (who was still alive when Herzen lived at 25 Euston Square) someone had stuck a handbill saying 'Royal Free for the Cup', and an empty sherry bottle rested at his feet. Newspapers drifted around in the gritty wind that flowed about a dismal modernist fountain.

Not only had Herzen gone from this place, and all trace of him been expunged, but all trace of his age had gone as well. It's as if the modern world believes it can free itself from history, no longer carry any burden of culture by carelessly destroying the past from which only it could be derived. Crumpled into the Newspeak of Inmarsat, preoccupied with Cup Finals, blinking away the grit that swirls in the discarded rubbish, it now knows art, decency, and the real liberalism of moral choice only as a list of self-interested institutional names on an internationally approved lump of rubbish that had been negotiated by the Arts Council.

Herzen is dead. His world is dead. But it was once alive, and it could live again if we rediscovered the means of knowing it. Our own world, on the other hand, seems barely living, as though in a coma, or in a long, dark sleep in which experience is merely the impressions left by dreams or nightmares.

One of these came to me over a period of several days when Alice and I went to Nice to visit Herzen's grave.

It was only a couple of years after we got married, when I could still be persuaded to travel, 1986 or 87, I suppose. Herzen, having left England in 1864, went back to his beloved France, and after a period in Paris went to live once again in Nice. This was no longer the city of Savoy that it had been when he first stayed, but was now, as a result of the Treaty of Turin, a part of France. In other respects, however, it was unchanged, and far distant from the Parisian centre of Bonaparte's pompous, malevolent empire. Nice must have been full of melancholy recollections, but it was where he had established a family grave, and it was where he intended to end his days. He was fifty-two in 1864, and had less than seven years still to live. As luck would have it he actually died in Paris early in 1870, but his body was taken south, and laid to rest in the spot that he had chosen.

The grave was not hard to find. The cemetery of Nice is on a pine-covered hill, behind the site of the castle, and with fine views from its walled paths down on to the port, the Bay of Angels, and the old town. It is a place of great tranquillity, literally now a raised-up island in the sea of decadence and squalor that the tourist and industrial city of Nice has become. We walked along the mile of steep streets and steps from the Place Garibaldi to the north, past the church of St Martin and St Augustin, and then up the very lee of the towering hill and its summit walls.

Herzen was located towards the southern end, a white sepulchre set down low, unshaded, completely exposed to the sun, already hot, though we were there in the first week of May. On top, rising amid a little spacious forest of crucifixes, white angels, and the miniature turrets of rather grander tombs, is an almost life-size bronze statue of the man himself – black and green from oxidation, flecked white here and there by the gulls. He wears those baggy, high trousers and dirt-scuffed boots of the mid-century urban bourgeois, the frock-coat of a gentleman, and the folded arms and huge high-browed, bearded, glaring face of a story-book philosopher. Someone had been there a little ahead of us, and put six fresh red carnations at his feet.

I do not find, as some must, tombs to be places of consolation. The deaths they contain and record speak to me of despair, not hope. On the front, beneath Herzen's feet, are the words:

A Alexandre Herzen
Moscou 1812–1870 Paris
Sa famille, ses amis, ses admirateurs

To the left-hand side:

A la mémoire de Louise Haag
et de
Nicholas Herzen
péris en mer le 15-XI-1851

To the right-hand side:

Natalie Herzen née Zakharine 1817–1852
Liza Herzen 1858–1875
Lola Boy et Lola Girl 1861–1864

Enough sorrow here to fill an entire lifetime, though it was crushed into his last twenty years. Reading the simple words made me heavy with fatigue, and I sat down in the gravel under the shade of a tree while Alice took some photographs.

'Max likes this place,' she said suddenly. 'He told me about it.'

The words were blown through me on a freezing wind. A sense of loathing spread through my body, both heavy and ethereal together. Not even Herzen was free to be mine but Maxime Vinteuil must have him too, indeed, have had him first, and been picked over with Alice in my absence, idly no doubt, as I might talk to her on a Sunday afternoon walking on the Meadows, or musing aloud in bed just after we have put out the light. Nothing, absolutely nothing, belonged to me any longer. I was cornered. Denuded. And all this in the sunlight of a French cemetery on a morning in early May. With no one, and nothing, to notice.

'Did he contribute the carnations?' I said.

Alice gave me one of her looks that said, 'I do wish you'd grow up.' I felt myself being pulled into a black place of resentment, filled with the most bitter of jealousies, but silenced, unable to speak. It was impossible to say anything since all of the things that I might have said began with odium and grew worse. Mentally employing words, I wanted to tear at Alice and flay myself simultaneously: punish her for my imagined hurts, hurt myself for the desire to punish. Black dog.

This mood, so suddenly present, was always extremely difficult to shift. It persisted through lunch – presumably a disagreeable occasion of which I have no recollection – and into the afternoon as we drove east across the border into Italy, and then eventually north to the little Piedmont town of Alba. Here we found a small hotel, ate at a restaurant, and went to bed. Exhausted by the day, and expecting, indeed longing, for the balm of sleep, I now found myself instead suddenly wide awake. Alice put her arm round me, begged me not to be silent, but the black pleasure of resentment was in not responding, and I lay still in the dark, rehearsing my anger, punishing myself, and extending my hatred from one to all of the many women, the 'rotten bitches' as I thought of them at such times, against whom, in my mind, I commissioned the repeated acts of violence against myself. Was this meant to be revenge? The feelings are impossible to analyse at the time because the living of them leaves no room for detached thought. And analysing them later is useless, because the logic that seems so obvious and so austere at the time decays into a recognizable madness afterwards, and leaves nothing to analyse.

And in any event, it is axiomatic that feelings cannot be recalled.

'There's nothing between me and Max. He's just a friend.'

She repeats this every few days, and I see Natalie Herzen with Herwegh in the garden of the villa in Nice, close to where we have just been at her graveside. Did Herzen believe her? The prospect – the certainty of there being no certainty – is unbearable. For him too? Until she finally ran off? It is the cause of my feeling that my life is coming to an end. Every time I think of Maxime – now long since gone from our lives – I think of Alice's stoicism and stubbornness. She has defences in depth, yields nothing. Following her parents probably.

On a deathbed, hers or mine, depending on the sequence, she will tell me all the truths she has so long concealed, and call the revelations of deceit a reconciliation.

I had no memory of sleeping, but was awake at 5.20, sobbing. No idea why. No recollection of a dream. A deep sense of dread, with loneliness – though Alice was asleep in bed beside me – and anxiety fears hurting every part of my body. Alice was snoring very softly, a metaphor for oblivion.

Not dreaming, even in shallow sleep, is peculiar. It's as if the subconscious has been cut off, like a parrot with a blanket over its cage, unable to speak back its little bits of garbled verisimilitude. I wonder if this contributes to making my imagination worse, my fantasies, terrors, and narratives of pain, more vivid. I can't dream out my fears, shed them in sleep, so I have to live them awake, when all the powers of invention, logic, narrative, and design in the execution of effect can be brought to bear. It is a horror, and one that I fear, like love. I call them, these fears, my Furies, the Eumenides.

Why was I so low, that morning in Alba? Alice's comment by Herzen's grave was one thing. The evidence that Maxime was always with her no matter where we went, like a snatch of song heard in your youth that memory cannot dislodge. Was the obsession with him hers or mine? Or both? Had she made love with Maxime? I think Maxime always wanted her, not love necessarily, but the pursuit of desire. When I asked her once if he'd ever suggested it to her she didn't answer directly, but said, 'I think Max was too badly burned by what happened before to want to go through all that again.' The formula of her reply was strange: 'too badly burned'. It's a Maxime expression, proof of a Frenchman speaking fluent colloquial English. He also used to say 'cricket is not my cup of tea'. Worst Fury of all — well, no, perhaps not; but bad enough — did Alice want him, and he declined — 'I've been too badly burned'? I see them, the Furies edging imagination to work, embracing by a hotel bedroom door. They are clinging to each other, but he says they must be sensible, and she reluctantly agrees. Or vice versa. Or not at all.

Another thing is reinforcement: how the sadness of depression strengthens itself. Once the mood is embedded the mind goes in search of its reasons, and there is never a shortage of candidates. Betrayal makes us angry, but the anger turns inwards when it meets denial, and the pain of the active imagination, with nowhere else to go, is released upon itself. Maxime's presence at Herzen's grave is merely a trigger: the item that releases everything else. It's as if my vulnerability, raw at every turn, is my gift to Alice for all the wrongs I've done her, all the harm that I can never rectify.

Alice was silent throughout the next day, tired of my black temper, distant and cool. When we walked she kept slightly ahead of me, her arms folded. Grim criticism, the imagined 'rotten bitches' of the day before, gave way to mere unhappiness, and this in turn to remorse. A flood of light after the dark, and equally painful in its own way. Not talking much we drifted down by back roads to Turin, and booked into an hotel in the central arcaded area of the city, a place of soldiers and prostitutes. Over dinner we started to talk again. Later, when we turned out the light, she asked if I wanted to make love and I said 'Yes' but if she was too tired then it wouldn't matter. She said she would like it, but might be 'a bit slumped – if you don't mind'. I didn't. She was warm and soft, and turned towards me, hooking her leg over my hip. I caressed her back, lower and lower. Quite suddenly she let out a little moan, like – it seemed to me at the time – a soft cry both of recollection and rejection, turned on her back, closed her legs together, and became passive. I asked her if something was the matter. What had her little moan meant? Why had she uttered it? She said she was unaware of making any sound at all. I let it go. Slowly she became responsive again, and we made love very beautifully. Afterwards she cried. Then we slept.

When you've been in an Oxford college long enough, the one thing you fail to notice about it is that most of the time it's so quiet. No traffic, no scampering, shouting people. Just silence, with noises so ancient they seem to be part of nature or architecture: chimes, fountain water dribbling, hooting or scuffling birds, the swish of a gardener's hose or gravel under his rake. It's so focusing, so undistracting, the mind dwells only on itself. This is why Oxford has so many philosophers and historians, and why they do the sort of linguistic philosophy and intellectual history that they do. The mind examines the mind, and tugs endlessly at the knot, wondering which end of the string is the real beginning, and which a real end. Herzen must have felt the same, down there at Nice, wondering why the silence gripped everything so at night, when the house was full of children, servants, visitors, the sea lapping beyond the garden, the trees full of crouching cicadas waiting for the day. Why did Natalie go with Herwegh? What had that truthless sycophant to offer? His truthlessness? His sycophancy? His bad poetry? His fake radicalism? An iron lark is like the curate's egg. An oxymoronic politesse, more damning even than it seems. Herzen wasn't a baby or a saint – he never really liked Florence, all those Della Robbias turning their palms to him, swaddled in lunettes, glazed-eyed on portico walls – and his own betrayals were terrible. But Natalie with Herwegh? That was different in kind, as well as in degree. Or is it that all betrayals are equal?

Infidelity in a marriage has a special quality to it. Do other people feel this too? All the thousands who divorce every year, failed in their promises, uncontrite in their dreams? Perhaps only the first time. The shattering of permanence is troubling even so. 'It's like a smash-up on the motorway,' Vita told me once. 'Or a cot death, or having a son who turns out to be a child molester. It's something that always happens to someone else. Until it happens to you.' I used to think I'd never be able to write this down, that I'd eventually be able to talk to Moser about it, and have him understand. But thinking about Herzen and Natalie, Vinteuil, Gradle and Alice changes things. Some-one said (Keats?) that good art forgives bad character. Poets can do anything they please because art matters more than morality. But does it?

And what if the infidelity is fictive? Lives only in a mind full of fears, or in the fractured imagination of the terminally ill? None the less real, but invisible, with no tangible co-respondent to hit on the chin? Or to be hit by? Metaphorically, that is. Unlike Moser, who though tall was tough and solid, not stringy, I am still, even at forty, the seven-stone weakling of the Charles Atlas Sunday newspaper advertisements of my childhood, sand kicked in my face. Is the quality of betrayal still the same? For me, that is? Even though there's been no opening of legs, no furtive, hasty caressing, no motorcar entanglements or weekend humping in Saltzburg or Bali or Libreville – wherever this month's financial deal is being worked. Limousine, pied-à-terre, beach hotel, no matter. The legs are firmly closed, no even half-promises, pouts, blown-out matches lingered over. The betrayal is mental geometry, a torture test, mind control, the laundering of opinion, brain-washing, they used to say.

'You said you'd be home around eight.'

'The plane was delayed.'

'Dammit, it's midnight, gone midnight.'

'Do you want to ring the airport and see?'

'I did. Six-one-nine was on time.'

'The meeting finished early. I just managed to catch an earlier flight, but it was delayed at Frankfurt. Very bad luck.'

'For whom?'

'Look, if you don't . . . Well me, actually, since I had to do the hanging around, and tomorrow is a work day, and I have to be at the office early . . .'

'I was worried about you. You could have rung.'

'I wanted to give you a surprise. Then we were stuck on the tarmac for hours.'

Early afternoon

I was distracted from this reverie by sharp footsteps on the stairs and a military rap on my door. Jesty came in. The college shit, shitty as ever. Conrad Jesty is a short man, stocky as Picasso, and with a little bit of the same jaunt or strut. Someone pointed out the Picasso similarity to him once, but apparently it wasn't news because he gave the chap one of those gimlet stares and said, 'Only someone not a member of my *tertulia* would dare to say such a thing.' Jesty is an economic historian. No wife, but a large collection of mountaineering memorabilia which he purchases at auction. He and I have little to say to each other. Though actively anti-Marxist, I think he holds the view that philosophical ideas are pretty much simply the product of their time, and so not worth much outside of historical context. I suspect him of being a Tory reactionary because he wears cavalry twills, and went through a phase of talking loudly about union 'barons' and 'she who must be obeyed'. I suppose he thinks of me as a middle-class radical – 'long on rights and short on obligations', as he once put it. He likes to 'have no truck with poseurs' – an attitude Felix described as 'self-hatred'.

Jesty stood up erect just inside the door, and looked very hard at me, as though disapproving, doing his best to forgive, and regretting his inability to do so. He had a newspaper rolled up under his arm, like a swagger stick, and I thought for a moment he was going to start barking commands.

'Sorry about Reg,' he said.

I blinked at him.

'Haven't you seen? I thought you might not have.'

And he passed me the newspaper, a copy of today's *Times*, open at the obituaries. 'Reg Moser: radical chemist', it read.

'Some sort of pun I suppose,' said Jesty. 'Poor taste. Thought you'd like to have it, though.' He paused, while my eyes seemed to him, I suppose, to scan the article, when in fact I saw nothing but a blur on the white paper alongside a photograph that didn't seem to me to be much like Moser. Taken at a conference, I expect, some years ago. He was wearing a tie, and his hair was pasted down. I went as if to give the paper back to Jesty but he waved it away.

'Keep it,' he said, turning as if to leave, but then stopping and giving me another glare. 'And for what it's worth, I'm sorry about Moser. No friend of mine, of course, but he was a solid citizen.'

And he left, shutting the door firmly behind him, the sound

of his steel-tipped shoes clicking down the stairs and across the quad. I made some more coffee and sat in an armchair.

Reginald Xavier Moser, the unorthodox and courageous evolutionary scientist, died in Oxford last Sunday at the age of 39.

Reg Moser, as he always preferred to be known, was born in Whitehaven, Lancashire, in December 1956. His father, who ran a bicycle repair shop, and was ambitious for his son, sent him to live with an aunt in Clitheroe so that he could attend a grammar school rather than the local comprehensive. Though erratic, he was brilliant from an early age, and easily won the Eglinton Prize Scholarship to Gresham College, Oxford, where he graduated in Natural Sciences in June 1977. After a brief spell at M.I.T. to master electronmicroscopy, he returned to Parks Road, where he joined the gifted team then being assembled by Professors Jonard and Washtiler for research into the structure and formation of antibodies in the human immune system. He graduated D.Phil. in 1980, when he won the Newhelm Prize Medal for his thesis on 'C1 Protein Chains in the Complement Pathway', something he later deprecated as a 'piece of merely descriptive science'. The modesty may have been a mite thespian, since he was well aware that his work formed the scientific foundation for innumerable subsequent developments in both the prevention and the pharmaceutical treatment of disease.

He then took up the offer of a fellowship at Harcourt College and embarked on a series of research papers on the biochemistry of complex metabolic pathways which were both ground-breaking and provocative. On the strength of these penetrating papers he was elected FRS in 1986, before his thirtieth birthday. Dr Moser always liked to distinguish between two types of scientist: the 'payroller', who worked in a laboratory at the small incremental tasks of 'normal' science, and the 'prizefighter', who took the big theoretical risks in punching his way to either failure or the Nobel Prize table. There was never any doubt as to which of the groups he thought he belonged. Driven, as he liked to say, by 'the patterned but undesigned complexity of matter at the molecular level', he rather surprisingly began to identify the great edifice of Darwinian evolutionary theory as his principal adversary, arguing that it was inadequate to explain how molecular structures might have come into existence. In its place he proposed a theoretical notion which he called dynamic selection. Unsurprisingly, this radical stance put him at odds with much of the scientific establishment, calling into question the mature discoveries that his early, brilliant promise had seemed almost certain to guarantee. At his inaugural address to the Royal Society, he gave his now notorious lecture in which he characterized adaptation by natural selection as a second-order explanation for which a first-order theoretical account of the origin of species was still awaited. The controversy stirred by this perhaps misdirected attack spilled from the placid realm of science into the rather more turbulent waters of political discourse in general, and conflict over educational priorities in particular: developments that were widely regretted.

A man of strong conviction, Reg Moser was scrupulous in playing his part in these affairs. He devoted the rest of what was to prove an all-too-short career to the technical elaboration of his views, and the search for a unifying theory that would justify his rejection of natural selection: a quest regrettably still unfulfilled at his death. In recent years, perhaps fuelled by frustration, if not despair, at his inability to solve the problem he had set himself, his naturally placid and agreeable temperament occasionally deserted him. When he found it hard to attract colleagues to work with him, and harder to raise funds to support his increasingly unorthodox research activities, he might give vent to his feelings in unworthy ways. 'Science projects,' he once said of the Medical Research Council, in a newspaper article, 'proceed according to unnatural selection.' It was possible to be hurt by a tongue that was as eager as it was eloquent, but much could be forgiven by those who knew of the pain and the passion that lay behind it.

There is some uncertainty as to the cause of his death, which an autopsy is to resolve. He would have been forty on Saturday. Reg Moser was married to the well-known and much-admired concert pianist Vita Margolis, who died, also tragically young, three years ago. There were no children.

P. C.-Q.

I read this through several times, but could no more get it to match the Moser I had known than the photograph that accompanied it. Peter Campbell–Quaid seemed set not so much on the detached obituary of a distinguished colleague as on the diminution of a career of which he disapproved. Were even the facts correct? I never knew that Moser's father repaired bicycles. The man in the yellow pullover at the silver wedding party struck me as more like a provincial hotelier, or the proprietor of a small factory, perhaps manufacturing wire fences. It's true that Moser's research funds had almost completely dried up, and that he wrote a piece in the *Guardian* explaining why he thought this was happening, but it's also true that Campbell–Quaid chaired the main committee that repeatedly rejected his applications for research grants. And it wasn't true that he rejected natural selection, merely that he thought something else was going on that preceded it as an explanation of bio-diversity. Should people be told this? Does one reply to obituaries?

Moser used to say that certain areas of the life sciences were developing into a new religion, and that Campbell-Quaid was one of the cardinals of Darwinism. A few among the new generation of scientists were now seriously at risk of being thought heretical. Withdrawal of research support was excommunication from the sacrament, leading to loss of tenure and expulsion from the community of the saved. He talked occasionally of the remarkable American scientist, Lyn Margulis, and her work on the symbiotic origins of mitochondria, and how she had been shunned and ridiculed for years. 'She was lucky to be in America,' he said. 'In the far more closed and clubby world of Britain she'd have been beaten into surrender years since.' Herzen, as I pointed out to him, saw this coming.

An honourable union of science and religion is impossible, but there is a union, *from which one can draw one's conclusion as to the morality which rests on such a union . . . And all this is somehow a matter of routine, of custom: you may believe or not, so long as you observe certain proprieties . . . Think what you please, but lie like the rest.*

And that was written in 1862, just three years after the publication of *The Origin of Species*.

Moser, I'm certain of this, had no religious sense. In this we were absolutely alike. Its lack liberated him not only from the realm of gods, angels, divine providence and evil, but also from the more immediate temptation of theoretical orthodoxy.

Campbell-Quaid, on the other hand, was a Believer. He'd have been a Puritan in the seventeenth century, a Baptist in the eighteenth, a Manchester Liberal in the nineteenth. By the process which Moser used to call, not entirely as a joke, the natural selection of the approximately fittest, he was a Darwinian in the twentieth. And a popular one at that. His bestsellers have titles like *The Fit of the Fittest*; *The Accidental Orchestra. Harmony & Dissonance in Nature*; and *Dips in the Pool. Essays on Genetic Distribution*. In many ways he's the perfect exponent of orthodoxy because when he goes on television or the radio he manages to play both the austere and superlatively brilliant scientist, and the loquacious and amusing popular man of the people simultaneously. He enjoys bating bishops, but not so as to annoy the tolerant. His favourite targets, ones on which he likes to bring scorn and ridicule to bear, are Christian fundamentalists and creationists, who have little enough public support, and who, by a clever reversal of charges, he calls 'evil' and 'wicked' for knowingly spreading demonstrable falsehoods, thereby 'perverting' or 'corrupting' young minds. I think Campbell-Quaid was probably fearful of Moser because he knew him to be a true scientist. Behind his overbearing confidence in Darwinism as the explanation of life lay a need for a God, and a deep and understandable determination to ensure that his life-long investment in the orthodoxies of evolutionary science should not suffer devaluation. Moser was very amused when I told him that the Russian word *prav* means both 'right' and 'innocent'. Vita told me that he used to repeat the word to himself whenever he felt bitter, and it would restore his serenity. I wonder if it was the last word on his lips in the early hours of last Sunday morning.

Midnight

We had our Governing Body meeting at three o'clock. Another torment. Empty and tired, like the formalities of the occasion itself. Rawlinson was there – Senior Honorary Fellow – and he drew me aside before the meeting began.

'I do hope you're all right,' he said, his jowls shaking as he moved his head slowly from side to side in a movement that spoke of sorrow, concern and disbelief. I gave him one of my weak smiles. He has a deep, slow voice that seems to move at the same pace as the flesh hanging from his cheeks. 'Alice rang me this morning on the off-chance that I might be here for Founder's Dinner, which of course I will. She asked me to look out for you. She's very worried, you know.' I nodded, and must have looked rueful because he laid a hand on my arm, a banker's gesture of concern. Not unlike a priest. Both are interested in saving.

'Yes, I know. I talked to her myself. We were both very fond of Moser.'

'That obituary in today's *Times*. I do hope you don't . . .' But he was cut off here by the Master's entry, which was theatrically perfect. Sir Philip was wearing a light grey suit which showed off the black band on his left upper arm to perfection. He even seemed to have gone a little greyer at the temples, the events of the week ageing him. After some shuffling and coughing the meeting began. Governing Body brings together all the official fellows of the college, plus a handful of outside dignitaries, like Rawlinson, who have special connections with us. In his case money. He was an undergraduate here years ago, but now he handles the college's investments. The second law of the Moser/Leroux college code of conduct was Never Say Anything at a Governing Body Meeting. This was generally easy enough for me to observe. Philosophers want peace and quiet and a sensible library acquisitions policy. It must have been hell for Moser, however. A rationalist like him having to sit through interminable 'twaddle'. His word. 'Got it from me father,' he used to say, adopting a Liverpudlian whine. Nevertheless, he managed it a lot of the time, though the forbearance must have been a terrible strain. Under 'Matters arising' from the minutes, Jesty began to talk about admissions policy – always a chestnut at this time of year with entrance examinations and interviews beginning next week. Deirdre Weedon, our novelist, said he shouldn't disparage theologians. They keep the college 'sound'. Amelia Righoffer, Canadian originally, and a specialist in pre-Columbian Latin American literature, said she didn't want a sound college. She wanted a surprising, exciting, intellectually dangerous one. Don Povey, a physicist, who funnily enough has just recently published a book called *Time, Space and Eternity* all about God, asked if we couldn't just get on with the agenda because he had other commitments. Jesty smirked. Povey's book is on the bestseller lists at the moment, and his 'other commitments' involve dining with archbishops as well as doing media stunts. And so on. 'Another day at t'mill,' Moser would say in Lancashirese. Vita had asked him once if college life wasn't intrinsically interesting, and he had replied that anyone who took college administration seriously needed psychiatric help. Which is what Alice asked me the morning we left Turin, and were driving up into Switzerland. I wanted to see if I could find where Herwegh lived in Geneva.

'You mean a shrink?'

'Well . . . no, of course not. But seriously, a therapist or someone. Someone you can talk to.'

'Oh I see. A nice friendly neighbourhood therapist. And when I disagree with all the potty-training, Oedipal-loving, self-punishing, mumbo-jumbo, he can tell me I secretly wish to castrate Freud. No thank you.'

'You're not taking me seriously. There are alternatives. And I worry about you. So does Moser. You're hurting yourself, you're hurting me, it's not how I want to live.'

'Which is?'

'Just normally. To have ordinary life. To be happy.'

Alice often talks about 'ordinary life'. As though she wants to stay at home, have children, darn their socks, and make their dentist's appointments. But what really makes her happy is taking the noon Cathay Pacific departure for Hong Kong, business class, having discussions with colleagues, and flying on two days later to Manila for an agricultural investment conference before flying home via Caracas where she has to inspect Scorpion's fifty per cent interest investment in a Coca-Cola bottling plant. She's an exceptional person. The ordinary would betray her to boredom, just as the psychiatrist's couch would madden a philosopher's logic.

But occasionally it does seem like madness, even to me.

I catch at shadows, like a late-night business phone call to Alice from Gradle. What on earth does he need to talk to her about at midnight? And I turn it into the monster of torture and fear that I want it to be and wish that it wasn't. I daydream of the Warneford, a voluntary committal, the security of illness saving me from the degradation of wickedness. Mad, not bad.

'I am Dr Dymchurch.'

'The only doctor in this room is me. I shall call you Ralph.' This is yet another sign of my inadequacy, which the experts think I should confront. 'It's fear of being dominated that makes him autocratic. Like many authoritarians he is afraid of authority. His father probably. It may be why he took to philosophy: the need to prove dominance over the difficult and intractable. Or simply a masochistic pleasure in daily professional torture.' Dr Dymchurch is trying to ignore my slur.

'What drew you to philosophy?'

'What drew you into psychiatry?'

'Compassion and intellectual stimulation.'

'Then you can say the same for me.'

'Is there compassion in philosophy?'

'Is there intellect in psychiatry?'

'Dr Leroux, you are a voluntary patient here. The very least you could do . . .' Raising his voice. 'You are . . .'

'Unprofessional, yes. Not playing my role correctly.'

'You didn't have to come? What made you?'

Perhaps it wasn't a rhetorical question. I'm here, at least in my imagination, because I weep all the time, find myself crying without knowing why. I can't eat. Live on nothing but will-power, now almost exhausted. And then lack of sleep. Of course, there's Moser dead. He's a reason. But it's not new. It's been going on all my life. I'd wake at three in the morning, unable to sleep, attacked by mental images of distress: horrors, betrayals and lies. Very interesting how the imagination works on areas of ignorance. Some tiny flaw in Alice's account of her day or doings can become a gateway through which the imagination pushes any number of Trojan horses of the means to torture and sack my heart. I live these scenes of destruction with a clarity and a truth to life that leave me sobbing for them to stop. I try to think of other, happier things, of making love to her myself, but the imagination can't let go. I'd get up and walk around, the night cool, a breeze coming in through the windows. Then try to sleep again. A little success, but wished I hadn't, because it consisted of disturbed but dreamless, shallow sleep, followed by grim scenes when barely awake, and then more restless dozing, and so on. Like surfing on a cesspool. I'd drag myself out of it and lie helpless, so tired and so demoralized, for hours on end, unable to move, and weeping for myself, my incompetence, my love for Alice,

Alice herself, the love for me which she has and which the Furies, my Eumenides, tell me she has betrayed. And what makes their account so plausible is that they appear to understand Alice's mentality so well – just as I do myself, in fact – so that they are torture to listen to. I feel defeated, close to being broken, and in this state would eventually drag myself out of bed, though having no idea how I'm going to get through the day. Any sense of self-worth has completely eroded. We are walking the streets of Florence, like we did that happy time once before, out of season, bundled up and cold. Touring the Bargello she says I look like Brutus, but I feel like St John. She holds my hand, talks of the past, of how she was younger than me, my being her tutor and she in awe, of the piles of my thesis on my study desk, nearly finished then like Herzen now. Another mountain of words, stores against future want. What does she do? I only half understand. She said something clever about it once: 'Rationalization in industry is much like philosophy. You make sense out of promising ideas by bringing principals together.' I hate puns. They are a form of corruption. Like the idea that your books are your children, or that death is a sleep, or that mind doctors know better than you. I go back to taunting the imaginary Dymchurch.

'I'm sorry?' And I blinked round the table. Felix had jogged my elbow, bringing me back to the meeting. Jesty was grinning at me – a courtier's privilege to find the embarrassed amusing.

'A brief item about Moser,' said Sir Philip. 'I'm sorry.' And he settled his kind, grey eyes upon me, dropping his gold-rimmed spectacles on to the neat pile of papers in front of him. 'I have spoken to, er,' – he glanced down and squinted – 'a Belinda Moser, apparently his older sister, and she said that both she and her brother would appreciate it if we, that is to say the Court, were to take responsibility for funeral arrangements and so forth. I consulted Bearsted in the coroner's office, and he said there would be no impediment to our proceeding next week if the autopsy showed death by natural causes, which is, in the circumstances, what I'm sure we all hope for in this tragedy. The autopsy will be finished on Friday. Since we have candidates coming into residence for entry examinations on Tuesday, I thought we might proceed on Monday. Sharrock Brothers have agreed to look after everything, and the crematorium has been reserved for two p.m. There will be announcements in Saturday's papers.' He looked round the table, pausing for discussion and dissent. There was none. Unity in death. I had never encountered unanimity on Governing Body before. At least one person, usually several, would abstain if not vote against.

'It's agreed, then,' said the Master. Another silence. A bit like an auction, the hammer raised. Then Jesty spoke.

'Perhaps, Master,' he said in that voice of his that counterfeits reflection, 'perhaps we could minute that, as usual, Moser would have voted against had he been here. In this way we may avoid a troublesome consensus.'

The table rustled with sighs, papers being turned, coughs, the click of tut-tutting, little snorts above wry smiles. The Master retrieved his spectacles and returned them to his nose. His secretary turned the page of her short-hand book. Maurice Singleton took out an enormous white handkerchief, unfolded it, examined it, folded it once more, and put it away. The next item on the agenda was broached. Life, leaving death in its wake, moved on.

Cremation is the fire this time: a final rendering. For some reason it is not done to preface the final slide to the flames with silence. There has to be limited ceremony. We think instinctively of the music to be played, poetry to be read, a speaker or two to give, if not orations, at least appreciations

– a little of the dead's flinty humour and appetite for life. That sort of thing. The bits and pieces of the proceedings are, so to speak, bound together by the deceased's empty but presiding presence. The music is the music he liked, the poems were his favourites, the speakers were his friends. When Vita was cremated Albert Bressler played the piano, three of the *Fantasiestücke* by Schumann, and Ravel's *Pavane pour une infante défunte* which Vita herself had played at her first concerts when she returned from cancer treatment. The irreducible complexity of these apparently simple pieces was thought somehow to recapture Vita herself, to re-establish her presence among us for a fleeting moment, and then to let her go again, in the way that music is captured between two silences, born out of one and released into the other.

For Moser we ought to have philosophy and *haute cuisine*. Someone could read a particularly ironic bit from the *Tractatus* to be followed by the instructions for *Pigeonneau rôti en crapaudine au poivre et au persil simple*. Something bird lovers might enjoy together. Then a bite from Jeremy Bentham, whom Moser compared with a McDonald's hamburger – vulgar, cheap, bad for you, and enormously popular. After which, by way of counter-point, we should read something from Bocuse, his *Pêches du bocage* perhaps, or the instructions for *Soufflé glacé aux cerises*. There is great work to be done, Moser liked to say, in the biochemistry of cooking. From the physical precursors, through component specificity and minimal function, a truly great dish is a cascade process of ingredient interaction from which emerges the *Purée d'oseille à la crème*, or the wonderful *Escalopes de ris de veau Maréchale* which one finds in the Aveyron. The natural history of the biochemistry of proteins and the supreme art of great cooking were proof that there was only one world of learning. At La Napoule Moser said that philosophy was the bridge between them, but later he changed his mind about this image, and said rather that philosophy was the web, or net, in which all the great spheres of art and science were both held, and held together. This was not a view that I could ever contest since I knew (know) so little about his field. Generally, however, he disliked analogy, and would steer his pupils clear of it. For instance, he said that recently in the United States it had become fashionable in some scientific circles to describe the biochemical systems that 'are now known to be the basis of life' (as one commentator put it) as 'machines'. But of course they are not machines, they are sequential biochemical processes, and omitting the word 'like' before 'machines' does not make the incorrect assertion any less of an analogy. For one thing, he said, we actually don't really know that the biochemistry of proteins is 'the basis of life'. It's simply what we can see with an electron microscope. Some other instrument, in the future, may enable us to detect processes of which we are, right now, quite unaware. And since this has, for hundred of years, been the way in which our scientific knowledge has grown, it is hard to see that Moser wasn't right.

These meandering speculations were interrupted by movements of paper at the table, and I found myself looking at a guest list and table plan for tomorrow's gaudy. Papers put round by Kirkup, the Dean. He's a botanist whose love of taxonomy makes him ideal for this kind of college work. The Founder's Dinner has occasionally been a subject of controversy. Some students, even some senior members, regard these functions as improper, and think they should be abolished. Unfortunately, or fortunately depending on your point of view, our gaudy is compulsory, and has to be held on the first Thursday of December each year, because the statute of Parliament by which the college was established requires it. An act of piety and remembrance. The last time this became controversial was in 1968, long before I came here. On that occasion, after some unpleasantness, the college agreed that it was appropriate that fellows should each pay his or her share of the cost. This was such a considerable cost, however, that it had also been agreed, I think at the same Governing Body meeting, that stipends should be increased by the amount owed for the dinner. Anyone choosing not to attend the gaudy – or absent from it for whatever reason – would have an equivalent sum clawed back on battels. Of course there was never any question that the college paid for guests.

This year Campbell-Quaid was on the guest list, but this was no surprise. Moser had arranged it long ago, hoping to exploit the occasion to mend fences. There were two government ministers down: Preggett, the minister for Science and Technology, another alumnus I think; and Monica Summerton, junior minister at the Foreign Office, responsible for Africa and for Overseas Aid. The usual bevy of visiting academics: London, Cambridge and the US mainly. Kirkup had got Felix sitting opposite me, and had put me between two guests, an American woman from Princeton called Spekeleiner, and the director of something called the Chrysalis Project in Berlin, Herr Dr Rolfe Ludwig Gartz. It doesn't look very promising, but at least I'll have Felix, which is no doubt what Kirkup intended. Anyway, most guests are usually so intimidated by a college gaudy that they are rarely threatening. Silverware, claret, old masters and an army of scouts will generally subdue all but the most obnoxious.

I paused to look at the time: well after one and no sign of any desire to stop writing. Then the phone rang. It was Alice in Singapore, just had breakfast, heading for a meeting.

'I feared I might wake you, darling.'

'I was writing.'

'I'm sorry to interrupt. Are you all right?'

'Yes. No. Not really. Down a bit.'

She didn't seem to hear.

'Is there news of Moser's autopsy? What happened?'

'None.'

A silence, neither of us helping the other.

'I wish you'd say something,' she said eventually. 'Talk to me. Tell me things. Let me help.'

'What do you want me to say?'

'I don't want you to say anything. I just . . .'

'Well then.'

'Now you're interrupting me . . .'

'First you want me to talk. Now I'm interrupting. What do *you* want Alice?'

I had begun to cry again, and she must have heard a sob or something.

'Oh Philip. *Please* let me help. I do so want to.'

'You're in Singapore.'

'It doesn't matter. I can be there for you if you'll only let me.'

'I'm going to cash in my ticket for Florence. Moser's cremation may be held on Monday, and I'll have to be there.'

'Do you want me to come too?'

'Only if you want to.'

'I want to do what you want of me.'

'Do you, Alice?'

'You know I do.'

We are silent again, me locked up once more, walled in by the screens of fear, alienation and stubborn resentment; she far away, invisible and unimaginable, on an island in the concrete tropics.

'Look, I've got a meeting now, and then . . .'

'With Gradle?'

'Damn Gradle. For God's sake, Philip, he's not important.'
'To whom?'
'Oh will you please stop. I love you. Just . . . Oh damn!'
And she rang off.
It is night once more, and once more I am alone.

5

Thursday

'Life is infinitely more stubborn than theory, it goes its way independent of it and silently conquers it.'

No sleep again, so I got up at five to write this. Infinitely dark outside, and cold probably, because I can't hear the fountain. They stop it when the forecast is for freezing weather. I wonder if there's any escape from this. The most surprising part, perhaps because least talked about, is the pain. Is it peculiar to have so much physical pain without there being a physical cause, a wound or an illness? My body aches, not as though stiff, but as though it were one great tender bruise. Inside there is a pain of longing in my stomach, and the tight cold grip of isolation on my heart. These are real hurts, not at all imaginary. My arms are sore with their emptiness, and my fingers creak and crack as though old and arthritic. Time crawls by, tormenting me with its lethargy. And all the while my Eumenides scrounge at the fringes of the mind, picking on weakness, hounding suspicion, ripping at the imagination. Trying to fend them off is exhausting, the constant effort unavailing. The reasons for this sink into the swamps of statement and half-statement. Alice says – she told Moser this – that she's afraid to talk to me about her work friendships. Realizing this, I press her for details. In response she tells me some things but not others. Seeing her reserve, my suspicions flourish, feeding the Furies. But their appetites are inexhaustible and they love the flesh of insincerity. These things are mad. I know this. But then I set them beside what I know from experience, observation, intuition and imagination about the secret areas of the heart, its affections and desires.

Alice is a passionate woman. Also open and generous. 'I like helping people,' she said apropos of the *Vom Anderen Ufer* muddle. If a hand wants holding, or a head needs resting on a shoulder, she will oblige. She likes to feel close to others, in harmony with them. I imagine she believes in empathy, which I do not. These things could easily make her a victim. They pull her towards a sort of abstract romanticism when the charm of a particular moment might turn what is abstract into an almost tangible force. She also has a sentimental desire for perfection, which she always hopes to find in the future. So she will say, 'I do so want to be happy,' when she could or should be saying, 'How happy we are now.' It is always the future that offers the promise of an impossible ideal, and it may be what draws her to other men. They have to be exceptional – Maxime, Gradle, who else? Moser probably – because it's their exceptional virtues that hold the promise of perfection: Maxime's casual brilliance and his connections; Gradle's – well, Gradle's what?, since I know so little about him – but I imagine his cleverness, his worldly knowledge and *savoir-faire*, and a need to confide, so that she feels special with him – and Moser's decency, his genius, his humanity. In a sentimental way perhaps she longs for another life, or lives, where perfect, permanent, stable happiness can be found. Of course she knows that really this is absurd, but rationality won't ease the tug of longing, and this tug is what makes her vulnerable, and puts her *real* happiness at risk. Even at thirty-eight she still doesn't seem to understand the motivations of most men, their urge for sexual conquest, and the endorsement of their egos in the submissive collaboration of a woman in the acts of sex. Some of them, of us, the nicer ones, also give perhaps a little of themselves, so that some sort of temporary relationship gets erected. But most, certainly by middle age, want no such thing. They are counting and surveying. How did she compare with Julia or Margot? Hunting is a cynical sport, and at its end a kill.

I suppose Alice would be appalled at these thoughts, but I think there have been such experiences in her past, and that they have brought her to the brink of great hurt. An American here at Oxford called Whittaker. A man, no name to me, at a conference in Norway in 1983 who took her dancing all night. I pointed out to her that dancing was a ritual that preceded the making of war, rain or love. Which was it? She did not react well. Maxime more or less all the time, of course, until he left the bank. Now Gradle. Does she fantasize about him? Imagine for herself a perfect future of a different life, lived in a different way, composed of quite different elements, and where I no longer exist? Does everyone live this kind of psychic alternative existence, founded on someone in the real world, but imagined in another one, not parallel, but on the other side of some sort of boundary?

Here there is fear, shame and remorse.

Vita came to see me in my rooms on a Tuesday early in September three years ago. It was the middle of the afternoon. Moser was away at a conference in Leipzig, and was going from there to Harvard to give some lectures. Alice was on what she called a 'swing' through Asia. Vita's concert season was opening in London in October, and after that she was going to Amsterdam, Paris and Milan. Vita didn't often see me on her own, though occasionally we'd have a walk together, or drink tea. She gave a little curtsy at the door. She was wearing a long yellow dress that followed the curve of her body beautifully, and she lifted it an inch or so up her shins by holding it on either side between thumb and forefinger.

'Is the thinker thinking? Or may he come for a walk?'

It was a beautiful, hot afternoon. Late real summer. Still not term-time, and the tourists dwindling. I put on my old floppy, white, wide-brimmed cricketer's hat, took a stick, and we went down via the canal out on to Port Meadow.

After the apparent gaiety of her invitation Vita was quiet, seemed happy to walk along beside me in companionable silence. A common enough sight in Oxford. I asked after Moser, how his trip was going, and she said a few things about his response to the sudden changes in the former East Germany. She said he wanted to talk to me about catastrophe theory when he got back. The trees by the canal were just beginning, here and there, to turn, but when we reached the Meadow, and set off to cross it towards Wolvercote, the sun was hot, and the long grass like flaxen straw. Vita was wearing a wide-brimmed sun-hat that matched the grass around us, and with a broad ribbon of the same yellow material as her dress which hung from hat-brim to shoulder in the windless air. The usual large herd of cows was lying down, chewing slowly as we passed. I asked her about her music, the programmes on which she was working for the autumn: Saint-Saëns and Prokofiev, Debussy and Ravel. But she said she didn't feel like talking about music. In the silence that followed this I remembered the almost two years of her cancer treatment, long since successfully concluded. Of her extraordinary serenity and fortitude. The cruelty of losing her baby, then of knowing that she would always be sterile, then of losing her hair. She had a painful recovery from one operation in which lymph glands were removed, and twice was hospitalized in London for complete blood transfusions when her white-cell count fell right away. The chemotherapy made her sick, radiation treatment left her weak and with a terrible feeling of dessication. The operation to remove a tumour from her back revealed a carcinoma the size of a golf ball. Drugs for lymphatic cancer sometimes deprived her of her sense of balance, and sometimes of control of her bladder. On one occasion, always funny in the telling of it, when they were staying with her family in the Sancerre, both happened at once. They had been to dinner in a restaurant in Auxerre and outside, on the cobbled street, she suddenly started laughing out loud, her hand clasped over her mouth as she shrieked. Moser looked and saw that she was peeing. Then she swayed and, still laughing and peeing, though harder at both now, she fell to the ground. Passers-by, the good bourgeoisie of Auxerre, thinking she was drunk, stepped aside, muttering deprecating comments, which only made her roar the louder with laughter.

When the specialists finally cleared her, and she moved on to a regime of six-monthly check-ups, nobody could remember her ever having complained. She returned to full-time practice, and resumed her concert career. Moser told me that actually, though he had never said so to Vita, the five-year survival rate for patients diagnosed with similar cancer conditions was only about thirty per cent. Thinking about these things made me unprepared for her question.

'Do philosophers have much to say about the difference between the mind and the brain?'

'Far too much. It's a growth area. The philosophy, that is.'

'You don't approve?'

'It's not approval territory. Philosophers will do topics whatever, whether or not anyone approves. It simply, to my way of thinking, lacks interest.' She was silent, which in the manner of a tutorial makes me feel compelled to go on. 'The latest thing, out of California, is a proof that birds, trees, rocks and household thermostats all have consciousness.' Vita laughed at this, so I became mock solemn. 'Seriously. Bloke called

Chalmers. It's all the rage, conferences and stuff like that. Bloody silly really, of course.'

When we reached Godstow I sat down on a post and watched a family manoeuvring their riverboat through the lock.

'Was there some special reason you asked?'

'Mmm?'

'About mind and consciousness?'

'Yes, there was.'

Vita had sat on the grass, but now she lay flat on her back, putting her straw hat on her belly, and laying a forearm across her eyes to shield them from the sun. Vita, it is almost pointless to write it, had very beautiful hands, the fingers long and thin, thumbs slight and energetic, the palms and backs muscular and mobile. For some reason I always associate her voice with her hands, perhaps because they were alike in so much: capable of a huge range of expression, force and tenderness under control, unity, thought and action, so to speak, in harmony. Vita's physique was splendid too. At thirty-four she still had the figure and flesh of a twenty-one year old. But on this occasion, lying back on the lock lawn under a perfect sky, she was composed entirely of voice and hands.

'I went to the UCL clinic this morning,' she said. 'They told me that I have an inoperable brain tumour. Only a few months to live.'

I remember sitting, looking at her, being wet with perspiration, but I can't recall saying anything. And I can't recall anything that I felt. Convention would have it that I was devastated, that I felt my heart clench, and that the world blackened into horror and despair. But I honestly don't now know. There were yells and calls from the river. A young boy and a dog, releasing the last rope, jumped aboard their boat as it chugged through the gates, heading upstream.

'Apparently it's not uncommon with skin cancers. You can have a sort of run of them, removed at intervals, and then one gets going in the brain, and that's it.' She rolled over on her side, propping her head on her hand. 'Don't say anything,' she said. 'There's nothing much to say, and I know that you're sorry.'

'Does Moser . . . ?'

'Not yet. I had the first signs of this a few weeks ago, found I couldn't write some words, felt suddenly angry and hot for no reason, a bit of dizziness. I wasn't due for a check-up until November, but I went in and they did some tests, took some spinal fluid, ran an MRI. They warned me then. This morning was the results and the pep talk.'

'Remission . . . ?'

She nodded and gave me a grim smile, a sort of widening of the mouth without parting her lips.

'Miss Margolis, remissions are always possible, and we never give up hope, but it would be improper and a disservice if I did not emphasize the extreme gravity of your condition.' She dropped the grey, formal voice. 'What I have's called a leptomeningeal metastasis. Inoperable. Far advanced. Quick growing.' She was waving the sun-hat backwards and forwards over the grass, making shapes with its shadow, watching them lengthen and shorten. 'I'm conscious of it. Of going to die. But somehow my mind resists. Hence the question. Or perhaps it's that, in my mind, I know I'm going to die soon, but I can't yet consciously feel, sense, believe in, its imminence.'

'The sensible position is that the brain causes consciousness, but that the mind, itself a product of consciousness, by working on conscious phenomena, makes itself free, and therefore independent of it. Descartes is dead, long live . . .'

I have written this as a conversation, but I'm not sure why. I can't, in all honesty, recall precisely what either Vita or I said, and subsequent events made it even harder to recall. I certainly didn't say that last bit about the phenomena of consciousness. At least, I'm pretty sure I wouldn't have said it. I would probably have said something rather duller but more professional about mental states. I find myself instead wishing that I could remember the name of the riverboat in Godstow Lock. It would make the occasion more solid somehow. Give it a fact that could be checked and verified, like the name of the little boy whose cries of pleasure intersected with Vita's death sentence confession.

It would be nice to think that philosophy was useful at times like this, but the thought is a popular delusion. For some reason almost everyone likes to have the security of believing that some great thinker has endorsed his or her views in the past. Right-wing politicians grasping at Adam Smith or Karl Popper; earnest moralists wheeling out Kant; argumentative young iconoclasts abusing you with Wittgenstein; smug micro-economists who imagine themselves perched on the utilitarians' shoulders. They are all deluding themselves. Almost nobody actually reads philosophy. Even undergraduates who supposedly have three years in which to do nothing else very rarely read the texts which confront them in the syllabus. Philosophers are crutches on which, for the most part, the more or less intellectually crippled lean for support.

Kicking away the crutches is an Oxford game. Felix told me a while ago about Leminovsky, in All Souls, who got a former government minister going at dinner about his deep admiration for Adam Smith. When he'd finished his encomium, Leminovsky quoted him some passages from *The Wealth of Nations* about the need for intervention to correct market failure, and said how interesting he'd always found it that Karl Marx had also, on the basis of great study, been an admirer of Adam Smith. The former minister turned away and wouldn't speak to him again for the rest of the dinner. Mission accomplished presumably. Moser used to say that philosophy was to practical affairs what the safety net was to high-wire artists. It didn't make what they did any easier, but it helped them to feel a bit more secure. However awkwardly, in the end they would make a fairly soft landing in a bed of muddled ideas that they believed explained both the extent of their success, and the reasons for their fall.

Vita wasn't like this. I don't think I had ever heard her talk about philosophy before that afternoon at Godstow, though it used to amuse her to listen to the theoretical arguments among other pianists, like Alfred Brendel and Charles Rosen. She said that she had difficulty understanding what they were talking about a lot of the time, but that it was fun to read or listen to because it always had a musical quality. When we walked back to town from Port Meadow she apologized, was sorry to have told me her bad news. She needed to share it, she said, and she couldn't tell Moser over the phone. There wasn't anyone else. Only me.

I was feeling so bleak that I couldn't even bring myself to contest this surely quite false attribution, but, as if in the knowledge of what I might have said if I'd been able to, she began to talk about her training, her early years as a student of the piano, and her recent career as a concert artist and celebrity. She told me about her grandfather, a Beaumont, who was a piano-builder in Tours. A man with a huge beard, dark black eyes, and fingers like Strasbourg sausages, who first taught her to love pianos. He had a show-room and workshop full of them: mechanical pianola-players, Bechstein grands, Challen uprights, old Pleyels, even an ancient Broadwood, lots of Beaumonts of course. On Sundays and saints days when she was there in the summer, or at Christmas and Easter, she would spend all day in the workshop, playing the pianos, or watching the keys 'play' the pianola rolls by Paderewski, Saint-Saëns, Rachmaninov and Scriabin. She started piano lessons in London when she was six, but she could already play, as children learn to speak before they can read. When she was eleven she went to a full-time music school, a transition that seemed obvious as well as effortless. She was playing the piano for six hours a day, studying music for another two. She wanted nothing else. At sixteen she won a scholarship to the Royal College, and at the end of her first year there discovered something surprising, something that had never occurred to her before. She was lonely. Outside of her family she had no friends other than her pianos, and only one other person to talk to privately – 'in secret' was what she said – another girl of her own age called Clara, a superb pianist, 'far better than me'.

When she got to Clara, Vita stopped talking about her student days, and started reflecting aloud on what it had been like to give public concerts. The fear that no one might come. The intensity of practice. The dream-like quality of concert-day itself. Different methods of relaxation in the last hour or so before performance. And finally the sense of detach-ment, of isolation on the platform, of being remote, unap-proachable, untouchable. 'A sort of harmonious alienation' is what she called it.

I remember this only as fragments. It was a hot afternoon. I suppose that Vita's news must have stunned and appalled me. Drugged with misery, already imagining the pain of her death for Moser, partly astounded by her serenity and stoicism, partly incredulous that this lively, beautiful, intelligent young woman should be mortally ill without showing any sign of it, wrapped in my own dismay, I remember only trudging silently along beside her while she talked. When we got back to the flat that she and Moser had in Bardwell Road I asked her about treatment. She was making a jug of lime juice in the kitchen, rattling ice cubes, and I was standing in the doorway, turning my hat in my fingertips. The picture of this is fresh in my mind, like a still, though I'm stepped back now, an observer of myself.

'Bethany Laidlaw – she's my oncologist – said there was radiation and chemotherapy available, but she didn't sound optimistic.'

'And?'

Vita sighed. 'I declined, Philip. I couldn't go through all that again. It'd be worse this time too.' She asked me to pour some juice – 'I get too wobbly sometimes' – and I took the tray through to the music room, where it was cool. Vita sprawled on a sofa. 'Bethany said she fully understood. It looked hopeless. The principal tumour – there are several – is very fast growing. She suggested I discuss it with Moser and see her again on Monday. We'll both go. But I know what I want now.'

'How . . . How much time does she . . . this Bethany . . .'

'Two, three, four months without treatment. Six or eight with. Perhaps.'

'Will you be able to play in the meantime? Make recordings?'

She shook her head.

'That's how I first knew for sure, really,' she said. 'Ataxia. I sat down to play a Schubert Impromptu one morning – a favourite that I play to warm up and loosen my fingers – and found that my coordination had gone. No timing. A muddle.' She drained her glass of juice and lay back on the sofa. 'I was telling you about my friend Clara. I haven't told anyone about her before. Not even Moser.'

Clara was the same age as Vita, also the product of a 'mixed' marriage. Her mother was German and her father French-speaking Swiss, but they were both dead by the time that she and Vita met at a summer-school music camp in Annecy when they were seven. They became fast friends immediately and, because of Clara's status as an orphan whose guardians in Geneva were, though tolerant and well-to-do, not especially interested in her, began spending a lot of time together. Clara came to visit, first in the Sancerre, then in London. They spent summer holidays together, and over a few years Clara's visits lengthened into whole summers. When they both turned eleven Clara enrolled in the same music school as Vita, and they were together constantly.

Vita said that Clara was everything, to her girl's mind, that she herself wanted to be. A superb pianist – 'her hands were bigger than mine' – with the innate ability to deposit the same weight on each digit, a technical skill that normally takes even talented players many years to acquire. They practised together and, at least during the holidays, played duets 'in secret'. Duet-playing by students was forbidden at the school because instructors believed it resulted in students learning each other's bad habits. 'Though Clara didn't have any bad habits. Her musical instincts were quite pure.' Also she was strong-minded. Sensitive and loving, with great delicacy of feeling, she combined these traits with a purposeful sense of her own future as a musician, woman, lover, wife and mother. Vita said she used to imagine Clara being able to manage life with a difficult partner – perhaps someone equally gifted as herself but less stable, more moody – and all the while emerging as one of Europe's pre-eminent concert artists, with great works written specifically for her, and all the great concert halls vying for her performances. All this lay in the future. As girls of fourteen and fifteen, 'What we did was talk, telling each other everything, sharing our jokes and our secrets, our fears and aspirations. We played together, ate together; shared a bedroom; did each other's hair; swam in the river together in the summer;

shopped for Christmas together; made all our decisions together.'

Vita stopped talking for a little while. The afternoon heat was subsiding in an evening breeze that moved the leaves very slightly on a sycamore outside the open windows. Again I had the sense of an epiphany, a moment that preserves a whole area of meaning not in, but in despite of, time.

'Everything changed at the end of our first year at the Royal College. It's true what I said earlier. At the beginning I discovered I was lonely. Despite Clara. It wasn't Clara's fault. She didn't make friends with anyone else especially. It wasn't jealousy or anything like that. I just saw all these other people – the teachers and professors as well as the students – who all seemed different. Larger. More to grips with everything. Do you know what I mean? I felt little, a bit scared, wanted to hide in the shadows. Inadequate, I suppose. I talked to Clara about this of course, and she pooh-poohed it, said I was being 'adolescent'. 'Hormones and puberty', she called it, and said I should read the *Guardian*. What actually happened was that we spent even more time together. Withdrew almost completely. I found I couldn't even practise without having her in the room with me. I became quite ruthless about this – I can be, you know, when I want to be – insisting, refusing to let her leave to do her own work. We had some terrific rows. Shouting matches. She called me the most horrible names, but in the end she always did what I wanted. I was very intolerant.

'This was how things were when I met Moser, that summer eighteen years ago when he left his glasses in my uncle's car, and then we found you both by coincidence on the Boulevard St Michel in Paris.'

Vita turned a little on the sofa so that she could look at me, hitching her dress up to the knees and plunging her hands

149

down between her thighs. When Vita talked she had a very slight, and very attractive, impediment in her voice, not as pronounced as a lisp, not as self-conscious as a crushed *r*, but a sort of indeterminate mid-Channel suggestion of something foreign, a continental background, something a bit romantic and out of the ordinary. She had such a firm presence that I found it, and do still, though even more so today, impossible to imagine the world without her. Irrational, of course, since it is.

'Was Clara with you that evening?' I asked. 'In the car?'

Vita nodded. 'In the back. She always travelled in the back.' She turned away from me again and returned to staring straight ahead, at the far-end wall, one half of which was fitted with shelves that held her scores, and the other half, in shadow at that moment, but occasionally lit, especially if there were visitors, the backdrop to two pencil and ink landscapes by Samuel Palmer. 'Scores too,' Vita used to say of them. 'If you know how to read them.'

Clara had been with her all summer, Vita said. She was in the Roman arena at Lyon when Moser and I were there. They had gone on to Toulon the next day by train. They were both on the jetty at Cannes the morning that Moser chased ashore after her, scattering millionaires. And they had both run away from him. They had both driven north with her uncle at the end of the month.

'I remember the amphitheatre at Lyon so clearly,' said Vita. 'I had been there a long time that evening, sitting in the shadows, when you and Moser came in. Clara and I fell in love with both of you instantly. You were like, this was Clara's idea, two beautiful, smooth white pebbles being driven up out of the sea on to black sand. We literally held our breath and watched you go and sit down. Neither of us spoke. I knew it was a miracle, and of course I knew that Clara must think the same. I didn't want to break the spell, just sitting in the dark and looking at you both was heaven. I was seventeen. The moon shone on you both to make you silver and white. My mother had said that I had to be back at the hotel by 10.30, and it was already long past it when I eventually got up the courage to stand, walk across the arena floor knowing you would be bound to be watching, and leave. I longed for you to speak. To call to me. But I'm sure I would have run away. I was thrilled with fear.'

'And Clara?'

'Hopelessly in love with Moser. Always will be.'

'Poor Clara.'

'Yes. After we saw you both in Paris I wanted to send her away. But she wouldn't go. She came to stay permanently, and I tried to forget about her.'

'You mean, she . . .'

Vita laughed gently. 'You know, for a thinker you can be remarkably dense. Of course Clara never existed, though she was real to me. I invented her. It's the story of my childhood.'

'And it was she who loved Moser.'

'Deeply. Unshakeably. Still does.'

She turned her eyes to me once again, dry and hot is how I remember them, as if feverish.

'Whereas I was in love with you.'

Although I remember these events of that warm September afternoon and evening, it would be wrong even to infer that I can still recall the *feelings* they engendered. Someone said that memory of past events was almost useless because one could never remember the motivation that had led you to be involved in them. I'm not sure that this is true. What happened between me and Vita that day did not spring from motivations on either one side or the other. Not motivation, at any rate, in the sense of purposeful intent. It was all a question of feeling, and in addition to not being able to know Vita's feelings, I can no longer claim to know what mine were either. Consciousness is transient, and the nature of our feelings, not open to renewal, is for ever being lost.

Afternoon

Interrupted by Mrs Wharton, very upset at the state of my study, and telling me to attend to what she calls my 'housekeeping'.

'I suppose you've been up all hours not sleeping,' she said, flinging open my bedroom door and clicking her tongue at the mess she found. 'And I'll be surprised, I'm sure, if you've had anything at all for your breakfast, and you not touching your dinner last night either according to Mr Laurent as I saw not twenty minutes ago in the buttery, and him worryin' about you full steam. It's no way to carry on, as you know. I'll fetch you a nice cup of tea.'

This she did, and nice it was. But the college butler, Laurent, is right. I've no appetite. All the desires seem to have folded, or perhaps been switched off is a better image. I have a clear sense now of what a sensible position nihilism is. Nothing is worthwhile. Nothing matters or makes a difference. Death is, as Moser too must have come to see, the antidote to the disease of life. Even the energy and vigour of a Mrs Wharton cannot conceal the progress of the illness. Once she had brought my tea – along with a plate of biscuits large enough to feed a cricket team – Mrs Wharton set about my bedroom, shaking sheets as though they were demons, plumping the duvet and my pillows like an avenging angel shattering graven images. All the while, as she folded, stored, dusted and tidied, she kept up a stream of correctional advice. 'Now you've your gaudy tonight, and it's not right to 'tend a college occasion out o' sorts. All that wine and brandy sauce, I seen the pheasants this mornin' coming in, and it's a feast in store for yer, that's a certainty. Now I've ironed you a stiff front, and you'll be wanting a bath at about five, so my advice is you 'ave lunch . . .' and much else besides. Mrs W. talks because she is shy and is frightened by silence between people. If I wasn't here, she would play her radio and talk to it while she worked. Today what she was feeling particularly anxious about, and too shy to ask outright, was Moser's funeral on Monday. She had got word of the arrangements, as college servants always do, and wanted to know if the ceremony was going to be 'open, you know, so's that me and Mrs Nettleburn can come, like. Or is it private, family only and that?' She was very tense. I reassured her that even if it had been family only, which it wasn't, she would still have been welcome. 'Dr Moser thought of you as his college mother, Mrs Wharton.' She gave a sniff to cut off a tear, said, 'Thank you I'm sure Dr Leroux and I'll tell Mrs Nettleburn who'll be that pleased, I know, and you make sure and 'ave that lunch today, and then a rest and a proper hot bath before your gaudy. It'll work wonders, you mark my words.' Once outside the door she could be heard rattling brush and broom sharply on every step of the wooden staircase, obliterating her misery in the clatter of vigorous work.

Tea was enough, and I had no hunger either for lunch or for the company of others eating it, so I put on my overcoat and went out for a walk. I had been right earlier: the fountain was not running, the long, wide pond had a thin surface of ice, and the surrounding lawns were white with frost. My breath came out like steam, and I tied my scarf in another loop round my neck. Went over to the Broad and up past the Sheldonian – a mansion of ghosts. Even Turgenev, the very first Russian to receive an honorary degree from the University, had graced this building. It's become fashionable to say that Oxford, as a university, was asleep in the nineteenth century, and that it has only really awakened since the 1960s. But I don't think this is entirely true. The more you know about the nineteenth century in Britain, the more there is to forgive. Understanding lies among the details, just as it does in the relationships between people. Take Turgenev and Herzen. Herzen wounded Turgenev deeply with some of his comments about and criticisms of the novelist's political and social views, but Turgenev never retaliated, and was eager to forgive. Perhaps – his novels suggest so – he understood the direct connections between guilt and accusation. That those who have blame to lay are suffering Joyce's 'agenbite of inwit'. Like a sufferer from paranoia projecting his own guilt on to others, and fearing their retaliation.

After the emotional drain of Natalie's elopement with Herwegh, her return, the drowning of his mother and son, the stillborn child, then Natalie's death, Herzen was surely crushed. This is surmise, because even the things that people write about themselves may not be true, or entirely true, but instead committed to paper for effect, and we have no other witness but Herzen himself. In 1853 he wrote:

> I see a grave, a wreath of dark-red roses, . . . torch-light,
> a band of exiles, the moon, a warm sea beneath a moun-
> tain; I hear words spoken which I cannot understand,
> and yet they tear my heart. All, all, has passed away!

He was suffering, grieving, and the bruises from these blows were never to leave him. They were supplemented by guilt. He had done too little to make Natalie happy, driving her into the arms of Herwegh, ruining both her peace of mind and her health. He had stood helplessly by while his own mother and son drowned before his eyes. He felt himself worthless, denigrating his writing, abandoning, one by one, his hopes. And then there was his oldest friend, Ogarev. His

Moser, so to speak. The only man with whom he had been at one, and to whom he felt bound.

Nicholas Ogarev deserves a sympathetic and thoughtful biography to rescue him from the calumny of the odious Carr's portrait in *The Romantic Exiles*. Carr calls him 'Poor Nick', and never misses an opportunity to heap scorn on his actions, ridicule on his misfortunes. Ogarev was, like Herzen, a democrat and an honest man at a time when, in Russia, neither democracy nor honesty were valued. Perhaps they never were, and never will be. The pressures under which he lived must have been atrocious, but Carr gives no thought to them. He portrays Ogarev as the typical bourgeois son of a wealthy landowner, a youthful idler, his head full of silly ideas, and living immorally on the back of serfdom. In Carr's book he is indolent, self-absorbed, corrupt, hedonistic: the sort of young man that revolution would sweep aside. (Read: 'And a jolly good thing too!') When, in the summer of 1839, at the age of twenty-five, Ogarev liberated the 1,870 serfs on his estate at Belo-omus, and effectively gave them the entire property (he sold it to them for a pittance spread over ten yearly instalments), Carr says it was because he had 'no taste for agriculture' and 'a soft heart'. When, ten years later, as the result of a divorce and other misfortunes, Ogarev lost the remainder of his property, Carr describes him as becoming 'a beggar and a parasite'. Ogarev cannot win with Carr. To have property is to be a parasite, just as it is to have none. I think that Ogarev's real offence in Carr's eyes was to have been a principled democrat who believed in liberty for others as well as for himself. One result of this was that he suffered terribly at the hands of people who were prepared to exploit his tolerance. His first wife, Maria; the sister and her husband of his second wife Natalie; eventually even Herzen himself. Diabolically. And Herzen was his best, and in many ways most loyal, friend.

The body matters greatly in biography. Geoffrey Keynes told Robert Skidelsky that biographers should take the physical conditions, especially the frailties, of their subjects far more seriously. He is surely right in this. Carr manages to pass over the fact that Ogarev suffered from epilepsy with hardly a comment. The causes of this frightful – indeed frightening – disease were completely unknown in the nineteenth century. There was no treatment. Worse, it was widely believed that the manifestations of the illness were evidence of, at best, mental illness, and at worst, diabolism. In addition to this disability, Ogarev was also sterile, though not impotent. Carr manages at one point to imply that Ogarev's sterility was the consequence of a juvenile sexual indiscretion – which may have been, indeed, what Ogarev himself believed – but few modern medics would pay credence to such an assertion. Carr seems determined to imply that Ogarev's physical disabilities were the product of his degeneracy, both social and mental, so that he might stand in a crude sort of way for the degeneracy of an entire class. And it is a well-understood feature of Western moralism that the degenerate get what they deserve. A biographer less driven by Carr's motives (all the more important for being unstated) would have taken a far gentler and less censorious approach. And, in any event, Ogarev was a marvellous amateur pianist, which makes it difficult for any amount of calumny to convince me of his hypocrisy.

Having diminished Ogarev in every way that he can, Carr then treats him as a fool. Ogarev and his second wife Natalie Tuchkov arrived in London in the summer of 1856. Natalie Tuchkov had known the Herzen family well, because as a young woman of nineteen she had accompanied them to Germany, France and Italy in 1848/9. Natalie Herzen had been close to her, and she, Natalie Tuchkov, felt a particular obligation to Herzen's two surviving children, Tata and Olga. Tata, who was eleven in 1856, had been only four when Natalie last saw her, and Olga, who was born in November 1850, she was meeting for the very first time. On arrival in London Ogarev and Natalie stayed with Herzen. She was twenty-seven, Herzen exactly twice her age. She was beautiful, devoted to Tata, liberated, and longed to be a mother. Herzen was widowed, virile, solid, industrious and lonely. Ogarev, his best and oldest friend, whom he was to support financially for the rest of his life, was gentle, generous, sick, sterile and apart. An observer. A man of deep affections who refused, or did not know how, to oppose or condemn the happiness of his friends even when it entailed his own misery. Natalie and Herzen became lovers, and she bore him three children, all called Ogarev on the birth registrations, but all clearly Herzen's own. Elizaveta, known as Liza, born in September 1858, and the twins Alexis and Helen, known as Lola Boy and Lola Girl, born in November 1861.

Carr's malicious account of these events depends largely on Natalie Tuchkov's diary, but she was, in addition to her strengths, an hysteric, and the contents of her diary, betrayed by its style, are less than reliable. Ogarev might be a better witness, but he was not in the lovers' embrace, and his view of the unfolding events was distorted by his own emotional suffering held in check by his generosity of spirit. Love and friendship committed him to an ideal of noble behaviour which his suffering made it impossible for him to realize in practice. In this way, guilt was combined with his grief. These do not yield altogether useful tools for the biographer, though they offered Carr almost boundless temptations for ridicule, which even great intellect made him incompetent to resist. His claim, in the preface to the first (1933) edition of the book, that he has 'refrained where possible from judgements of [his] own' is, in the circumstances, a quite astounding conceit.

I had gone as far as Magdalen College deer park while thinking these thoughts, and finding myself there I leaned over the railings, searching for signs of the herd among the trees. It was cold, and although still early afternoon, the sky was leaden, nightfall not far away. No sign of the deer. I went through to Addison's Walk, down to the Cherwell. The river wasn't frozen yet, but it moved sluggishly under the black tree branches, dark and slothful. The absence of leaves, the crunch of the gravel under my feet, the sheet of frost that turned grass and weeds alike to white, brittle crystal reminded me of Tata, Herzen's daughter born in Russia, raised abroad, forever a foreigner, alien and in exile. She survived to a great old age, eventually residing in Lausanne, and dying there at the age of ninety-two in 1936. When she was seven, living in the villa in Nice, she had a pet goat to keep, and thinking of her tending this delicate and gentle creature – there is a painting by Guiaud – always reminds me of Herzen himself. Briefly I could see the three of them, the goat, the great bulk of Herzen, and the little child holding his hand and skipping by his side, as they make their way down the short hillside to the edge of the Mediterranean sea.

As I walked back up the High Street to college it began to snow, not the usual sleet and dirt of an English December, but a steady, heavy, barely eddying dense cloud of flakes that stuck and soon collected on every surface. There was very little traffic. The shops all brilliantly lit, but few pedestrians. I realised that for days I had paid no attention to the 'outside' world, and that this snow-storm may well have been forecast and anticipated, with me the last to know. Sitting here I can see it collecting on the window-ledge, already several inches deep. Beyond that is invisible, but for the glow of lights in rooms on the other side of the quad, because snow obliterates everything.

Later: 5.30 p.m.
Followed Mrs W.'s instructions and took a bath. Bit of a surprise looking in the bathroom mirror. Couldn't have shaved since last Saturday, hair dishevelled and in need of a wash. Can't remember whether I've even had a shower since Moser died. Were there any other things I've forgotten, things that I did but shouldn't have, or things that I didn't but would have? Impossible to say, and no one to ask. I suppose people are avoiding me. Too embarrassing. I may even have fallen asleep in Governing Body – yesterday? I certainly just fell asleep in the bath. I shaved in the bath too, but it wasn't a very bright idea because I cut myself on the chin and couldn't stop it bleeding. In the end I stuck a tiny piece of lavatory paper over it to get it to dry up.

Coming back to my desk, I turned over some pages of the biography, looking for the passages about Ogarev that I'd been mulling on in town earlier. Found and read one, but disheartened by it. Poorly written and unpersuasive, prose dead on the page, lifeless descriptions, pompous judgements, contrived anecdotes. You need style to write a good biography, otherwise why would anyone want to read a life when they could be living one? People will laugh at my Herzen when it's published.

There ought to be an ethics of biography: how to approach it, what can be said. I remember reading a piece by someone in which he described how, in the course of writing the biography of an American poet, he set up an interview with one of his subject's numerous lovers. When they eventually met, the woman maintained that she and this chap had just been friends, nothing more. Only then did the biographer

159

reveal to her that he had already read her letters to the poet, and that these told a different story. Caught out and embarrassed, the woman had to change her tune.

This is the tabloid approach to biography, petty, impertinent and vain. The author, when he first wrote to this unfortunate woman, should have stated that he had read her letters, which were located in such and such an archive, and that he would like, if he could, to discuss her relationship with the poet. These were her letters, after all, to which she presumably still owned the copyright. Such an approach would at least have offered her some fair alternatives, like going to re-read the letters herself, or just telling him to get lost.

When biographers start to think they are God, then they inevitably do the devil's work. Ulick O'Connor, otherwise sensible, believes that there is nothing that someone might have done that can't, with the right formula of words, be set down in a biography. It's hard to agree. People wound each other, and many wounds never heal. They leak a life away, or turn septic and kill. Some actions, kept secret, long buried, cannot be turned over into the light, because of the destruction they might wreak on the still living. Biographers have responsibilities, and not only to the truth.

They also have ambitions. Is all ambition vanity? Herzen came to think so after the decline of his newspaper, once influential but marginalized in the politics of Russia in the second half of the 1860s. This coupled with the growth of his pessimism. I imagine he believed that he might have been able to make a difference if only he could have *been* there, but his return to imperial Russia was completely impossible. Was it true of Moser, who wanted to build another storey on the great mansion of natural science theory? Or Vita, trying to still the nothingness of silence with her own music – the anarchy of sound, Moser called it at the end. I thought her love for me was the purest thing I had ever encountered. She came over to me from the couch, took my hand, and led me up into a loft room where there was an open skylight and an unmade bed. She kissed me on the mouth, and in one swift, slightly clumsy movement, losing her balance for a moment, she peeled the long yellow dress over her head. She still seemed hot and feverish, but was sensual now too, not embarrassed. She got on the bed, her legs splayed, and grinned at me, pleading. In that moment, was she any of the things I had thought her to be? I remember it, but can't remember what I thought, or rather how I reacted, since thought would be too precise a word to describe the turmoil that I sense now that I must have been feeling then. If I had been a man of action, surely I would have left. Anyway, the moment passed. She returned to herself. The beauty, stillness, complexity and honesty of her love acted like a field of magnetic attraction. I could not leave. The thought came quickly that this was a truth, and therefore it could not be repudiated. One might deduce, from other principles, how it came to be true, but its truthfulness could not be undone by reason, only by death. And Vita's death was exactly what was, shortly, to extinguish the truth.

'And Moser,' I said to her weakly.

'Will always be loved by Clara, who is everything I am not, and far better than me.'

We made love. Unnecessary to write it really, except that I want to be able to remember what it was like, the shape and touch of her body, the warm, wet places, the pressure and strokes of her fingers, the curves and almost-planes, the ridges of pelvis and clavicle, and the distant lustre of her eyes. The words on the page kindle the longings of desire, but do they return her to me in memory, revive her being in my own? What I recall is a shadow of the moment, like dark figures thrown on an illuminated wall, yet detailed, identifiable. And

I am there and not there, because although it is me that I can so to speak see, it is me doing the seeing – observer, spectator, voyeur. The act of memory will not unite me with the experience, only remove me from it. I am sitting on the edge of the bed, naked, and she is standing in front of me. She removes her panties, then presses my face against her belly, her hands, those fingers, playing in my hair. I could smell her womanness, but that is an odour, a perfume, that is gone, for ever, released and dispersed. I can see this, but there is no feeling, only a sort of maddening overture. She straddles me on the bed, and I fall back under her beauty, the weight of her and her grace. She moves her lips, settling me inside her, leaning back, her eyes closed now, hands behind her neck. I lie awake at night and watch this, see her rise and dip, contracting and pulling, revolving her hips slightly, releasing, contracting and pulling, again, and once more, and again. Her eyes open and she smiles. She folds forward into my embrace. We sleep. And all the while, I watch.

We stayed like this for three days. Vita made up the bed in the loft and I went out to fetch food, but in the silence of that late summer, the half of a week apart went by in love-making, the whispered conversations and exchanges of intimacies that mark the giving and taking of love. We agreed never to speak of her illness and approaching death because that was part of time, and we had stepped aside from it. Neither of us mentioned Moser again, nor Alice. We abandoned clocks, forsook hours, sleeping in the afternoons, eating after midnight, making love at dawn and in the evening like the first time. When it was over, on the Friday night, I went back into college. Alice came home on Saturday, Moser on Sunday. In the middle of the following week he told me that Vita had a brain tumour, had, with his agreement, declined further treatment, and was going to die, probably before the end of the year.

I saw her three more times. Once in late September when I sat on the edge of her bed and she held my hand, and told me very solemnly about all the things I must do to look after Moser once she was gone; the second time three weeks later when she was almost unable to see, suffering acute pain, and rambling in her speech, which was coherent in itself, but leapt from topic to topic in an apparently unguided way. A lot of it was about Clara, and I had to tell Moser, when he asked me about it, that I didn't have any idea who this person was. The last time was two days before she died. She was in a coma, but I like to believe that I can remember her squeezing my hand when I sat with her and said goodbye. She died at eleven o'clock in the morning of 10 November.

Moser told me later – I think at the New Year, when he came to stay with Alice and me in Jericho for a few days – that Vita had been a different person in her last nine weeks or so of life. Even in the first couple of weeks after his return from Harvard, when they were back and forth to UCL and she was in many respects quite her old self, he could tell how much she had changed. 'The brain in transition, under pressure, transforming consciousness, changing her feelings, her imagination.' This was when he coined his phrase 'the anarchy of sound' to describe her attempts to play the piano. Something of the harmonies and the structural fabric was preserved, but in a jumbled and discordant form, the direction and the timing gone, transitions muddled, but the sounds still haunting. The music of Eden.

I was tempted to put this, by analogy, into the biography of Herzen, because it is a metaphor for life. We live by time's arrow, from birth to death, the pages of the calendars turning one way only from infancy to senility, the pace of the clock no different at the end from the beginning. But this is not how we experience it. And I don't mean by this mere trivial things, like summers that seem to last for ever in childhood, or the speeding pace of the seasons in middle age. Rather, the character of experience itself is formed of and shaped in the memory, and the memory does not move in a linear way, but rather by reference, stray connection, allusion, smell and sensation. It colludes with an unconscious self, autonomic, laid down in the brain but constantly shuffled and reformed like an infinite celestial pack of cards. We strive to control and direct it, but it, as we say, wanders from old paths to new trig points, down tracks once lost and briefly rediscovered, past old half-remembered monuments next to new signposts that point back at experience once fondled, but since decayed for lack of use. The true nature of experience lies here, and it is what eludes the biographer, and leads me to seek shelter in facts and events, letters and diaries, places and dates. Vita's anarchy of sound was thus an apt rehearsal – what I expect she herself called a *répétition* – of her short distinguished life as a virtuoso, all the many *moments musicaux*, the movements of sonatas and concertos, the preludes, scherzos, studies, noc-turnes, sarabands, fugues, polonaises and gymnopédies of the soloist's repertoire recalled and reformed not according to the lines of the staves on the score, but now, the partitions gone, according to the logic of the unique individual who had played them.

When her dizziness became so great and her coordination so poor that she could no longer stand up, Moser said Vita asked to have a bed made up in the music room. The piano was closed and locked, like a gate. From her bed she had a view of the two Palmers, and of the sycamore tree outside the window. As it shed its leaves in the autumn rain she lost her sight. In what he said had been their last conversation coherent enough to make sense, she had held his head between her hands and told him how much and how deeply she, Clara, had loved him, and how he should be glad, 'for Clara is a far, far better and stronger person than I'. And she fell back exhausted on her pillows, begging for morphine, which he gave her.

Moser wept when he told me this.

6

Friday afternoon
Cranham St, Jericho

'Just as conspirators try to conceal their secret with a transparent veil of mystery and an eloquent silence, so do the phanerogamous try to display and blurt out all that is in their hearts . . . One's eye is so used to seeing them that one involuntarily looks for them at every street row, at every demonstration, at every banquet.'

The snow was already about six inches deep. Porters were clearing and salting a pathway from the lodge to the Senior Common Room when I walked over for pre-dinner drinks. The Oxford gaudy, an occasion for joy, is one of those invisible features of English life, like country-house weekends and private recitals. In essence one gaudy is much like another, a feast at which dons and their invited guests celebrate their own distinction with fine wines, elaborate dishes, and good conversation. They begin early with pre-prandial drinks in a brightly lit common room, and end late with coffee and brandy by fire- and candlelight. In practice every gaudy is different, because each college has its own form, its own architecture, its own traditions, some of them quite and surprisingly recent. All Souls gaudies, held in the magnificence of the Codrington, are like state banquets, and about as interesting. In Balliol and Merton they are still trying to recover from the legacy of Richard Cobb, who single-handedly made both colleges infamous for greed and the malice of his conversation. Exeter's gaudies are said to be a little prim, those of Univ. noisy, and the House decorous – like a committee of dowager duchesses planning rather than having a gala. The general public's knowledge of these things, in so far as it has any at all, has been shaped, one imagines, by mystery thrillers and comic novels, neither of which does anything to illuminate the darkness of ignorance, since gaudies are not thrilling and never funny. Here at the Court I think we have a reputation for being earnest and informal, without surrendering the niceties. The niceties include evening dress, academic gowns, the accumulated silverware of four hundred years of hoarding, thirty-year-old claret and one-hundred-year-old port, and the civility not to mention or to draw attention to these things.

High-stepping my way through the snow to cross the quad, skirting the now invisible pond from which the silent, frozen fountain projected like a petrified Alsatian stork, I slipped and fell. The snow saved any great hurt, but I twisted my wrist and grazed my knee, though it struck me as funny at the time, and for a moment I lay in the snow laughing quietly to myself as the flakes fell heavily on to me. It was thinking about Moser and Campbell-Quaid that did it – Campbell-Quaid's enmity of Moser was thought-provoking, possibly mind-consuming, certainly distracting – that, and the glass of scotch I'd had while scribbling after my bath. I went into the SCR cloakroom to get myself cleaned up, and found that I'd torn my dress trousers at the knee that was grazed and bleeding. I sponged off the knee, and was relieved to discover that if I kept my gown wrapped around me, I could conceal the rip in my trouser leg.

Campbell-Quaid, C.Q. to his friends and intimates, is a tall thin man with steel-grey hair, a long, white, pointed nose over a receding chin, and a sharp, narrow voice of reed-like intensity. One wonders whether he keeps a sharp knife in his pocket to trim it with. He is slightly round-shouldered, with long arms and large hands, simian indeed: a feature that gets observed rather in the way that people note the likenesses between dogs and their owners, because Dr Campbell-Quaid, FRS, holds the Darwin Chair in Evolutionary Science at Cambridge. And everyone agrees that Darwin and monkeys go together. I have seen Campbell-Quaid several times before at Oxford, dinners and so forth, and once went with Moser to hear him lecture. His topic was Eldredge and Gould's theory of punctuated equilibrium. The details of his argument elude me now, but what I do recall most vividly was the relish that he took in the demolition of the theory, the sarcasm that he heaped upon its authors – whom he clearly identified as adversaries – and the delight he appeared to experience not only in scotching their theory, but in diminishing them as people. It all seemed rather far from textbook accounts of the scientific method. Given that I knew what he thought of Moser, I felt apprehensive of him, hoping to avoid him.

No such luck. I recognized him as soon as I came into the common room. He was talking to the Master, who nodded in my direction and then indicated with a finger that I should join them. Sir Philip introduced us, but Campbell-Quaid's body language brushed the formalities aside as we shook hands. His high eyebrows were raised, as if in some surprise, or disbelief, as he looked into my face, as though it were most peculiar the sorts of persons one encountered in college these days. (I suspect him of being the sort of misguided pedant who would say persons instead of people.)

'I wrote Reg's obituary in *The Times*,' he said, returning his face to an oval of gravity, pointing his nose directly at mine, and intoning the words 'in *The Times*' in the way that a stage clergyman would say, 'Let us pray.' The obit. page of *The Times* is a pantheon of sorts for some.

'I realize.'

'I hope you liked it,' he went on, releasing my hand.

'In what way?'

'That it was factually accurate and fair. Isn't that how we all want to be remembered?'

Politeness prevented an answer, as it often does. The piece was inaccurate and unfair, but the best I could do was deny him the satisfaction of my being agreeable. The Master rescued us by indicating the scout at my elbow with a tray of drinks, saying simultaneously, 'I always think myself that the ideal obituary, which is not, after all, merely an epitaph, nor a biography, not only gets the outline facts of a life right, but also gives the reader – who's most unlikely, *faute de mieux*, to have known the chap – enough to chew on in the way of controversy, so that he gets a slice of recent history as well as the life of the individual. A man in his times. Don't you agree, Felix?' He turned to Cunningham, who had come up to join us. No umbrella for once. The common room was filling up now, conversation quite noisy.

'I always assume,' said Felix, pursing his lips, raising his voice above the hubbub, and looking vaguely in the direction of the ceiling, 'that obituaries are intended to reassure the nearly-dead, like me, that death is not the great leveller. Some are greater than others, and continue to be so, even in rigor mortis.' He managed to make the Latin 'of death' sound like brick cement, which it may be, I suppose. He and the Master began conversing about something else, and Campbell-Quaid turned back to me.

'You were Moser's friend, I believe. Close to him. Sir Philip was telling me.'

'Yes. We had known each other . . . a long time.' I had almost, thoughtlessly, started an account of how Moser and I met, the course of our friendship, the solidarity we shared. But at about the word 'other' I realized that Campbell-Quaid was no longer paying any attention to me, but was looking past my shoulder at the crowded room, his eyes flitting from cluster to cluster of black-gowned figures, from doorway to window-seat, from corner groups to fireplace groups, and so on.

'Very interesting,' he said, in his dry, reedy voice. 'And a great pleasure to have met such a good friend of Reg's. How we shall miss him. Tell me, isn't that Milton Pestich over there, the palaeontologist from Stanford?'

'Yes, he's been here this term. Would you like me to . . . ?'

'No need.'

And he was gone, touching my elbow in an English gesture of sympathetic brotherhood as he edged away into the crowd. Must be *learned* English, however, because his name is Scottish. Though he doesn't talk like a Scot. For some reason, at that moment, Campbell-Quaid reminded me of Gradle, whom I've never met but whom I think of as playing a role in my life similar to that played in Moser's by Campbell-Quaid. A figure with the power to break you, before whom you are helpless. And someone who is quite sure that use of the power is necessary and legitimate – regrettable perhaps, 'Look, I'm sorry about this', and so on – but none the less very present astride your path, like a bully, or a personnel manager with a grudge against you. I began to wonder whether champagne was a good idea, right on top of scotch. And how long was it since I'd eaten? The champagne was excellent, however, Drappier 1980, good old Laurent, and I drained the glass, giving Felix a cue to turn back to me with a replacement. Robin Foxton was with him, a nice, very gentle physicist, a recent appointment to a full fellowship, and attending his first gaudy. By his side was a tall, handsome woman, thirtyish, round-eyed behind big round glasses, and wearing a low-cut body-hugging full-length green dress, with a rather imaginat-ive slit up one side.

'Philip,' said Felix, 'may I introduce you to one of our college guests, Dr Tanina Spekeleiner from Princeton? Dr Philip Leroux.'

'I'm learning some of your crazy nomenclature,' said Ms Spekeleiner. She had one of those shrill voices that Moser used to call *taille-pierre* – stone-cutter. It sliced through the common room like a laser beam through space, leaving a silent path behind it, and augmenting the volume of noise from everywhere else. 'Are you an official fellow? Or a professorial fellow? Or a dean? Or the Visitor. Or a don? Or what?'

'Philip is official,' said Felix. 'We have unofficial philosophers, like young Foxton here, who's in solid states, but Philip is our official philosopher. When Philip thinks we listen. What Leroux deduces today the rest shall think tomorrow.'

'Oh wow! And what does Leroux deduce today?'

'He deduces that he is being made fun of,' I smiled, shaking her hand. Smiling made my chin itch. 'But I believe you and I are sitting together at table opposite Cunningham here, so we'll be able to get our own back over the pheasant.'

'Pheasant!'

'According to my scout.'

'Pheasant according to what . . . ?' screeched Ms Spekeleiner just as Laurent hammered on his gong to announce dinner. Silence fell.

'Awesome,' shrieked Ms Spekeleiner. 'Scouts . . .'

'Dinner is served,' said Laurent, his voice soft in the silence.

'Oh God almighty, have mercy on our souls,' said Felix under his breath. Talk and the shuffle of feet obliterated all embarrassment but mine – or so it felt – and we all went through to Hall. Tanina Spekeleiner was to sit on my left, and it was only after grace, and getting her settled in her seat, that I realized that my chin was bleeding again, so that it was with handkerchief pressed to my face that I had to introduce myself to the guest on my right, Rolfe Gartz from the Chrysalis Project in Berlin. Robin Foxton explained across the table, where he was sitting on Felix's left, that Chrysalis was an EU venture to stimulate the development of hi-tech industries in countries of the former Soviet Union. Robin himself was involved in 'the research end of things'. I introduced Herr Gartz to Tanina Spekeleiner across my chest, and she told him that she was in Women's Studies but this didn't mean that she wasn't interested in men too. 'Especially if they're official men like Phil here.'

With this we began our soup. Or at any rate most of us did. Poor Herr Gartz, attempting to pull his evening-dress shirt cuffs down below his jacket sleeves, must have pulled too hard, or had too slight a grip, because his fingers jerked free, and he back-handed his mock turtle soup across the table where some of it poured into Felix's lap. The rest spilled across the table top.

'Oh soup ... er, soup ... erlative, soup ... reme,' said Felix, rising to his feet, dabbing with his napkin, while an army of scouts surrounded us, cleared several square metres of table, wiped them clean, and relaid the surface, all in the space of about five seconds.

'No harm done,' said Felix, subsiding once more into his chair as a fresh bowl of soup appeared in front of Herr Gartz. He was now as red in the face as a cherry tomato, and was presumably searching the Euro-lexicon in his head for an appropriate apology. This, and the mortification from which no one seemed set to rescue him, served to keep him quiet for a while.

'That was really something,' said Ms Spekeleiner, referring, I think, to the scouts' performance.

'We are gratified by your admiration,' said Felix. 'Tell us, Ms Spekeleiner, is this merely a tour of inspection you are making? Or can we hope for some greater purpose? A sabbatical year to be spent among us, perhaps?'

She started to talk about her graduate students, the need to bring a 'cross-national dynamic to gender studies' which were apparently stagnating in the doldrums in the United States. 'I wanna get my kids really plugged in to what gives with feminist issues in Britain and on the Continent.' Apparently she had been at San Diego formerly, and there they had 'done some neat stuff cross-nationally in Taiwan and Mexico', and so on. I phased her out in order to concentrate on the Meursault, which was far better than most conversation could ever be. Moser always used to complain that Laurent kept wonderful wines for first courses, and then served the food so fast that one was barely able to enjoy the wines before they were gone. This turned out to be true of the gaudy. Soup gave way to fish and a far less extravagant Muscadet. Felix and Dr Spekeleiner, whom we were apparently to call Nina, were in conversation head to cleavage across the table. And since Robin was now rescuing Herr Gartz from the embarrassment of his gaffe by talking about the potential of flat-screen tele- vision in the Russia of the future, I let my eye and mind wander the rounds of the Great Hall. Every seat was taken, two hundred and fifty people or thereabouts, a steady, pleasant, rumbling rhubarb of conversation, the clinks of glasses and silverware, scouts scurrying. Laurent was at his post behind the Master's chair at the top table, from where he caught my eye and raised his eyebrows briefly in a silent greeting. Sir Philip had the government ministers on either side. Next to Colin Preggett was the dapper, diminutive figure of Randolph Partiger, the head of the university's publishing business, and a thoughtful, loyal man who surely deserved better than the awful Preggett at a dinner like this. Next to him was Rawlinson, looking reflective, head cocked to listen to Partiger's points, nodding occasionally in time to the movements of his knife and fork. Scorpion at rest. The banker as scholar's friend. He reminded me of Alice and our last, hopeless, telephone conversation. Well, I didn't feel so bad now. Not even about Moser. Campbell-Quaid was at one end of the top table, deep in conversation with Conrad Jesty, who seemed to be laying out something with his forefinger. There was a light breath in my left ear.

'Mr Laurent's compliments, sir.' It was Morris, one of the older scouts. 'And he would appreciate your drinking a toast for him to Dr Moser. In this, sir.' He set down a clean glass and filled it from a freshly opened bottle of the Meursault, which he then put down on the table beside my place. 'Seeing as 'ow Dr Moser always appreciated Mr Laurent's service, sir.' I glanced in Laurent's direction, but his face was a mask while listening to something that the Master was conveying to him. I didn't see him look in my direction again until much later in the evening.

As requested, I silently offered up a toast, *requiescat in pace*, to Moser, whose struggles were now over. I wondered if Campbell-Quaid had ever been beset by doubt in the way that Moser was when his presumption – after all, he repudiated the idea of 'belief' in science – that Darwinism was the full and complete answer to the puzzle of the origin of species began to crumble. You need a tremendously strong ego to tread a lonely theoretical path in the natural sciences. At his low points Moser used to refer to Geoffrey Burnstock at UCL, whose courage and tenacity he much admired. The trouble with questioning aspects of Darwinism was not so much that you were alone as that you appeared to be in such bad company. The creationists, of course, mad hatters at the tea-table of science. But Moser was less worried by them than he was by apparently well-qualified scientists like Kauffman, Doolittle and Behe, whose arguments ranged from what he called the impenetrable to the mystical without passing through scientific reason. Like Robert Shapiro in New York, Moser favoured a scientific search for a scientific explanation of such phenomena as irreducible complexity. Unlike everyone else, however, he believed that the breakthrough to this new territory would have to be conceptual, and would necessarily entail the creation of new terms, a language appropriate to a new theory. The present discourse involves comparisons with 'purposeful', 'intelligent' design. Biochemical systems, like the cascade process of protein interactions that create blood clots to staunch bleeding, are often described as being 'machines'; neurotransmitters in the brain 'plug into receptors rather as a key fits into a lock' (but do keys 'plug' into locks? Usually it's plugs that plug into sockets); while glia functions 'much as does a trellis in a rose garden'. The language is of machinery, keys and locks, transporters, electrical super-highways, receptors, messengers, manufacturers, libraries, cascades and tuning. But these terms, as Moser used to complain, do nothing to advance our knowledge. They merely obscure by analogy. Biochemical processes are just that: biological processes in which chemical transformations occur. How they came into existence is a scientific problem that will be solved by theoretical means, deduced from, and refined by, empirical thought, coupled with speculative experimentation. For this to occur there need to be new terms, an expansion of language.

'Do you plan to share it with us, Philip,' asked Felix, 'or to keep it all to yourself?'

'Are you interested in the linguistic philosophy of science and the origin of species?'

'Not especially, no. But the Meursault is a different matter.'

Scouts were clearing away the fish plates, though I hadn't touched mine. About a third of the Meursault was still there, however, so I shared it round.

'We are drinking a toast to the memory of a colleague,' I said to Nina. 'Moser. A scientist. And a great man. He died last weekend.'

'To Moser, then,' said Felix.

Nina was about to say something, but she jumped a little and said, 'Ouch. Hey!' instead, and then blushed. Strange woman. Peculiarly innocent in a way. Felix was smiling. I turned to Herr Gratz on my right. He was far younger than I had previously been aware: fair, with a blond moustache, and close-cropped hair. A little on the fat side of overweight. Too many EU lunches perhaps.

'Are you, Herr Gratz, in favour of broadening or of deepening the European Union?' I asked him. This was the sort of thing college gaudies are for, after all.

'Both,' he replied, blinking at me as though it was inconceivable that anyone might think differently. 'Zer are certain difficulties. But it is too late to turn back ze watch.' Foxton was nodding enthusiastically.

'Herzen – did you know this, Robin? – was a great Europeanist too. Are you familiar with Alexander Herzen, Herr Gratz?'

'Pleez. Forgive me. Wiz who?'

'Alexander Herzen. He's at the European University Institute in Fiesole. Philosopher, historian, political scientist.' I turned to my other side. One must share conversation at a gaudy. 'And a great supporter of women's causes too, Nina. Almost one of us . . .'

'But not official.'

'No. Not official enough. Off the record really, because the modern world . . .'

Felix butted in here. 'Philip's pulling your leg, Nina', that sort of thing. 'Herzen, dead since eighteen something-middling . . .'

'Seventy.'

'. . . is Philip's hobby-horse. Speciality. He's just finished the biography, which will be out soon, and will make both him and the college famous.'

'Ah. Congratulations,' said Herr Gratz. 'Now I understand', which was manifestly not true. This man was fun to be with. 'I know so little of the European Universitat Institute because they have not physics there, I think.'

'No. That's Princeton. Isn't that right, Ms Spekeleiner?'

'Nina, please. Um . . . I'm not sure . . .' She had a fixed smile on her face, so broad that it was dislodging her glasses upwards into her forehead. Her eyes flickered from Felix to Robin to Herr Gratz. 'I . . . well, yes we do . . . that's to say there is physics at Princeton.'

'You see. Just as Herzen predicted.'

'Philip,' said Felix, giving me a look across the table. My minder for the night. I took Nina's hand between both of mine and gave it a squeeze.

'Dr Spekeleiner . . .'

'Nina, Philip.'

'. . . you're a sport. You should come and join us here at the Court. We need people like you. Your breadth, your acumen, your interests, your remarkable . . .'

'Make way for the peasants,' said Felix, spreading his arms to indicate the arrival of the meat. Mrs Wharton had been right, pheasant was the *plat du jour*. In its wake came a huge 1964 Clos de Vougeot which made Nina cough and Robin blush. Felix raised his glass to me, saying *sotto voce*, 'To caution', and I gave him, in return, one of my agreeable, compliant smiles. I ate the potato chips, which were excellent, and went well with the burgundy. The Great Hall seemed greater, its ceiling higher, yet the pictures on the far wall much closer. Sir Percival Wendover, all mutton-chops and waistcoat, the second and most generous of the Wendover family whose connections to the college had brought us so much money, and so much splendid ill-will, gave me a wink from behind his sheet of varnish. He would have known what to do next. I was filled, thrilled, with the same, limitless possibilities.

'Tell me, Ms Spekeleiner. Is there a Mr Spekeleiner?'

'Four,' she replied.

'Four. Goodness, you barely look . . .'

'My father, my uncle, my older brother, and my younger brother.'

'But no . . .'

'If a Mr Spekeleiner was my husband that would hardly be my father's name. And in any event I wouldn't take it. But I am married. My husband's a psychometrician.'

'How interesting. And what does he do?'

'What *are* you Dr Leroux?'

'Philip, please . . .'

'I zinc,' said Herr Gratz, apparently eager now to show his range, 'zat Dr Spekeleiner's husband may be an analytical statistician working in ze feeld of psychology. Is zis not so, *Fraulein?*'

'Ah, I see,' I said. 'A sort of calculating shrink. How very interesting. Bit like a computer with feelings, eh Felix? It must . . .'

'Philip,' said Felix, looking terribly serious, and taking off his glasses. His forehead was glistening with perspiration. 'I don't think this is fair to Dr Spekeleiner.' He directed his gaze from me to her. 'You must forgive our colleague, Nina. A lot of strain recently, and . . .'

'Oh come on, Felix, it was only a bit of fun. Nina enjoys a bit of fun, don't you Nina?' I was pleased to see that she looked none too certain of this. 'You know, Nina, I'm married too, and I don't take my spouse's name either, so we're equal there. Alice, that's my wife, she's a merchant banker, flies all over the world' – and I put out my arms and half stood up to illustrate what this entailed – 'and simultaneously she's a Marxist, wants to put an end to capitalism, from each according to his – or indeed her – no sexism in twentieth-century Marx, eh? – means, to each according to his needs. For centuries I've been merely trying to understand the world. Alice, however, is going to change it. Good old Alice is one of the great contradictions of late capitalism, so it's not odd or peculiar to me that you should have a mathematical trick-cyclist for a husband. There's nowt so queer as folk, as me mother used to say.'

Dr Spekeleiner looked a bit stuck at this point. At any rate there was a morsel of pheasant hanging from her lower lip, so I wiped it off for her. Oddly, she seemed upset at this, so I turned to Herr Gratz.

'Are you married, Rolfe?'

'Yes. But my wife is not like yours, interesting . . .'

'Oh come, come . . .'

'She a technical in a medical laboratory is.'

'A technical. Fascinating. I think everybody has wanted, at one time or another, don't you agree Robin?, to be an adjective. Not just a cannon, but a loose. Or a glorious rather than a singer. Even a morbid. Nina here could be an exemplary, or a transitional, or a delectable. Hello, viewers. Tonight we are privileged to have a dreary with us in the studio.' I produced an imaginary microphone and thrust it under Ms Spekeleiner's chin. 'How does it feel to be a dreary? And when do you expect to become a brilliant or a shining once again?'

Nina sat there with her mouth open, a forkload of pheasant suspended just below the microphone. She seemed to have no sense of how to handle an impromptu media interview, when I thought that all Americans got training for this sort of thing in high school.

'You're an unusual man, Phil,' she said eventually. 'Aren't you going to eat your food?'

'Oh, how rude of me. Do forgive me,' I replied, withdrawing the microphone and passing it to my German assistant whose wife, the technical, had, after all, started this conversation. 'I'm being a very bad host. Of course you must have it if you want it.' And I went to scrape the pheasant from my plate on to hers. For some reason Felix reached across to stop me, locking my wrist in his strong grasp, and fastening his eyes on mine.

'I think Dr Spekeleiner may have had enough,' he hissed.

'No, no, I don't think so. What she just said was . . .'

'Yes, yes, plenty thank you,' said Nina, shielding her plate with her hand.

'Ah,' I said, wringing my arm free of Felix's grip. I distinctly remember thinking that if Felix hadn't been a friend of mine, and this an important formal occasion in the college calendar, and snow falling outside to make everything look picture-book Oxford perfect, I would have punched him on the nose for his impudence. I was only trying to help this ridiculous American woman get what she wanted, or at any rate deserved. Sort of thing a good host does. I thought I'd better calm Felix down by changing the subject.

'You know,' I said, 'our colleague, my friend, Moser – the one who just died – he used to call Bertrand Russell "*Faisan farci à la Souvarov*" because he was rich, rare, and liked to get stuffed with tasty morsels. Do you read Bocuse, Felix? He is to cooking what Moser was to biochemistry. An artist and an innovator. A scientist of victory over the oppression of boring food.' That's a joke which no one will get.

'No. But I ate at his restaurant once. In Lyon. Marvellous.' And he began to talk about the food, and the city of Lyon, and the countryside of the Rhône and Saône valleys.

The place-name of Lyon brought me to an abrupt stop, though the world continued to move around me. The sounds of talk and eating were louder. I felt terribly hot. There were tears pressing pinpricks into my eyes. Was everything spinning? Was I about to fall down? Someone was banging a spoon on a glass to secure silence. The Master was on his feet. He wanted, he said, to make a few remarks before the dessert, and he proceeded to do so, though I'm blessed if I can remember what they were. Mention of Moser and Lyon returned me to the Roman arena, the lost sensations of crowds and cries, dust and dismemberment; of Vita alone with her bosom friend locked inside her; Moser dancing, and then on his knees in the sand of the hot, still night. So unlike this one. I was there again, and loosened my bow tie, released the stud in the top of my dress shirt, drank another glass of the miraculous Clos de Vougeot.

Seeing Moser on his knees was a reminder, paradoxically, of his strength of will, even then. Almost all progress in science and the arts depends on, or comes from, the force of will exercised over the power of necessity as expressed in our genes. Genes are the source of potential in talent. Environment – which is apparently everything else, after all – is the context by means of which talent, stimulated, provoked and shaped, finds expression. A new thing – a score, an idea, a formula, a way of seeing – once created, is itself a part of the expanding environment, available to shape new, emergent talent. But it is the human will to create which breaks the hold of the past on the future. Decline, decay and death are the triumph of genes over the conscious life of the mind. Works of revolution-ary art and scientific discovery are the victories of the human mind over the limitations of the gene pool. Darwinism is not so much the theory to account for the origin of species in life, as that of the origin of death among the proliferation of species.

These views of Moser's were always going to get him into hot water with the scientific establishment of our day. For them, the high priests of Darwinism, no aspect of the human species can be free of genes which, by definition, are the building blocks of life. The mind is a construct of the brain, which is determined by our genes. A pure Darwinian, like Campbell-Quaid, would expect in due course to find a combination of genetic material that accounted for strong-willed people. No doubt recent discoveries that show, for example, that any individual's particular pattern of brain neurons, receptors and dendrites is a consequence of early experience, learning, and exposure to knowledge, would itself yield eventually to the discovery of those genes that controlled and determined the potential for this development.

Moser used to laugh about this sort of endless reductionism. What worried him far more, indeed occasionally even angered him, was social Darwinism. The people who took over Darwinian terminology and used it to explain human social behaviour. Like birth-order studies where children 'adapt' to family pressure, and find 'niches' in which they can succeed by being different from their siblings. The whole point of Darwin's theory is that individuals don't adapt. Geology, climate, geography – circumstance, so to speak – favour particular adaptations, which in turn permit individuals to survive, thereby strengthening the gene pool for those adaptations. If the individual has got to do the adapting, it's already too late.

Darwinism is a new religion, but like all the great nineteenth-century theories that sprang from the lap of Hegel, and the shadow of necessity, it is dying of its own weight. It wants to explain (away) free will – which it cannot do – and it has no answer for the incredible, beautiful, natural irreducible complexity of life at the micro-biochemical level. What we need is a superior theoretical account of the origins of human life, not one endorsed by an inferior social and pseudo-science of human behaviour. Modern man is not born free. Everywhere he is shackled by Darwin's chains. For centuries scientists have sought to explain this. Our intention, however, is to set him free.

People started to applaud, which seemed appropriate, but on focusing it turned out to be for the Master sitting down and the minister of Science and Technology, the Rt Hon. Colin Preggett, PC, MA, standing up. When the clapping subsided he said that he had a message for us. Britain was changing. And it was changing for the better. Changing not because the government said it must and told it how. But changing because the government had learned the hardest lesson of all, self-restraint. Now people were free to choose what they wanted, to compete how they liked. He believed in the new Britain that was springing up at our feet.

I could see that this kind of self-congratulatory nonsense was going to take a while, so as quietly as possible – perhaps not wholly successfully – I got to my feet and slipped out of Hall. Downstairs at the main door – Axel's Gate, it's called – there was that wonderful and peculiar stillness that comes with heavy snow. Nothing moved. The snow itself had stopped falling; the sky was black above; it was cold and windless. The pathway shovelled from the porters' lodge was bordered by mountainous banks of snow, and beyond these the quad spread away like a flat, white field, every feature levelled, the pond invisible, and the former stork fountain now quaintly smoothed into a shape resembling a bishop in his robe and mitre. I sat down on the steps, feeling a bit sick. Campbell-Quaid's features came back to me, thin and pinched. A white man with his burden of knowledge. Snow White and the seven dwarfs of the Medical Research Council Grants Committee. Moser's last submission, an application for a grant to finance research into the puzzle of how proteins are formed such that they may fit together in certain ways, had been returned to him at the end of last week. The peer reviewer, instead of writing a note about it, had scribbled comments all over the application itself, recommending, on the final page, its rejection. 'Low priority' was the official formula. Moser told me that he recognized the handwriting. It was Campbell-Quaid's. This inclined me to the view that Campbell-Quaid was, in one sense, responsible for Moser's death. People don't commit suicide for nothing. Moser had no real family. No children of his own. Vita was dead. His research career was blocked. And I had failed to talk to him.

There was the sound of movement, chairs scraping overhead. The transition to dessert was under way. I went back up the stairs and joined the throng making its way through to the Old Common Room, where we took our places at a new table arrangement. Some colleges, like Nuffield, can't accommodate dessert in a separate room on grand occasions, and gaudy celebrants have to hang about in the corridors or the common room, or shiver in the quad, while the scouts sweep and re-lay the tables. We have none of those sorts of difficulties in the Court. As usual Laurent had ensured the preparation of our traditional dish: a delicate meringue in the shape of a swan, the centre, between its wings, filled with a *crème brûlée*, and the whole floating like an *oeuf à la neige* on a little sea of *crème anglaise*, the surface flecked here and there with minute dashes of a dusky chocolate. One of these delicacies adorned each place at the table, a reminder of the time when the Court shared ownership of Isis's swans with the Crown – a privilege lost at the Restoration for reasons of political intrigue. Jesty likes to say that it was revenge on the part of one of Charles II's concubines, who formed a passion for the then Master of the Court – a Puritan lawyer called Sir Geoffrey Flavell – who declined to satisfy her lust. 'The only known occasion when the college has failed to prostitute itself in defence of its privileges,' Jesty would say, with a 'Ha!' followed by a crisp sniff. The details may be false, but they illustrate a truth nevertheless: that college life is sustained by shaping and preserving close relationships with the political forces of the day. Hence Colin Preggett and his insufferable clichés.

When I eventually found my seat neither Dr Spekeleiner nor any of the others from Hall was anywhere close to me. They were all whisked away to new, distant company. Now I found myself wholly among college colleagues. Ben Gould was opposite, looking more than ever, in his evening suit, like an Italian concert pianist. Next to him were Jesty to his right, and Maurice Singleton, looking pained, to his left. There must have been some others too, but I can't now remember who they were. There was a Gewurztraminer to drink with the swan, a beautifully spicy dry one from Dambach-la-Ville, a drink for Voltaire, if only they'd made it then. Had they? A quaffing wine, I thought. Not for sipping. Moser called Voltaire the French endive: sour, difficult to soften, but healthy.

'Been talking about your friend Moser with Campbell-Quaid,' said Jesty, attacking his swan with a fork, and demolishing it into its *crème anglaise*. Eating heartily, he dropped powdered meringue down the front of his dinner jacket.

'Ah,' I said.

He sniffed. 'Not Campbell-Quaid's favourite natural scientist, I gather. "Very forceful personality," he said, which I believe is a euphemism for headstrong. "Not a good team player" was another . . .'

'Egotistical.'

'. . . I imagine so. "Too confident of his own judge-ment" . . .'

'Imprudently presumptuous.'

'Exactly. A nice man, C.Q. I liked him. I think he had old Moser's measure, could smell the rat and so forth. Moser was a decent trooper in the Court, I told him that, but a bit phoney I always thought. Never did like phoneys. C.Q. has invited me to be his guest at a Royal Society meeting. Ha! (*sniff*). But what of you? I hear you've been entertaining a charming American scholar with your English wit.'

'I had the honour to sit next to a truly brilliant young feminist, yes. Her name is Deirdre Spikehurler and she is a founder and co-editor of the women's collective journal *Spit*. She helped organize the Gay Crusade Day march on Nashville and has a weekend breakfast programme on PBS TV called *Ambush*. Her volume of reminiscences about growing up on a goat farm in the Appalachians with a castrato for a father and a cocaine-sniffing alcoholic mother who went to the same primary school as Bill Clinton is called *Battlefront* and is pub-lished by Amazon. It's been on the bestseller list for months. She's a star. She even has one of those stone-cutter voices they get by having a micro-amplifier installed in the throat at the same time that they have the braces put on their teeth when they're twelve years old. I liked her. She has invited me to be her guest at the next meeting of the *Spit* collective.'

Jesty put down his fork and looked at me over the top of his demolished swan.

'Are you taking the piss, Leroux?' he said.

'Not out of you, Conrad,' said Ben, his jowls and ears moving in unison. Defusing things, as ever. 'Only that poor American girl.'

'Don't worry Conrad,' I said, for some reason ignoring Ben's implicit offer of help. The Gewurztraminer really was excellent. 'I'm not yet ready to compete with you for the position of college shit. You grace it too effectively.' Jesty's eyes darted backwards and forwards round the table. Maurice Singleton suggested that perhaps I should 'Come, come, Philip', do up my bow-tie and eat my swan. Jesty was pushing his chair back, but Ben had his hand on his sleeve. I felt very strong and excited. I'd had enough.

'You come and tell me these insidious things about Moser, as if I didn't know Campbell-Quaid's opinion already, diminishing a great man, far greater than you or your C.Q. will ever be, with your tittle-tattle, and your insensitive, needling, nasty, provocative gossip. And then you imagine yourself wounded and insulted because you've succeeded in provoking me, but unlike the usual occasions, when your victims stick to the rules and behave themselves, and don't rise to the bait, I did, and do. So now you think yourself entitled to be outraged. But you're not. The only outrage that's been committed so far this evening is the outrage of two second-rate academic time-servers daring to impugn the reputation of a far greater man only five days after his death, and coming to an agreeable consensus about his inadequacies. You'd have done just the same sitting next to Ms Spiteflinger: making yourself oh so agreeable, and then wrecking her reputation behind her back . . .'

'Much like you, Philip, from what I hear,' said Ben, almost under his breath, but loud enough to be heard. A lot of the rest of the table had gone very quiet. Jesty was still sitting down, but his eyes were blazing, and he looked as though he wanted to fight.

'No, no, Ben. I wasn't agreeable to her at all. I behaved very badly, I'm glad to say. Tried to make her as uncomfortable as possible. I shouldn't have, but I'm . . .'

'Drunk,' said Maurice.

'Ah! (*sniff*),' said Jesty, relaxing a little. Perhaps being drunk is all right. Not like being bereaved. I slumped back in my chair and closed my eyes. The Old Common Room swayed gently, rather pleasantly, I thought, in the candlelight that illuminated it beyond my eyelids. My pulse was beating at a terrific rate. Scouts were clearing the sunk swans. New plates heralded nuts, candied fruit, fresh fruit, dates and Turkish delight. The port and madeira began to circulate. There was a gleaming, winking bottle of Cadillac, one of the really great dessert wines. Moser used to say . . . Dear God, is there nothing Moser didn't once say? Will I live the rest of my life with his voice in my ear, his opinions on my tongue, his ideas revolving in my brain? It's as if he has come to inhabit me, has forsaken his own body in favour of mine, and wants the same freedom with me that he once took with himself. I've read that biographers often feel like this. Ackroyd denied it about Dickens, but his Blake read differently: the old seer got to him, I think. Had him reinventing Great England. And Jessica Douglas-Home in *P.N. Review*, wondering if Violet Woodhouse would ever 'float free of this earth and so free me'. It works in reverse as well: Ted Hughes, pursued by careerists and the hounds of feminist criticism (one has to employ the male dog in these circumstances or be thought illiberal), as though he were 'a picture on a wall or some prisoner in Siberia', robbed of his own past and present self, replaced by others' mendacious fantasies about his relationship with poor, sick Sylvia Plath. Biography is a dangerous medium.

Is this why I *feel* so threatened? Was it why Moser *really* was threatened? He wanted to rewrite the biography of Man, so to speak, and . . . Someone was nudging me in the ribs. It's important to stay alert at dessert because you have to keep the port circulating.

'Rejoining us?' asked Maurice, though not with any

enthusiasm. Can't say I blamed him. This was to be his last gaudy, and I suppose he felt a bit down about it.

'I was,' I lied, 'trying to compose some suitable toast to you, Maurice. In memory and praise of your past as a colleague, guide and friend; with hopes and best wishes for your retirement. Happy and long-lived.' I raised my glass. Others did the same. A little, ragged, hoarse but audible cry of 'Maurice' went up from our part of the long table as more glasses were raised. Maurice beamed. For a moment I thought he was going to reply with one of his vague, worried speeches, but the possibility was butchered by Jesty, who was proposing a wager with someone down the table, and calling loudly for a scout to bring the Betting Book. The subject turned out to be how long Yeltsin would survive. A case of champagne the wager. Maurice played both chess and bridge, so he knew a lot about odds and end-game strategies. He'd expect to be an item in the Betting Book himself soon enough.

What happened next is a muddle. Somehow – though I don't remember actually moving – we were all back in the SCR drinking coffee and/or scotch, or something, and I was in a group with Monica Summerton, the abrasive, rather shrill junior minister at the Foreign Office. She is young, and blonde, and has a rather ruthless husband who once did something in the Treasury but now does it in a City accounting firm, something like that. The magazines keep writing her up as the next female British Prime Minister, and unlike everyone else she has come to believe it. I remember that she asked me what I did, and I told her that I was a philosopher, and I think she must then have said something quite sharp, perhaps about the general utility of philosophers to the future of Britain, that sort of thing. I can't recall what I then said, but I suppose that I may, indeed must, have said something a bit brusque, perhaps even mildly offensive. From what I've been told, she bridled, and someone tried to pull me away. I remember resisting briefly, but I can't believe that it could have been particularly strenuous because the next thing I remember is the cold air in the quad, and Felix struggling to put up that enormous umbrella of his because it had started snowing very hard again. I was finding this quite amusing, and had started to develop a line about how Felix's umbrella wasn't a real umbrella but only a virtual-umbrella, the sort that exists in every way except reality, a sort of *eidos* umbrella, Platonism revisited, the return of the Greeks, the celebration of the Games, boys as superior to women, Sodom and the junior minister at the Foreign Office, snow on Olympus as Nina Spekeleiner administered – as the sociologists say – a questionnaire to the perishing cold peasant ladies of Katerini. All that sort of thing, logical in its own way, when out of Axel's Gate came the Master accompanied by Preggett, the minister, deep in conversation with Campbell-Quaid.

'Ah. I'm glad to find you out here,' said Sir Philip, looking serious but benign. 'And feeling better, I hope? Less, what shall we say, down?' I noticed that he was wearing gumboots, his dress trousers tucked inside them. 'And what an extraordinary night!' He waved his arms at it, like a conductor getting the orchestra to rise, as though this was something rather wonderful that he had perpetrated personally, but for which he was reluctant to take full credit. Felix at last got his umbrella up, though one of the spokes was broken, and poked up through the material.

'Who's next?' I said, looking at Preggett and Campbell-Quaid.

'I'm sorry?' said the Master, beginning to look concerned. More people were emerging into the quad, overcoats being pulled on, voices raised in wonder at the snow.

'Not you, Master,' I replied, keeping my eyes fixed on Campbell-Quaid. 'Remember item three of the code of college conduct. Never Tell Anything to the Master.' I stepped up to the minister and his scientific companion, slipping a little on the cobbled pathway. 'These two. Who's next for character assassination?' As I said this last word – actually one of the things that I do remember rather well is how difficult I found it to say – I slipped again, this time my legs going in opposite directions. Campbell-Quaid reached out to steady me, but he was too late, and down I went. The problem is, or was, that just as a drowning man grabs at and clings to the swimmer who is trying to save him, taking him down as well, so I managed to crash to the ground with Campbell-Quaid gripped between my arms.

Our fall was very neatly broken by the wall of snow erected by the porters beside the cleared path. It parted beneath our weight and we went down into its soft pillow. Campbell-Quaid, it must be said, was not nice to hold in one's arms. He was thin and spiky, all ribs and elbows, and as we toppled into the snow I pushed him very firmly away. I may have done this rather more forcefully than I intended, or perhaps I had my knees bent under him, and in straightening them they acted as a catapult, but whatever the cause he sailed on past me, facing away, but turning very slowly as he went. There was a plop as he hit the snow. Something was still making me laugh, though I agree now, in the light of what followed, that this was inappropriate. Staggering to my feet, I went to try to help Campbell-Quaid, but he appeared to interpret my approach as a threat, and, getting unsteadily to his feet, lurched away from me. The Master, struggling to surmount the snow wall in his gumboots, called out something in a voice of alarm. Several others, including Felix, who must have impeded them somewhat with his umbrella, also started towards us. I could see the danger – the concealed and frozen pond somewhere at Campbell-Quaid's back – but he was alarmed, and possibly craven, as well as oblivious to this particular feature of his predicament. I reached out to hold and steady him, but rather than grasp for the security that my hand might have offered, he ducked and swivelled, as if to avoid a punch. Once more unbalanced, he staggered away a pace or two, and then fell flat on his back. For a moment he gazed up at me, his long, mean shape silhouetted very neatly in the snow like a fossil in a rock. Then there was some creaking and a good, loud crack, the concealed ice beneath him collapsed, and, like a Swiss pocket knife in the half-open position, he went through into the water, bottom first.

Several other things then happened. The Master pursued Campbell-Quaid into the pond in his gumboots, and started to try to pull the unfortunate Darwinist to his feet. His posture did not simplify the effort. Various upstairs windows on to the quad opened, revealing the faces of dons, guests and scouts eager to catch a glimpse of events. They looked so festive, the lights behind their heads, the snow tumbling through the dark, blinking and white against the grey college walls, that they made the gaudy, at its end, somehow truly joyful, so that I found myself smiling and waving. Then Conrad Jesty and some companions, having extricated themselves from Felix's umbrella, also reached us. Robin Foxton and a couple of others went to help the Master, but Jesty – who may have mistaken my innocent role in this affair – came straight for me, and struck me in the face.

There was no time for restraint. Reaction was instinctive. Also, to be frank, pleasurable. A sort of expiation. I hit Jesty as hard as I could on the cheek, which hurt rather (me, that is – my sore wrist from falling in the snow on my way to dinner), and then even harder with my other fist on the other side of his face, except that he'd turned his head, so that his nose took the full force of the blow. He staggered, beginning to curse me, and bleeding very colourfully in the snow. Behind him, Campbell-Quaid was rising very slowly to his feet, like a beast being pulled from the deep by the combined efforts of the Master and his helpers, chief amongst them now, the minister, Colin Preggett. Jesty was still standing up, which in the circumstances seemed to me to be quite wrong, so I hit him again, this time in what I hoped was the chest. Once more I was mistaken, and the blow fell rather lower. Jesty doubled over, winded, gasping ineffectively for breath. First he crumpled to his knees, like a cringing supplicant, then as the air returned to his lungs and he gasped it in, he fell backwards. As he did so, he grasped for support at something, anything, but only managed to get his fingers through the tear in the knee of my trousers. As he went further backwards, and toppled into the pond, taking the Master, Preggett and Campbell-Quaid (once again) with him, he completely tore off the bottom of the left leg of my best dress suit.

I turned away, hot and jubilant. All of a sudden there seemed to be dozens of people milling about, figures being dragged from the pond, scouts with blankets, lights everywhere, Laurent's voice from somewhere nearby issuing instructions for a fire in the Master's rooms, hot cocoa, brandy and a tray of glasses. I was light-headed and giddy. Legless in Gaza, at the pond with serfs. Felix said something to me and I turned away, thinking that I'd better go to my rooms.

Someone was standing on the path, just inside the quad from the porters' lodge. All alone. Quite still. Away from the muddle and bustle of the bedraggled party now making its way through Axel's Gate. The snow was falling heavily all around her, but by an effect of the lights to either side, she seemed to be apart from it. An area of warmth that glowed in the dark and in the snow. She had a scarf round her head, a handbag over her wrist.

'Oh Philip, Philip,' she said. 'What *have* you done?'

It was Alice.

Passion and madness are talents of a sort, and do not come at will.

7

Saturday morning

'You think that when you have understood what is going on,
your desire to act will pass? But that would mean that what
you wanted to do was not what was wanted.'

Moser didn't commit suicide. My doctor rang this morning
to say that he'd talked to the coroner, and the cause of death
was a massive heart attack. 'All over in a second,' he said.
There would be no inquest. The coroner's office had already
informed the college, so the funeral would go ahead on
Monday as arranged. I asked about the aspirin bottle, the note
to Vita. Coincidence, apparently. No sign of aspirin in his
blood or liver. The envelope with Vita's name on contained
letters written to him by Vita. He must have kept them by
his bed.

Alice said that she was glad, and that I must be too.

Am I? No, there are no signs of gladness. Humiliation,
misery, remorse. The horror of not being able to speak. When
I saw Alice there at the Court, in the snow, I wished I could
collapse, hand myself over to others to be cared for, but I just
stood there, crapulent and ashamed. She came and embraced
me, touched my face where the mark from Jesty's blow was
turning to a bruise, and where my own incompetence with
the razor was once again bleeding.

'How did you get here?'

'I'll take you home.'

Apparently she had spoken to Rawlinson from Hong Kong
after talking to me on Wednesday night. On his advice she

flew to Paris, took the train to London, and was met at the station by one of Scorpion's drivers, with a four-wheel-drive vehicle fitted with snow tyres. It took them four hours to get to Oxford. The chauffeur and car were still waiting outside the Court, and took us home to Jericho.

I was slow to remember all this when I woke on Friday morning. I had a splitting headache and a sick stomach. '*Une crise de foie*', they say in France. A hangover will do. It was only in the afternoon that I managed to get up, and since Alice had gone out to make an 'arrangement' – a mystery I couldn't even be bothered to think about at the time – I had a few hours to myself for scribbling. The therapy of words.

I am going to have to say goodbye to Moser, but I do not know how. I needed to talk to him about Vita, and assumed that I had plenty of time. Like a couple of old men at the end of a French film, we'd sit on a bench in the sun somewhere, and with thirty or forty years since Vita's death behind us, I'd explain to him, he'd accept and forgive, grant absolution of a secular sort, and our friendship would be in some fundamental way complete. Now he is dead, and I am alone with this terrible unexpiated crime.

Too harsh? If she loved me, and I loved her, isn't it, wasn't it, purified? Does love legitimize passion? I imagine that most people, at least in the West, believe that it does. Or rather, by a three-step process, love brings beauty to sexual congress, beauty is truth, and truth is the one legitimate aim of all endeavour. Ergo . . .

This won't wash, of course. Somehow one has to deal with the question of obligation. Do commitments exchanged constitute obligations such as to restrict future alternatives? Well, what else are they for? Worse – or at any rate more difficult – do the commitments or actions of people thought to be normal, though at some later time shown to have been ill, entail obligations at the time they are made equal to those of people who may not, later on, be shown to be ill? Or at least not ill in the same way? And if the commitments, by their very nature, entailed reciprocity, does the later negation of one liberate the other? That's the only question I've been able to pose so far that offers me even a glimmer of hope of salvation. I mean peace of mind, of course.

Moser used to talk occasionally about Vita's last weeks of life. He had found them shattering. She had strange fantasies, he said. Ideas of being in love with other men, quite a few of them, one an Indian at the Economics Institute whom she met with Alice; another a Japanese pianist; and so on. None of it was true. As her brain tumour grew it put great pressure on the amygdala, now known, he said, to be the location of our consciousness of the significance of emotional experience, enabling us to make judgements about it. Her fantasies were quite real to her. She had made love with these men. Moser said, 'Except for the fact that she hadn't, she had. The experiences were quite real for her. If you had to write it, you would be compelled to call these encounters a part of her biography.'

Were they, then, those of them that I think I can recall, also a part of mine? If they weren't authentic, didn't they cease to exist as the acts that they seemed to be at the time, and become some other sorts of acts, acts that were not purified, but merely stained by illness? And is illness, as a feature of error — or, to be frank, immorality — less or more justifying than rank bad faith, *mauvaise foi*, the usual basis of betrayal?

God knows I cannot answer these questions.

Another one. Not so hard. Why is it better — for him? for us? at any rate for Alice? — that Moser should have died of a heart attack rather than an overdose? Is it because, if he had killed himself, someone would have had to take the blame? Campbell-Quaid, for instance? Or me, if he'd found out? Or the college, say in the person of Jesty the Shit, or Sir Philip the Smooth, as representative of an uncaring world that soon forgot how deeply he mourned for Vita, how passionately he cared for his work, how desperately he needed the liberty of his own research? In a suicide there's always plenty of room for guilt.

Or is it because one senses that the suicide, if he'd survived the attempt, would receive the kind of attention that would make him unlikely to try again, and that his success on this occasion was, therefore, a kind of accident, or mistake, that might have been prevented if only one had knocked on his door at the right moment? Whereas a massive heart attack, well, that's an event that absolves us all.

Elizaveta Nikolaevna Ogarev, known as Liza, Herzen's child by Natalie Tuchkov, born on 4 September 1858, committed suicide in Florence shortly before Christmas 1875, when she was seventeen. Five years after the death of her father. Carr saw in this terrible act a convenient way to end his book on *The Romantic Exiles*, thus demonstrating that, at least at the level of cynical exploitation, not every suicide is in vain. It may be put to literary use. Herzen and his circle, Carr means to imply, exhibited a kind of adolescent intellectualism, immature and lacking in solid worth, a dilettantism that died of its own volition, having nothing substantive, nothing concrete, to offer the world. Liza's self-destruction in a villa on the slopes below Fiesole, before her life had even really begun, seems, by its finality, to mark the termination of Herzen's own struggle for truth, dignity and peace. Carr called Liza's suicide an act 'of precocious despair, adolescent defiance and childish mischief'.

One reason why history can seem so unforgiving is not simply that all its judgements are provisional, but that so many of its practitioners so often forget the fact. There is arrogance where one ought to find humility. Surely no serious scholar writing in the 90s would describe the tragedy of the suicide of a young woman of seventeen – however beautiful, talented and well-connected – in the terms employed by Carr writing in the early 30s. We have known too many suicides, and suffered them too dearly. Nor would we now assume, presume, that the causes of her death lay on the mere surface of events. Suicide goes deeper, far deeper, into a concealed territory of terror, betrayal and fearful exhaustion. We know so little about the living. We can confirm nothing about the dead.

To have used Liza's suicide, in the way that Carr does, as a convenient symbol with which to brand her father a failure may seem careless as well as shabby. It is worth stating, therefore, that I don't believe for one moment that it was careless at all. Carr is clearing Herzen out of the way in order to make the Russian revolution the inevitable result of the rise of Marxism – a hard-edged science of society which he compares with Darwinism – 'the most influential product of Victorian science'. Disposing of Herzen left him free to write his monumental historical justification of Leninism and the tyranny of the Communist state. In a sense it is a mark of the respect that he secretly harboured for Herzen's influence in the wings of the Russian political theatre of the mid nineteenth century. Unless Herzen can be disposed of, written out of history much as old Bolsheviks were airbrushed out of photographs by Stalinist *apparatchiks*, his presence might still be felt. An alternative to repression, Party dictatorship, and state madness.

A mere eighty years later, not much of the great Marxist-inspired upheaval seems to be left. When I was an undergraduate one of my own philosophy tutors told me that he had himself once been taught by Ernest Teale, a sort of mole of a man so old that he could remember G.E. Moore and the 1910s like yesterday, and so unworldly that in the 60s he still claimed to be a Platonist. No doubt he knew what he was saying, too. Ernie told my tutor that before 1917 nobody, but nobody, took Marx seriously as a philosopher, economist or historian. It was the events conducted in his name that made his work interesting. Great minds like Plamenatz, Popper, Kolakowsky, would never, but for Lenin and the Bolsheviks, have bothered with Marx. 'It will all fade again,' Ernie used to say. 'Dreary stuff.'

Now that it's going, Carr's demolition job on Herzen ought to go too, for history has not done with Herzen. His ideas might still be Russia's ideas. And I don't mean by this that the particular policies that he advanced should now, nearly a hundred and fifty years later, be resurrected, put into effect. It is, rather, a matter of stance. How we confront the world. How we engage both in and with society. Herzen understood that democracy is not a thing, nor yet even a set of institutions. Rather it is a method. An outlook. A way. It relies on procedure and on tolerance. But it must reach and involve everyone, because one of its fundamental axioms is a respect for all human life. Herzen represents – in his freedom from place, his exile, his steadfast independence and generosity – the *attitude* of free, democratic man, failings as well as triumphs. It is why his life cannot be separated from his work. His biography is a philosophy: a serenity of temper. Even when pessimism overwhelmed him in the 1860s there was proportion in his depression. '[T]he greatest sorrow in the world –' he wrote to Turgenev in 1862, 'that of the old man, young in heart, surrounded by a generation growing more and more shallow.' Not anger. Not bitterness. Not rejection. Sorrow. The greatest sorrow in the world.

The date of this letter returns me to Nice, to the graveyard on the hill above the Mediterranean, to the small words on the side of the Herzen family tomb: Lola Boy et Lola Girl

1861–1864. These were Herzen's youngest children, twins, born to him by Natalie Tuchkov. They died of some perfectly ordinary nineteenth-century childhood malady – measles or whooping cough or meningitis – before their third birthday. Herzen's love for his children, his affectionate pleasure in them, his unusual liberality towards their domestic and scholarly upbringing, shines from his letters, his essays, even his political writing. The twins' nicknames suggest the same: though christened Alexis and Helen, their baby gabbling at an early age suggested the onomatopoeic 'lola', and so this they became. Lola Boy et Lola Girl. I think that when they died, the light went out of his life: the pose of pessimism, until that time more an affectation than a deeply held position, became fixed. In weeping for his children he wept for mankind, and most especially for his beloved Russia. And he was right. There was much to weep for in the century that lay ahead.

If, today, we were looking for a symbolic way to end Herzen's biography, we would end it surely, not with the suicide of Liza, but with the deaths of the two little Lolas.

Symbolic endings are, however, untrue to life, which has a shape in itself. The symbolism, such as it is, resides in the perceptions of others. I think this must have been what Moser felt, a week ago tonight. He had come up to my rooms in the afternoon, quite animated as I remember him now. He talked about two concepts in biochemistry and evolutionary theory called 'minimal function' and 'component specificity'. He explained that he was trying to apply them to a feedback process in the anatomy of the human brain that controls and directs the production of hydroxycorticosteroids, which are essential to life. Without them, we die. In short order. He said the 'exquisite orchestration' of this process, as one writer had recently described it, which involves the production and secretion of sequences of different hormones to trigger the production and release of others, simply could not have come into existence according to the principles of evolutionary theory. For one thing, they actually appeared to play a part in regulating genetic processes within the cell nucleus itself. For another, they depended on at least two interrelated feedback processes. When something is regulated by its own feedback within a cascade process of hormone production on which the immediate survival of the organism depends, how could it have arisen as a result of single-step mutation over time?

Moser didn't doubt the capacity of evolutionary biologists – the C.Q. ideologues of their field – to come up with a complicated explanation complete with 'uncertainties' that would require 'more research'. And the allusion reminded me of the skill with which Russian Diamat-Histmat theoreticians could pummel any historical or current event into the Marxian framework that suited the glorious Marxist-Leninist state. Except that they got up one morning in 1991 to find that it had disappeared.

Moser knew that we cannot fly in the face of history. And he understood his history of science. There would have to be a quite new, simple, elegant explanation for the origins of biochemical sequencing. 'It *has* to be the case,' he said. 'It *must* be. It *must* be.'

Perhaps he was on the edge of it. He was very tense and excited. But there was sorrow in his voice too. The sorrow of a scientist young in mind, surrounded by colleagues growing more and more shallow. Homoeostasis is our way of maintenance. When someone has a heart attack it's because the organ of the heart, for whatever reason, has become rigid, and is no longer able to regulate the flow of blood according to the needs of mood or activity. Homoeostasis has been lost. Moser was, at the end, unbalanced by something. Perhaps some great discovery. Some insight. Unbalanced, but not in the mind.

Later

Alice came in and I had to stop. She had Felix with her. Apparently she'd found him outside in the snow trying to make our doorbell work. He looked pretty solemn, asked how I was feeling, and declined Alice's invitation to stay for tea.

'Have to get back,' he said. 'Things to attend to.'

He reached inside the satchel over his shoulder and passed me a small brown paper parcel. I opened it. It was my floppy cricket hat. My name inside. Ever since the fourth form. It had been missing for three years or so.

'We got Mrs Wharton to clear out Moser's rooms this morning. Bursar wanted them for exam candidates next week, and we've promised to let Moser's sister have his personal effects from the college on Monday. After the funeral. Wasn't much there, but she found this hat of yours, said you must have lent it to Moser, and knew you'd want it back. I thought I'd drop it round. See how you were.'

'I'm OK,' I lied.

'And you'll be there on Monday.'

I nodded, blinking back my sense of annihilation. The emptiness, and power, of the vacuum.

Sometimes I think I'm a freak. The one part of the human anatomy that cannot experience pain is brain tissue, but I seem to have a pain in my brain more or less all the time. The worst pains are Vita, Moser and Alice. And they get worse with death. This is death's contribution to human understanding. There is another place, unearthly, where we imagine the dead to be located, but with which we are not able to communicate. In our helplessness we talk to ourselves. In severe cases, doing so, we imagine ourselves to be communicating successfully with the dead. It is a form of hysteria.

I told this to Dr Kahn last night. He is the psychotherapist who emerged from Alice's 'arrangement' yesterday afternoon. She had made it through Rawlinson and the Master. Sir Philip felt, he told me on the telephone, that Governing Body would want to support my continued presence as a college fellow if I undertook appropriate treatment for my 'very understandable recent difficulties'.

Alice made an appointment for me to see Kahn at his home just before supper. One of those huge north Oxford houses made of yellow brick, with Cotswold stone cornices. Very quiet, though I could see a couple of Filipino housemaids in the basement kitchen when I arrived, and one of them opened the door to me when I knocked. She showed me into a quiet room with pictures on the walls, vases of flowers here and there. Kahn arrived moments later: a big, silent man. Six foot three at least. Bulky. Heavy glasses on a fat nose. Grey hair curly like Peter Ustinov's once was. No sparkle though – a grey man – grey pullover, grey trousers, grey jacket, grey carpet, grey upholstery. He hardly spoke the whole hour that I was there. He began by asking why I had come to see him, as though I was an intruder, or a completely unexpected and rather peculiar incident in an otherwise tranquil Friday evening. I was surprised by this. After all, I was there because my arm was being twisted, and surely he knew this already. I decided to give him a facetious answer, but instead I began to cry. Again.

Here for the time we will stop. Some day I shall publish the chapters I have omitted and shall write others, without which my narrative would remain unintelligible, truncated, perhaps useless, and in any case will not be what I meant. But all this must be later, much later . . .

Death isn't the other shore, of course. The farther shore is the one Herzen had reached when he arrived in Western Europe from his native Russia and discovered in his permanent exile that maturity was the liberty to seek and to know, free of all the barriers of the past. It was the shore that Moser was on before he died. Those who are lucky in life, like Alice, seem to know all along how to get there, and how to live once they do. A few, like Moser, get there as a result of work and intense struggle. Many, probably the great majority, never set out to make the crossing. Others drown in their own egotism before they arrive. A few of us, against our desire, are washed up here by accident. We do not know why. We are terrified by what we find.

NOTES AND REFERENCES

Prepared by Dr Felix Cunningham

Unless otherwise specified, all quotations in the text are drawn from the works of Alexander Herzen published in the following editions:

My Past and Thoughts. The Memoirs of Alexander Herzen, translated by Constance Garnett, revised by Humphrey Higgens, four vols, London: Chatto & Windus, 1968. Herzen's letters to Turgenev of 1862 and 1863 are in vol. IV.

From the Other Shore and *The Russian People and Socialism*, translated by Moura Budberg and Richard Wollheim, Oxford: OUP, 1979.

Childhood, Youth and Exile, translated by J.D. Duff, Oxford: OUP, 1980. (This and both the above works contain an introduction by Isaiah Berlin.)

Leroux refers frequently to E.H. Carr, *The Romantic Exiles*, which was first published in 1933. His own copy was the Peregrine Books edition, Harmondsworth: Penguin, 1968.

The work that is, surely, certain to become standard is: Philip Leroux, *Alexander Herzen. A Life*, London: Mullens, forthcoming.

Notes

Where only a page number is given, the note refers to the text displayed on that page.

Dedication: From a letter to Turgenev, 15 January 1863.

p. 1: *Childhood, Youth and Exile*, p. 65.

p. 23: *From the Other Shore*, p. 58.

p. 29: From a letter to Turgenev, 29 December 1862.

p. 35: *My Past and Thoughts*, p. 823.

p. 36: *Childhood, Youth and Exile*, p. 103.

p. 53: *My Past and Thoughts*, p. 706.

p. 55, 'Herzen's first real book . . .': In fact Herzen published various items in Russia before his departure for the West, including, in 1846, a novel, *Who is to Blame?* The word 'real' suggests Leroux's opinion of worth rather than precise historical fact.

p. 56: Turgenev, writing about Herzen, in a letter to Kolbasin, 17 August 1879.

p. 58: *From the Other Shore*, p. 79.

p. 67: Ibid., p. 68.

p. 68: *My Past and Thoughts*, p. 745.

p. 73: *From the Other Shore*, p. 114.

p. 76: *Childhood, Youth and Exile*, p. 269.

p. 80: Ibid., p. 69.

p. 89, '. . . the kind of human truth . . .': Richard Holmes, *Dr Johnson and Mr Savage*, London, 1993, pp. 4–5.

p. 101: From a letter to Turgenev, September/October? 1862.

p. 106, 'Cockchafers of the political . . .': *My Past and Thoughts*, p. 1156.

p. 107: From a letter to Ogarev, published as *Bazarov Once More*, 1868, and reprinted in *My Past and Thoughts*, pp. 1750–65. The quotation is at p. 1759.

p. 108: *From the Other Shore*, p. 68.

p. 124: Letter to Turgenev, 20 October 1862.

p. 132, '*Pigeonneau rôti* . . .': This delectable dish may possibly still be found at the restaurant 'Au Pressoir' in the Avenue Daumesnil, an unfashionable part of Paris, and just the sort of place where one might have run into Philip Leroux dining with Moser.

p. 132, 'Bocuse': Paul Bocuse, *La Cuisine du Marché*, Paris, 1980. A bible to Moser. Other suggested recipes here are drawn from Raymond Oliver, *La Cuisine*, Paris, 1981, a favourite text of Leroux.

p. 137: *From the Other Shore*, pp. 136–7.

p. 154: *Childhood, Youth and Exile*, p. 187.

p. 160: Ulick O'Connor, *Biographers and the Art of Biography*, Dublin, 1991.

p. 166: *My Past and Thoughts*, p. 675.

p. 168, 'Eldredge and Gould's theory . . .': Niles Eldredge and Stephen Jay Gould, 'Punctuated Equilibrium: An Alternative to Phyletic Gradualism' in T. J. M. Schopf, ed., *Models in Paleobiology*, San Francisco, 1973, pp. 82–115.

p. 174, 'Kauffman, Doolittle and Behe': Stuart Kauffman, *The Origins of Order*, Oxford, 1993. Russell Doolittle, 'The Evolution of Vertebrate Blood Coagulation: A Case of Yin and Yang' in *Thrombosis and Haemostasis*, 70, 1993, pp. 24–8. Michael J. Behe, *Darwin's Black Box. The Biochemical Challenge to Evolution*, New York, 1996.

p. 175, 'Robert Shapiro': Robert Shapiro, *Origins. A Skeptic's Guide to the Creation of Life on Earth*, New York, 1986.

p. 175, 'Much as does a trellis . . .': Peter C. Whybrow, *A Mood Apart. Depression, Mania and Other Afflictions of the Self*, New York, 1997, p. 123. Perhaps Leroux and/or Moser had read this remarkable book in MS, since it was published after their deaths. Alternatively they may have encountered the trellis image in conference papers or discussion.

p. 182, 'Like birth-order studies . . .': Most recently, see Frank J. Sulloway, *Born to Rebel. Birth Order, Family Dynamics and Creative Lives*, New York, 1996, which also contains an extensive bibliography.

p. 188, 'Ackroyd denied it . . .': Leroux told me that he heard Peter Ackroyd say that he had never once even had a dream about Charles Dickens while working on his biography *Dickens*, London, 1990. And it is true, as Leroux suggests, that one of Ackroyd's subsequent books *Blake. A Biography*, London, 1995, reads rather differently.

p. 188, 'Jessica Douglas-Home . . .': See her 'Violet Gordon Woodhouse' in *P.N. Review*, 108, March–April 1996, vol. 22, no. 4, p. 8.

p. 188, 'Ted Hughes, pursued by careerists . . .': See Janet Malcolm, *The Silent Woman. Sylvia Plath and Ted Hughes*, London, 1994, esp. pp. 126–30 and 141–3.

p. 194: From a letter to Turgenev, 10 June 1862.

p. 195: *From the Other Shore*, p. 95.

p. 204: *My Past and Thoughts*, p. 755.

PENGUIN ONLINE

READ MORE IN PENGUIN

In every corner of the world, on every subject under the sun, Penguin represents quality and variety – the very best in publishing today.

For complete information about books available from Penguin – including Puffins, Penguin Classics and Arkana – and how to order them, write to us at the appropriate address below. Please note that for copyright reasons the selection of books varies from country to country.

In the United Kingdom: Please write to *Dept. EP, Penguin Books Ltd, Bath Road, Harmondsworth, West Drayton, Middlesex UB7 ODA*

In the United States: Please write to *Consumer Sales, Penguin Putnam Inc., P.O. Box 12289 Dept. B, Newark, New Jersey 07101-5289.* VISA and MasterCard holders call 1-800-788-6262 to order Penguin titles

In Canada: Please write to *Penguin Books Canada Ltd, 10 Alcorn Avenue, Suite 300, Toronto, Ontario M4V 3B2*

In Australia: Please write to *Penguin Books Australia Ltd, P.O. Box 257, Ringwood, Victoria 3134*

In New Zealand: Please write to *Penguin Books (NZ) Ltd, Private Bag 102902, North Shore Mail Centre, Auckland 10*

In India: Please write to *Penguin Books India Pvt Ltd, 11 Community Centre, Panchsheel Park, New Delhi 110017*

In the Netherlands: Please write to *Penguin Books Netherlands bv, Postbus 3507, NL-1001 AH Amsterdam*

In Germany: Please write to *Penguin Books Deutschland GmbH, Metzlerstrasse 26, 60594 Frankfurt am Main*

In Spain: Please write to *Penguin Books S. A., Bravo Murillo 19, 1° B, 28015 Madrid*

In Italy: Please write to *Penguin Italia s.r.l., Via Benedetto Croce 2, 20094 Corsico, Milano*

In France: Please write to *Penguin France, Le Carré Wilson, 62 rue Benjamin Baillaud, 31500 Toulouse*

In Japan: Please write to *Penguin Books Japan Ltd, Kaneko Building, 2-3-25 Koraku, Bunkyo-Ku, Tokyo 112*

In South Africa: Please write to *Penguin Books South Africa (Pty) Ltd, Private Bag X14, Parkview, 2122 Johannesburg*

A CHOICE OF FICTION

The Beach Alex Garland

'*The Beach* is fresh, fast-paced, compulsive and clever – a *Lord of the Flies* for the Generation X. It has all the makings of a cult classic' Nick Hornby. 'A highly confident début ... this incisive novel may well come to be regarded as a defining text in the history of imaginative travel writing' *Daily Telegraph*

Love of Fat Men Helen Dunmore

'Helen Dunmore is one of the brightest talents around and these stories show the full scope of her talent ... Exquisite writing adorns every page, marvellous flashes of poetic insight' *Sunday Telegraph*. 'Dunmore's new collection of short stories have the crisp delicacy of a snowflake and a snowflake's piercing sting' *Sunday Times*

Felix in the Underworld John Mortimer

Writer Felix Morsom's existence is comfortable if uneventful, until he meets Miriam, who proclaims him the father of her son Ian, and he becomes the prime suspect in a murder case, encountering more drama than he could ever imagine ...

Chasing Cézanne Peter Mayle

Camilla Jameson Porter's magazine *DQ* drips with flattering portrayals of the rich enjoying their riches. André Kelly, her favourite photographer, is away in the South of France when he discovers a highly lucrative art swindle that involves a shady art dealer who just happens to be Camilla's lover ...

After Rain William Trevor

'Each of the twelve stories in William Trevor's glittering collection, *After Rain*, surveys a quietly devastating little earthquake. Tremors that ensue when pressure is put on a fault-line running through a marriage, family or friendship are traced with fine precision' *Sunday Times*

READ MORE IN PENGUIN

A CHOICE OF FICTION

The Memory Game Nicci French

When a skeleton is unearthed in the Martellos' garden, others rattle ominously in their cupboards. For the bones belong to their teenage daughter Natalie, who went missing twenty-five years ago, and the murderer must be very close to home. 'A beautifully crafted psychological thriller ... electrifying' *Harpers & Queen*

Gaglow Esther Freud

'[Freud] sweeps us back to Gaglow, to its tensions and mysteries, to three sisters who love their brother and detest their mother, whose adored governess vanishes into an uncertain world ... her fine prose holds the reader to the end' *The Times*

The Brimstone Wedding Barbara Vine

Unlike the other elderly residents of Middleton Hall, Stella is smart, elegant and in control. Only Jenny, her young care assistant, guesses at the mystery in Stella's past. 'Out of the mundane accessories of past existence, Vine fashions a tender, horrifying mystery ... The story, beautifully written, emerges delicately, yet with shocking, ironic force and breathtaking imagination' *The Times*

Grianan Alexandra Raife

Abandoning her life in England after a broken engagement, Sally flees to Grianan, the beloved Scottish home of her childhood. There she begins to heal, putting behind her a whole lifetime of hurt and rejection. 'A real find, a new author who has the genuine story-teller's flair' Mary Stewart

Shadow Baby Margaret Forster

'An unfailingly intelligent novel, full of lucid observation of a phenomenon, mother-love, too often seen through a gilded haze of false feeling and wishful thinking ... Forster is a fine storyteller' *Sunday Times*

READ MORE IN PENGUIN

A CHOICE OF FICTION

Quarantine Jim Crace

'A story-teller of unique gifts . . . One of the finest novels I've read in years' *The Times*. 'Splendid . . . a novel so original that its prose will ring in your ears, and its theme – man's potential for faith and brutality – will haunt you long after you have read the last page' *Daily Telegraph*, Books of the Year

Kowloon Tong Paul Theroux

'Hong Kong in 1996. Here, as the days tick away towards "the Handover" to China, two last-ditch Brits become belatedly aware that their time is running out . . . Theroux's taut tale quivers with resonance, menace and suspense . . . The work of one of our most compulsive story-tellers on peak form' *Sunday Times*

Distance Colin Thubron

Edward Sanders, a young astronomer, has lost two years of his life, his memory obliterated by a trauma. In the days following his awakening, one memory fades in and out of focus: his love for a woman he cannot name. But as the elusive image becomes clearer, so too does the terrible event that plunged Edward into his private abyss.

Libra Don DeLillo

'DeLillo's monumental novel *Libra* concentrates on the inner life of the people who shaped the Kennedy assassination . . . It's DeLillo at his chilling best: he constructs the very human faces behind a monstrous event, creating fiction which trespassed on reality' *Time Out*. 'As testimony to our crimes and times, this is an original, unignorable book' *Observer*

The Destiny of Nathalie 'X' William Boyd

'The intense visual quality draws the reader into a world where betrayal and fear are the dominant themes. This pithy and evocative style is reminiscent of the young Hemingway . . . a master of fantasy, farce and irony' *Sunday Express*